Edward A. Rand

A Candle in the Sea, or, Winter at Seal's Head

Edward A. Rand

A Candle in the Sea, or, Winter at Seal's Head

ISBN/EAN: 9783337253691

Printed in Europe, USA, Canada, Australia, Japan

Cover: Foto ©Andreas Hilbeck / pixelio.de

More available books at **www.hansebooks.com**

A CANDLE IN THE SEA

OR,

WINTER AT SEAL'S HEAD

BY

REV. EDWARD A. RAND

AUTHOR OF

"FIGHTING THE SEA," "LOOK AHEAD SERIES," "UP-THE-LADDER CLUB SERIES," "SCHOOL AND CAMP SERIES," "HER CHRISTMAS AND HER EASTER," "A KNIGHT THAT SMOTE THE DRAGON," "DOWN EAST MASTER'S FIRST SCHOOL," ETC., ETC.

New York

THOMAS WHITTAKER

2 AND 3 BIBLE HOUSE

PREFACE.

A FEW years ago, I wrote about our Life-saving Stations, and the title of the book was "Fighting the Sea." That subject not only interested my imagination and engaged my sympathies, but impressed me with a deep sense of the vast service rendered humanity by our life-saving crews. I have great admiration for it and the ability of its executive head, the Hon. Sumner Increase Kimball. While the service of the Life-saving Stations thus has impressed me, I have been deeply interested also in the work of our Lighthouse Board. Wisely is it directed at Washington, and brave, at times chivalrous and heroic, is the service rendered by our lonely light-keepers. I think of them at their often sea-girt posts with feelings of profound interest and respect. The country owes them a debt even when any accounts have been squared. I want the youth of our land to appreciate this work, to respect and admire the lonely hands that trim the wicks of these candles of the sea, our lighthouses. By reason of this faithfulness, those on the ocean sail more securely, and those on the land hope more confidently for the return of their hardy sailor-boys.

CONTENTS.

A CANDLE IN THE SEA.

CHAPTER I.

THE MAN IN THE WATER.

"B B."!
"B. B."! said the voice again.
"What's that amount to?"

The speaker was chalking these two letters down on a garret wall. He slowly but thoroughly rubbed out one of these letters.

"'B'! Just that left! What does that amount to?" he said, in a melancholy tone.

He had a languid, tired way. Making a lazy effort, he slowly rubbed out the remaining B.

"There!" he exclaimed. "That's what I amount to. 'Poor old Boardman Blake,' I expect they are all saying."

He now sleepily gazed about the old garret. He saw the dusty, musty bundles of old herbs suspended from the rafters. He noticed a rusty, discarded sheet-iron stove. His eyes wearily travelled from a broken antique bureau in one corner to a bedstead that in another corner looked as if it had kept on its weak legs as long as it possibly could, and now dropped upon its knees as if deprecating some worse fate that threatened to befall it.

"Everything going one way, all of us getting old! What does B. B. amount to? Nothing!" he exclaimed, here facing the vacant wall again, and listlessly, moodily contemplating the emptiness.

He now noticed a spy-glass on an adjacent shelf. Of course this was old. The tube was dented and scarred, and it seemed to say: "I have lived many years in this wearisome world and have seen rough usage."

"You're old too!" said its owner. "You have done good service though."

He here abstractedly took the glass down from its shelf. He felt the next moment an unaccountable desire to level it toward the sea which stretched in all its grand, awful solitude before the garret-window, a great disk of sapphire widening out into the east.

"Good old glass!" said the owner, pointing it affectionately at the sea and squinting carelessly through it.

"Good old glass!" he said, dreamily. The

next moment, he cried, "Zounds!" In an instant, a marked change came over him. He slammed the glass down upon its shelf. He turned abruptly away. His eyes snapping, his hands nervously working, he went vigorously down-stairs. With flushed cheeks he appeared in the kitchen. In a trembling, excited tone, he said:

"Lyddy!"

Lydia, his spouse, looked up from her sewing-work, over which she had been sleepily bending. Her dark eyes behind the spectacles which she kept scrupulously clean, shot out little golden arrows.

"Why, Boardman, what *is* the matter?"

"Matter enough!" he almost shouted.

"Matter? You scat me. You came down the stairs fairly a-stompin'. I haven't heard you stomp so for——"

"Reason enough! Where are my big rubber boots?"

The old man was now flying about like a big, fat bumble-bee, whose eyes have been put out and then is turned loose into a garden-patch.

"Boardman, *have* you gone crazy?" asked his bewildered spouse, nervously rising from her chair and in alarm gazing at that beloved husband's antics.

"Crazy? If I have, it's in a good cause. There's a man out there in the water? Saw him with my glass."

The old wife was now as excited as he. She flew about, exclaiming:

" Massy! A man in the water! Why didn't you tell me? Fly, fly, Boardman!"

For a fat man, this was no easy task, but he did his best.

Boardman flew very soon out of the house, but he did not go in the big rubber boots. He forgot these in the hurried search for his old overcoat, and wore his slippers. His wife followed him promptly, pulling an old hood over her head and drawing her red shawl around her shoulders.

Boardman was heavy and a little under the medium height. He walked off though, as if he were striding along in a pair of new seven-league boots.

He passed from the kitchen out through the store he had kept many years. How ancient it had seemed that morning, and its diminished stock of goods, how very unequal to the demands of a progressive generation! But now, the storekeeper's imagination was filling it with that great and superfluous stock of vitality aroused within himself. The capitals " B. B."

on the old sign too, above the door, faded and shrunken, now rounded out into their original size, and stared at him in their conspicuous prominence. He strode past a fishhouse where he had stored cod and halibut, hake and haddock, for a thrifty trade with the " country up back," but of late years this stock had dwindled more and more ; and the building in an almost conscious thinness and weakness had threatened to collapse. This old structure now seemed to strengthen and fill up once more. " B. B." here became big letters again.

In this mood of vigor, opulence and importance, Boardman Blake reached the white, sloping sands and was about to place two round rollers under the keel of a waiting boat, when a voice screamed out :

" Boardman, ain't ye goin' to tell the life-savin' folks?"

Startled, he looked up hastily and saw his wife.

" You here, Lyddy?"

" Sartin! The life-savin' folks——"

" There is nobody at the station till September, you know, and by the time I could go round and hunt 'em up at their homes, that man out there might drown."

" Then I'm goin' with ye," she replied, promptly.

He gave another startled look but acquiesced, and as he shoved a roller under the boat, he stooped and squeaked:

"Don't see why you shouldn't go as well as me! You are no older than I am."

"Guess I can steer. You forgit in our courtin' days when you rowed and I steered up to 'Goose Pint'—" She paused.

Although there was a man nigh unto drowning out in the sea, Boardman Blake laughed to recall this old courting-escapade, and he cried, "Come on, Lyddy! Want to shove on this boat? Here—now!"

Away went the boat on the rollers, while Boardman and Lydia ran beside it, laughing away, their hastily donned over-garments fluttering about them, vivacious as the two youths that once took a boat up to "Goose Pint."

The boat reached the water. "Lyddy" scrambled into it. Boardman gallantly and with strong hands shoved it out into the surf, beyond which it was quickly rowed. His wife had seized the paddle and with it was making a commotion about the stern of the boat.

"See him, Lyddy?"

"Not on 'Gull Rock,' is he?"

This was a ledge bare at low water. Her

quick, sharp sight of other days seemed to come back this morning, and she saw a man's form rise dark and pillar-like above the ledge.

"That's the place I saw him through my spyglass up in the garret."

"Do tell! It is the last place for a man to git!" This was not a reflection on the man up in the garret, but a surprise at the location of this man on Gull Rock.

"How do you s'pose he came there, Boardman?"

"Don't know! upset, dare say, and he swum there!"

The rowing and paddling all this time went on persistently, and toward the boat the man on the rock turned anxious eyes.

"Good!" he muttered, steadily keeping the rescue boat before his vision.

"Getting chilled—ugh! The water is cold. It has covered the rock and—bah—it may cover me! I thought nobody would see me. That swim tired me out.—Keep back there! What are you coming up any higher for?"

This was said to the cold sea-water now rolling in steadily upon every low sandy beach, over the flats on either side of the river's channel, up the creeks, twisting through the flat, green marshes. Would this same restless tide cover up a man on Gull Rock as mercilessly as it would flood the beach and the flats and the black muddy bottoms of the creeks? That seemed to be its purpose, for the rock, bare when the almost exhausted swimmer crawled out upon it, was now covered with chilling sea-water. This was also making its way up his legs. It had a cold, repulsive feeling under his pants. He thought of snakes twisting them-selves about his legs. Several times he lifted a foot out of the water and pressed upon his pants as if trying to force the snakes out of them. Once he entered into an ugly cal-culation whether the water would rise high enough to cover him. How high anyway did the tide in that part of the world generally rise? He cursed the tide and cursed too the moon, said to occasion the tide.

He thought of another contingency. The tide might not cover him, but could he main-tain his standing on the rock if the wind should blow hard and make a heavy sea, and—then —in the night, what if shifting about, he stepped off the rock—and——?

He now cursed the wind and the night and then the rock itself. But suddenly, he saw the flutter of a movement on the beach.

"A man!" he muttered.   "A woman!"

He then took out a handkerchief and wildly, excitedly waved it.

Those for whom this demonstration was intended, did not see it. The man signaling though, was comforted and encouraged, even as some other movements do not affect anybody save the makers of them, and these are wonderfully helped. The man on the rock now began to smile. He hummed a tune. He whistled. He felt so sure of relief that when the expected boat did not reach him as soon as he had calculated, his mood changed from satisfaction to grumbling and fault-finding.

"When will those two boobies ever get here?" he wondered. "Probably some old man and some old woman!" was his conjecture.

The two philanthropists were thinking only of the good they were doing and came on cheerfully, exultingly, persistently.

"Stiddy, Lyddy, stiddy! Does me good to see you use your paddle," cried Boardman; "but bring her to, easy—that is it, easy when we near the rock. There!"

"All right!" said the crew at the paddle. "I'll fix her."

Up to the pillar in the sea, to that strange, solitary, chilled being on the rock, Lydia Blake guided her boat, so that it rubbed gently against him. He eagerly grasped it, and without a word, was scrambling into it.

"Well!" said Boardman, the host, to his mysterious guest. "We are glad to give ye a welcome!"

"Yes, yes!" cried the paddler in the stern enthusiastically. "Poor feller! most chilled through! Wall, we will git you hum, and git you into dry clothes!" His face interested her. "Not a good face," she said, "but he is han'sum."

"Think it is about time something was done. Don't want to get on this coast again," said the stranger, in a petulant, ungrateful tone.

What?

Did the two rescuers hear aright?

The peevish lack of thankfulness chilled them, as if they were the ones who had got into that water out from which they had just taken him.

Boardman said nothing. He looked surprised, and silently pulled on his starboard oar, and turning the boat, headed it for home.

Lydia always found her tongue quicker than her husband.

"You ought to be thankful that anybody took so much trouble to come and git you," she remarked.

This aroused the man to some appreciative-
ness of the act of rescue.   He paid special at
tention to the fact that it was an old woman
in the stern of the boat.

"Of course I'm grateful!" he murmured.
"If you had been out here on this ugly rock—"

"Oh, yes! We understand that," remarked
Boardman, who was disposed to take a charita-
ble view of the man's shortcomings and those
of everybody else. "You had a hard time.
I could tell that as soon as I clapped my eyes
on you through my spy-glass. I was up in the
garret, and hadn't used that glass since my
nephew, Walter Plympton, was here one day—
he's in college, you know——"

Here the stranger acted in a very abrupt,
peculiar fashion. He swung round and sat in
such a way that neither Boardman nor Lydia
fully, fairly saw his face again. This he could
manage, for he had climbed into the bow of
the boat and taken a seat behind Boardman,
though urged to sit amidships. He now sat
with his back towards Boardman and Lydia
also. These two boatmen who were renewing
their youth, sat awhile in an astonished silence.
To a question which the stranger soon asked,
"What about that glass?" Boardman replied:

"Oh, I saw you through it."

"I am much obliged," said the stranger, though in a cold, undemonstrative way.

"You're welcome," replied Boardman.

The stranger now appeared to be smitten with a desire in some way to let it be known that he was not without his gratitude to his rescuers.

"The light-keeper at—what do you call it?"

"Over there to the nor-reast?"

"Yes, what you can see from here."

"Oh, Seal's Head! We say 'light at Seal's Head.'"

"Well, it isn't a man's head any way, that has charge there. I met him out a-fishing this morning. I talked with him about the light. He said he was going to leave it——"

"What, Silas Maxwell goin' to leave the light?" asked Lydia.

"He told me so, and that he made up his mind only yesterday."

"Indeed!" said Lydia, delighted to get hold of this fresh bit of gossip and carry it round like oranges and cake. She looked as if she wanted more, but she was not gratified. He only remarked, "That Silas must have seen me in the water after I left him—couldn't help it in fact—for my boat was upset not more than three-quarters of a mile from his— and he must have seen me——"

"Oh, might not!" charitably exclaimed Boardman. "They say Silas' sight has been a-bothering him. Maybe that is the reason of his quitting the light. Why didn't you stay by your boat and hold on to that till picked up?"

"It sank. Then I thought I might as well strike out for the shore, being a good swimmer, but it was much farther than I calculated. I got to that old rock out there, and I was so used up and the distance ashore was so great, I knew I could not do anything. I thought I might as well drown on that old rock as anywhere else."

"That old rock was a good friend to you," observed Boardman, who did not like the man's unwillingness to acknowledge an indebtedness to anybody or anything.

The stranger replied, "Your best friend is yourself," and after that maintained a sullen silence.

"Pig!" thought Lydia. "There he sits shiverin' and he might warm himself up a-rowin'. The queerest man I ever see! What is that scar on the lower part of his cheek? Looks like an old shark's mouth."

It was a singular scar, but if it had not been large as well as singular, Aunt Lydia would not have discovered it. Two minutes ago, she would not have seen it, but he had removed from his long neck a broad scarf, and the mark had been uncovered. It suggested the greedy gulp of an ugly fish.

"I could tell him by that, and by his eyes of faintish blue, which are big and have about as much color to them as a strip of my old blue calico dress out in all the sun and rain last summer. I want to see that face once more. Bad, and yet smart and han'sum! He's young, too!" thought Lydia. Neither she nor her husband had a chance to see that face again, for its possessor persistently turned it away from his companions. When they reached the shore, he abruptly said "good-bye!" and started down the beach toward the empty life-saving station.

"Won't you go up to the house and get some dry clothes?" called out Boardman, in astonishment.

The man muttered some reply that was unintelligible and pointed toward the station.

"It is shet up!" shrieked Lydia. That did not delay him. He shuffled ahead, his stiff, wet clothes clinging to him. It was the last seen of this man with "the faintish blue eyes" and the old shark-scar for many days. Boardman and Lydia stared at him in wondering silence until he had turned a rocky corner in the coast-line and then they proceeded to roll the boat up the beach.

"I call that the selfishest case!" declared Lydia.

"Don't he look odd a-shufflin' off, Lyddy, ha-ha?"

Boardman laughed one of his easy, good-natured laughs. When anything was a perplexity to him, if the case had the least humorous quality to it, he would express his feelings in a laugh. It might last a minute or two, beginning in a series of suppressed chuckles, continuing in a forcible explosion and ending perhaps in a "Well, well; it beats the Dutch!" These humorous manifestations of the feelings of her husband, did not generally make Lydia feel that way. It rather provoked her to say something sharp and disagreeable, sometimes.

"Now, Boardman!" she protested. "What is there to laff at?"

But all of Lydia's protestations, on the other hand, operated as a kind of feather to tickle more profoundly Boardman's sense of the ludicrous. These extra chuckles he tried prudently to repress, knowing the effect on his wife, but they would show themselves at the corners of his mouth and eyes. She saw every sign.

" He is a mizzable——

" Oh, let him go, Lyddy! We will go home and get some dry clothes and a cup of tea and——"

" I don't know 'bout that."

" Oh, yes! You did splendidly. Why, I don't believe when we went to Goose Pint that we made better time."

She was now moderating like a stormy sea when the wind changes and the sun shines.

" You think so, Boardman ? "

" Why, I know it, dear."

She was all right now. As she often said, Boardman knew how to " manage " her. Up to the old home they went, laughing. They entered it by a door on the kitchen-side of the house, Boardman first picking up an armful of the brush piled against the eastern wall of the shed.

" I'll start up the fire in our old stove, Lyddy, if you have a mind to make us a cup of tea," he said, cramming the light, dry brush into the stove.

But this stove did not now seem so old.

The fire began to crackle and flame with all the energy of youth. The stove began to rattle in a kind of juvenile flutter, and, as if in response, the sunshine streamed fresh and young, warm and golden through the small, old-fashioned panes of the windows. Soon, the teakettle began to sing that one tune for which teakettles are so famous and which I would not have changed, modified or exaggerated for any consideration. In this world where everything is so uncertain, so shifting, it is pleasant to know there is one way, even in the darkest night, by which you can always tell if a teakettle be on the stove—provided there be fire in the stove and water in the kettle.

"A dry shift is good," said Lydia, who was soon pouring a cup of tea for Boardman.

"And dry slippers, too! I went in my old slippers and didn't know it for some time," said Boardman, chuckling away. "Don't know when I have felt so young and nimble."

"Nor I," replied Lydia, cooling with energetic puffs a saucer of hot tea lifted to the level of her mouth. "Felt nimble as an eel."

For several minutes nothing was said. Boardman had the air of one who had gone into a brown study. He continued to sip his tea and he industriously broke off bits of toast from the slice in his hand. But he did this in an abstracted, mechanical way. He replied to his wife by nods, by hemming, and once by a dreamy " Jest so! "

" There, Boardman, do you know what you said then? I said it jest to try you, ' The snow is very deep. ' "

" Oh, did I ? " replied Boardman, waking up. " Some remark about the winter, I thought it was, but——"

" There, I knew you had gone off ! "

" Gone off," in Lydia's vocabulary, was the synonym for a meditation, a study, any season of profound reflection, and Boardman was rather inclined that way. This was especially true of the later days when " B. B." seemed such small letters.

" Yes, wife, I thought——"

" What were you thinkin' about ? "

" Well, I—I thought what a difference it made in this world whether a man had a purpose or not, something definite in view, for which he worked and which he tried to bring about. Now you and I had a purpose to save that man——"

" The ungrateful wretch ! Couldn't appreciate what my husband did ! "

"And my wife, too! Don't leave her out! But here is the *pint*. Lately I have not done all I wanted to and the store didn't bring in so much, and I don't know as it ever will——"

"Now they've got a new one agoin' below us. Pesky shame!"

"Oh, they had a right to. However, it does affect our trade, and I can't handle the stock of new goods they have got. However, I've been a-thinking. I felt I was a-getting old——"

"But I ain't, Boardman!" exclaimed Lydia, her dark eyes lighting up and snapping.

"You didn't act like it this morning, Lyddy. Well, I was about to say, I had a purpose this morning, and, I must allow, it surprised me to see how I flew round. And I felt as young and spry——"

"Jest like a kitten!"

This simile amused the fat, heavy store-keeper.

"However, I felt as if I could do some-thing——"

"And did it."

"With my wife's assistance. Now, this is what I was a-driving at. It seems to me the having of a purpose makes a great difference with folks in this world——"

"Of course——"

"A man says 'I have got something to live for, and life is worth living; I have a purpose.' Does not this make a difference between young folks and old folks? The young have a purpose in life. They keep it before them, a kind of flag, you know, and it leads them on. It stirs them up. It keeps them a-going, and old folks don't have that purpose. They feel that work is over and school is out. There's no more use in doing and living, only just a waiting and——"

"What old folks?" asked Lydia, a light kindling behind her spectacles. Boardman, though, did not pause to notice this. He was fairly aroused. He was making gestures, and eying Lydia directly, he went on: "——just a waiting, and they do nothing. Or, one may not be old, but a man or woman may have come to the conclusion that they are about useless, through drinking, say. They haven't a purpose that is good for anything, have they? A *woman* that drinks is worse than the *man*."

Lydia was now knitting her forehead. She was pondering a problem. What did her husband mean by this protracted delivery of his thoughts? It was something unusual. Boardman was given to meditation rather than expression. Here he was, though, talking volubly, in a very animated, forensic way. A dark suspicion made a shadow in her thoughts! She had asked him in the morning if he were crazy. She had not really thought so then, but—but —what was the state of the case now? Had the unusual strain of the morning's events been too great for the brain of Boardman Blake? She eyed him sharply, intensely, solicitously. He in return eyed her as directly as if she were a special audience convened to hear one Boardman Blake, a noted platform-speaker. He continued:

"To have a purpose is not that the difference between me to-day and when I was a young man? A purpose divides youth from old age. Now in our boat I put off—you helping me—and tried to save that man——"

"Most selfishest!" groaned Lydia.

"And how it stirred me up! I didn't know myself! Now what I want is a purpose. It will do me good, and having it, I think I can do some good to other folks. Now I tell you what I think of doing. I know I shall be sixty soon, but I am not there yet. I have had some experience, when I was young—about six months—and I think I can get the chance— and I think of applying for the light at Seal's

Head which Silas Maxwell is going to give up."

"What, Boardman? That's what you're drivin' at all this time you've been makin' that long speech? Why, you most scat me out of my senses. You keep the light at Seal's Head? Wall, *have* you gone crazy?"

She eyed him. Had that brain of Boardman Blake's broken down under the unusual strain of the day's events? Crazy?

"Me? I guess not. Do I look so?"

"But you really *mean* it?"

"Of course!"

"I thought you were drivin' at suthin' a long time. It seemed to me that cat had an amazin' long tail."

She was not fully satisfied with the evidences of his sanity. He had not manifested such energy for a long time. She was not wholly free, even now, from suspicion, and when he was not looking, scanned his face sharply, and once she seized his wrist and felt his pulse.

"Why, Lyddy," he inquired, "what are you up to?"

"Are *you* well? Do *you* mean it?"

"Mean what?"

"About goin' to the lighthouse, Boardman?"

"Yes, if you're willing and I can make you comfortable on shore. I shall have help, so that I can have a furlough every few days and come home."

"No comin' home on furloughs to see Lyddy Blake! If you're a-goin', I'm a-goin' too. Guess I—I'm as young as you are."

"You really will?"

"Sartin! don't believe you ought to be left to yourself or anyone else to help, except it is your wife—I—I—I——"

Her spectacles were directly pointed at this excited partner. She was still in doubt. Was he sane?

"You will go with me? Hoo–rah! Hoo–rah!" cried Boardman, fairly jumping out of his chair.

"Lyddy" thought now that all reason must have fled.

Boardman had gon . hopelessly crazy.

CHAPTER II.

STILL WANTED—A PURPOSE.

THEY were coming out of "prayers," the students in a country college. The low, serious tones of the president, leading in the brief, simple service, had died away. The tramp of feet disturbed the reverent quiet of the chapel and then class after class pushed out into the college yard. The grass was still green under the maples and elms, but the most extravagant imagination could not find any emerald tint in the autumn foliage overhead. It burned, it blushed; it was now scarlet, then gold; it was a single vivid shade of crimson and then a clump of rainbow tintings. It seemed as if nature, that had caught in the stained chapel windows the added brilliancy of the sunset-flush, wished to show what colors, what patterns she could introduce into the Gothic arches tapering up amid the framework of the trees, and so had filled these leaf-windows with color and set them up in this, her grand temple of worship.

Under those flaming, drooping masses of foliage, walked Walter Plympton. He was twenty-one and had just entered upon the studies of the sophomore year. He was tall, muscular and finely shaped. His large eyes matched well the long, dark, rich hair. He had a strong, clear, resonant voice. In temperament he was enthusiastic and sanguine, and in his attitude toward others generous and truthful. The last thing that could be charged upon him was cowardice. He was fond of adventure and any risky feat proposed to Walter Plympton engaged his sympathies, even if his judgment could not commend it. He had a quiet appreciation of the humorous, loved a joke, and, though he sometimes rushed into his jokes with a thoughtless ardor, yet no one ever twitted him with malice therein. He was written down as one of "the popular fellows" of the class. The careless scamps of the college had not discovered any side to his character that would shelter their extravagances, and he did not join in their escapades; but in the same "Walt Plympton" they felt that there was an element that understood them better than did the "staid old men" among the students of the little college. He was impulsive and he was venturous and he was enthusiastic, and though he managed to control his impulses, there was something in Walter that did not forget the restless nature of boys who were continually giving way to this and that foolish prompting, and as often getting into the thorn bushes of trouble. By the religious men of the college, he was classed as on their side and he stood there sincerely. He had made a profession of his faith a number of years ago. He had sometimes wondered what he would do in the future with that faith. Would he ever study for the ministry and preach that faith?

"Not good enough," he would murmur when that inquiry came into his thoughts. Still he hardly knew what else to do. The future was a surface upon which he had not written a single definite plan. He was waiting to learn what to do, listening, looking, to catch some voice or hint about his life-work. Then what about the coming winter? In vacation time he ought to be at work. Had he a school? What were his plans? "All at sea!" he murmured.

The subject was in his thoughts when he left the college chapel the evening of this chapter. It remained with him through the supper to which he went directly.

"A penny for your thoughts," said a fellow-student. "A-dreaming, Plympton?"

Walter smiled rather vacantly, laughed good-naturedly, and said nothing.

Thinking still upon this subject, that he must have employment in the vacation, that he could not afford to be idle, he left the table and sauntered down to the post-office alone. To go to the office was the invariable custom of many before they took up their work for the evening. To go alone was something unusual in Walter's case. His nature abhorred loneliness. He was the fellow that liked to have a chum in his room and a companion in his walks. Rules have exceptions. A lonely mood struck him to-night. He gave way to it wholly, as to everything interesting him.

"I'll poke down street alone and try to settle something by myself," he concluded. "Ought to teach to help pay expenses, or may be get a chance to do some copying in a law-office—no, I must teach, and there are three places I know of to-night, and I wonder if I had better write to any of them? Yes, have heard about three. Now, which one shall I write to? Must decide something."

A chance thought came to him: "If it is so much of a puzzle to tell about one's work for

a winter, what must it be when one has really
to tell about his life-work? Well, I haven't
got to decide that yet.   Thankful!"

When he reached the post-office, he
inquired in the old way, "Anything for
Plympton?" and then wondered if the postmaster realized how many important decisions he handed out when he passed their
mail to successive applicants.   Would anything decisive come to " Plympton " to-night?
Those small envelopes were like guideboards
set up along perplexing paths, lanterns lighting
up dark ways, voices calling back from fields
into which one may have wandered ignorantly,
and saying, " Here! you are to do so and so,
or go so and so!"   The postmaster, though,
in a very unappreciative, mechanical way, went
through his duties.   To-night, the agent in
the settlement of men's destinies, in a careless
way shoved through a little grated window to
this prisoner of hope, an old-fashioned envelope, superscribed in a small, crabbed hand,

"MR. WALTER PLYMPTON."

Walter took the letter, walked off, and
examined again the superscription.

" It is for Walter Plympton," he said aloud.

Then he opened the letter and read as follows:

"SEAL'S HEAD LIGHT, Oct. 10, 18—.
"DEAR NEPHEW :—

"I suppose you may have heard that I have been appointed keeper of the light at Seal's Head. I sought the appointment with some misgiving, but it seemed advisable to do so ; my store was paying little, and I did not have the money to enlarge my business and make the store pay more. I felt the need of something to do. Like good many other people, I wanted a purpose. I have got it now,— to keep this light. If you could see me—no, us I should say—your Aunt Lydia and me, sitting by the table before the stove, she on one side and I on the other, here in the light-house kitchen, I think you would say it was a very comfortable place to be in. Aunt Lydia is knitting, and sometimes—nodding. However, I mustn't expose her, but tell what is on my mind. I have an assistant, your old friend, Tom Walker. He is very much in need of a good, long rest. He got a bad cold fastened on him somehow, and can't seem to get rid of it. He has said more than once 'I ought to go home and nurse myself.' We were talking about you the other day, at the table. Tom said : 'I am thinking of your nephew, Walter, whom I know well. College chaps sometimes

like to do something in vacation, and I wonder
if he couldn't come and take my place, a
couple of months, say? He may have my
pay.' Your Aunt Lydia just jumped—almost
—out of her seat. 'Wouldn't that be splendid?' said she. I said kind of calm—you
know your Aunt Lydia is pretty wide-awake—
I said easy, 'That is quite an idea. 'Twouldn't
be a bad thing at all. I might write to
him.' So I have written. I venture to say
you would earn as much as if school-keeping,
and it would be a change and a kind of rest.
Now, supposing you think it over and write to
me, whether you would like to come here at
the close of your term, and stay awhile. Come
if you can. I think I can fix it with the lighthouse folks that manage these things. Aunt
Lydia sends her best love. I tell her she is
right there, to send best or none. She wants
me to say 'Come' for her. Think it over,
and I hope you will come.

  "Your affectionate uncle,
    "BOARDMAN BLAKE."

Walter gave several complacent chuckles,
crowded the stout letter back into the old-
fashioned envelope, and said: "The very
thing! I have got it! Much rather do it

than hunt up a school! Ha, ha! here goes the assistant-keeper of the light at Seal's Head!"

He stuck his thumbs into the arm-holes of his vest, tipped back his head, and laughed as he wondered if the college bookseller whose store he was passing, or the driver in the butcher's cart rattling by, or those sophomores coming toward him, Ben Hale, Palfrey Smith and Ripley Eaton, knew that the assistant-keeper at Seal's Head was actually, that moment, on the sidewalk and going toward the colleges!

One of these, Ripley Eaton, left his companions, approached Walter, and in his hearty way slapped Walter on the back, and said:

"Old boy, you look happy! Going to be in your room in half an hour? Want to see you.'

"Certainly! Yes, I'll be there. Come round, won't you? I look happy? Well, you wouldn't suppose that you were addressing an——"

"See you again, Walter!" cried Ripley, breaking away, for he had been suddenly hailed in a very urgent fashion by another student and Ripley turned to meet him.

"Well," thought Walter, lowering his head

and taking his thumbs out of the arm-holes of his vest, "I guess the world is not so interested in hearing about my going to Seal's Head as I supposed. Wouldn't Rip Eaton like to have my chance! Just the place for him!"

Walter turned to look back upon Eaton.

"Handsome fellow!" he exclaimed, "One of the handsomest fellows I know of! Just a pity that he is rich! Now, if he had to shove himself through college, had to go to Seal's Head or keep school, it would make him live low and be moderate in his ways. As it is—I don't know!"

Walter shook his head and then walked rapidly toward his room.

"We will have a little fire," he said, as he entered Number 30, North College. "There is no reason why an assistant light-keeper should not be comfortable. Ha! ha! Won't the boys envy me, those that have got to keep school, when they know of my easy berth!"

The stove was an open one, of an old-fashioned Franklin pattern. It had seen many years of service in college, had been sold again and again, and thus descending from student to student, had been bought this very fall by Walter, "dog cheap." The cheapness of the dog was due to a crack in its head.

" This or none!" said Walter, at the time of the purchase. "Can't afford to get a new stove."

Connected with each college room was a little wood-closet. The amount of wood in these closets corresponded with the amount of money in the students' pockets. The closet was a kind of finance meter. It said, " poor " or " rich."

" Don't know," said Walter, as he opened the door of his closet and proceeded to take a few sticks from the little heap of wood there, " don't know as I ought to be burning up this wood so fast, but really it doesn't seem right for an assistant light-keeper to go chilled. So we will have a little fire. Then I'll read again that letter."

The wood was kindled on the hearth of the stove, and flashed such a vivid light into the room, that Walter now noticed in the letter he had received from his Uncle Boardman a postscript.

" Didn't see that. It is on the last page and really escaped my attention," murmured Walter. "Can't just make it out and I must light my lamp."

His lamp disclosed to him this addition to his uncle's letter :

" Do you know a man who has on his neck a mark, shaped like a shark's mouth? The man may have had an abscess and this was the scar. Your mother said she told you about the man that Aunt Lydia and I fished out of the water. He had on his neck a mark, shaped liked a shark's mouth. Why I ask is on account of this fact, which your aunt and I did not notice at the time, but afterwards recalling all the circumstances, it seemed to us both very strange. We had been talking very socially, and suddenly I referred to a nephew at college, mentioning your name. You see I happened to be looking through a spy-glass and saw him out in the water. I told him of it and said I hadn't used that glass since my nephew, Walter Plympton, was at my house one day, and you, I added, were in college. Thereupon, he swung round, and didn't face us again. He seemed to be avoiding us. I didn't have a square look at that man's face again, neither did Aunt Lydia. He was very fine looking and very bad looking, also. Now, do you know any such person marked that way? Excuse me for being inquisitive, but it was a rather strange coincidence."

" Know a man that has a mark like a shark's

mouth?" soliloquized Walter. "What eyes my uncle and aunt have got! Folks have said that Aunt Lydia could see things when nobody else could possibly discover anything, but that is a slander on her. She is honest as the days are long. Man with a mark like a shark's mouth! A sailor who has been tattooing himself in a crude, heathenish fashion—Hark!"

Here came a slight tap on the door. It was followed by a fierce, loud one.

"Come in!" shouted Walter. That was college etiquette, not to rise and open the door to any caller, but to gather up your voice, make a ball of it, which was also a bawl, and then throw it at the door. In response to the yell, Ripley burst into the room.

"Rip, how are you! Take a chair, my boy! Got some holes in the cushion, but those only show what a quantity of soft padding is inside."

"Genuinely stuffed! When a man gets a hole in his character, maybe its real office is to show what a lot of merit is inside. That so? Relation of Holes to Character! How would that do for a subject at the next prize exhibition in college?"

"Might be worse, Ripley, might be worse! But sit down! Don't be afraid of it!"

Walter's silent thought was, " What a handsome fellow you are ! "

Ripley Eaton had a face of unusual beauty. The fine profile had a classical moulding. The complexion was clear and bright. The eyes were of a black that sparkled, and the flashes won your confidence at once. The dark hair had that perverse but attractive trick of curling, which gave to a face of marked regularity of features, a fascinating irregularity of frame and outline. His voice was rich and full, and his manner cordial. It seemed as if with such beauty must go a blemish somewhere, or it would not be human. The defect was partly within and partly without. There was too great a susceptibility to his surroundings to make all decisions reliable. Not because deliberately insincere, he might shout with a crowd in victory to-day, and to-morrow groan in sympathy with those who had been defeated. That which made him a very sympathetic companion might make him an unreliable ally. However, he knew his weakness. If to knowledge, he had only added serious effort to improve, there would have been much hope. The other deficiency was in Ripley Eaton's associations with a group of uneasy, dissipated fellows in his class, and one student in particular out of his class. This man's name was De Vere. His full name was John De Vere. Sometimes the college boys in irony called him St. John De Vere. He was said to look like Ripley Eaton, but not in this particular—Ripley's face did win the interest of people, attracting them at once; De Vere's repelled everybody. The difference was in the expression of the two faces.

While Ripley was a sophomore, De Vere was in his junior year. De Vere had acquired an influence over Ripley in a singular way. The two had gone to the river, flashing through the sleepy college town, and while bathing there, De Vere had saved Ripley from drowning. So De Vere asserted. Several students who witnessed the affair said that Ripley was unnecessarily alarmed and would have reached the shore unaided, but De Vere had gone to Ripley and made him think that help was necessary and had assisted him ashore. Ripley chose to believe that De Vere was the hero who had saved his life, and thereby he came peculiarly under the influence of De Vere's strong, magnetic will. Most of the students disliked De Vere, and the aversion of some was intense. Over a small circle, he had a peculiar influence. He could be very gener-

ous when he wished, and as his circumstances
were easy, this gave him an opportunity to
keep under obligation a small knot of poor
fellows who wanted to avoid him but found
it convenient to give him their confidence.
He had a very smooth, persuasive tone of
voice, when he wished to modulate it, and his
manner could be polished and courtly. Nobody so sympathetic as De Vere on occasions,
or would do more for a sick retainer, watching
steadfastly by night, and nursing him tenderly
through the day. He had read widely, possessed an entertaining fund of anecdote—not
always a nice fund—and was classified by his
set as " good company." He never was pusil-
lanimous or weak, and could furnish with back-
bone any number of lobster-shelled admirers.
He had much to say about " honor." This in
college is sometimes very peculiar and may be
of doubtful merit. In De Vere's mouth,
" honor " was a stock phrase. He liked what
was manly, preferred what was " heroic," and
doted on the " chivalrous." And yet under
all this seeming generosity, this persuasiveness
of voice, this courtliness of address, this socia-
bility, bravery and loftiness of air was—" the
devil."

So some of the boys asserted. Walter had

never seen **De Vere.** He had heard about him.   Ripley **had** spoken of De Vere to Walter, and De Vere's enemies had expressed to the latter their opinions.   Walter, who had attracted Ripley to his circle of friends, once felt it to be his duty to warn Ripley against De Vere.   Ripley had never carried the story of that warning to De Vere, but De Vere was keen enough to see that an influence different from his own had been brought to bear upon Ripley, and he had meanly wormed out of Ripley the fact that a college friend, one Plympton, had cautioned Ripley against one De Vere.

"I hate him," De Vere often said to himself. "When I get back to college, I'll pay that Plympton for his interference."

De Vere had been out of college Walter's first year, though not voluntarily. The faculty had sent him off to rusticate and improve if he could and would. He lived only a dozen miles from the college and Ripley saw De Vere at the latter's home several times during the year. Twice, influenced by Walter, Ripley had refused De Vere's invitation to take a glass of wine with him.

"It is that Plympton's doing, I know," concluded De Vere. This conclusion was correct.

On two other occasions, Ripley had taken the proffered liquor, vehemently pressed upon him by De Vere, and he came back to college the worse for this diabolical hospitality.

For some reason, Ripley did not get beyond the spell of De Vere's influence. In part, it was from a mistaken sense of " honor." De Vere never let Ripley forget that somebody "saved" Ripley, as he said. How could Ripley turn his ungrateful back upon so self-denying a benefactor!

De Vere was now expected back at college any day. He had not begun with the students the new academic year after his twelve months of unclassic retirement, because stricken down by fever. He had sent word lately to a satellite that he was now well and would soon be " with the boys."

Walter had heard of his intended return and was curious to see Ripley's evil genius. At the same time, he was sorry for Ripley. The night of this chapter, Walter wondered if Ripley were going to say that De Vere had returned, for after seating himself in the chair whose cushion suggested the relation of " Holes to Character," Ripley broke out suddenly:

" Oh, De Vere—— "

He halted.

" De Vere what ? "

" You don't want to hear about him ! "

" Why not ? He is not a mad dog to be avoided, is he ? "

" Oh, well ! I was only saying, or going to say that I expect him back any day."

" Very well," replied Walter in his open, sometimes blunt way. " If he is coming back I hope he will behave himself."

There was an embarrassing silence. Ripley felt that there was an abundance of room for the making of this remark, and yet he seemed in " honor " bound to say in defense something that could not be gainsaid, if he had the chance.

Walter's thought then was, " There ! I don't know as that was called for ! I am so impulsive ! "

Walter's voice was the first one heard when next anything was said :

" A penny for your thoughts? What's on your mind, Rip ? "

" Oh ! " replied Ripley, starting up as if out of a nap in which he had been caught. " What did I come here for ? "

" Because you wanted to see me, I hope," said Walter, laughing; " though that was not my question."

" Well——"

Ripley did not prefer to say what was just then in his mind; he was thinking about De Vere. For what had he come to Walter's room? He could talk about the purpose of this visit.

" Oh—oh—I felt like seeing you and getting indirectly your opinion."

" I will give it to you directly," replied Walter, whose frank, straightforward nature abhorred circuitous modes of expression or action.

" Well, I was a-wondering, Walter, if I had better go off with the boys——"

" Anything going on ? "

" I can't just say what."

" Well, good boys, or bad boys?   Now if you are going with the good ones to a service over at the church, no harm in that," said Walter, smiling, " or a walk, or a lecture, or——"

Ripley shook his head.

" Well, just what is it, Rip ? "

The caller shook his head again.

" Mischief, I know! Say, old fellow, there is nobody on these college-grounds that likes fun better than I do——"

" We know that, Walter, well as you. That is why some of us come to you and hang about you, when we know that some of the old men

like your room-mate, Logan, who is off teaching——"

"Logan is a good fellow," interrupted Walter
promptly.

"Oh, that may be, but stiff as a row of clothes-
pins on a wash line. Like all the rest of the
old men. Why, if we went to them, they
might preach a sermon at us——"

"That wouldn't hurt you."

"Oh, we get enough of that."

Here followed a pause. Ripley's face was
turned to the fire and wore a look of indecision.
The light brought this out and emphasized it,
as well as the great beauty of his features.
Walter noticed the look of perplexity that ac-
companies indecision, and he broke the stillness.

"Rip, I like fun, but I don't believe in the
fellows bruising round, breaking up property,
robbing hen-roosts, and making people miserable generally. I want money too badly myself
to see property damaged if not destroyed, when
I know it cost so much. Somebody has got to
pay for these things, and it may be fun for
some of the boys to tear round and break up
things, but it would be the honorable and manly
way to pay for the damage."

Ripley's face lighted up with a half-incred-
ulous smile as if such a course would be a nov-

elty in certain circles governed by a supposed
high "code of honor." Turning quickly to
Walter, he asked:

"Do you mean De Vere?"

"I wasn't thinking of him. I never saw De
Vere."

"He thinks you are down on him."

"I certainly never told him so, for I never
had a word to say to him in my life. When
will he be here?"

"Oh, he may get here any day. He may be
in his room now. He wasn't though just before
prayer-time."

"Well, let him go. You going off with the
boys to-night?"

"I haven't decided."

"You haven't told me what they are up to,
and I am not particular to know. My advice
to you is to stay in your room."

"Well, if it is done, there won't be so much
music round college for a few days any
way."

"Music?"

Walter thought in silence a moment and exclaimed:

"You don't mean the college-bell? Say,
Rip! That the music that is going to be
hushed?"

" Don't ask any questions about objects on land or sea, in earth or sky."

" However, my advice to you is to keep in your room."

Here Ripley rose, yawned lazily, shook himself and said, " Wish I knew what to do about matters and things generally ! What is life but a tangle? Where is the beginning of the thread you pull on and where is the end ? What am I here in college for, any way ? It seemed all bosh my coming here, and now I am here, what is the good of my being here ? When I get through, what am I going to do ? I don't know. Life is a sphinx. I can't make her answer my questions."

" Just the way I have felt, Ripley, and I am puzzled——"

" Oh, we dare-devils know there is something about you that can understand us even if you don't go with us, but I don't know what I am here for now, and after getting through college, it is all an enigma what I am going to do."

"I can tell you what I have in mind this coming vacation."

" School? That is what you steady chaps all propose to do. I would like to go to school to you first rate."

" Afraid you might regret it, young man.

If I should have to discipline you, say, for sending notes in school time to the young ladies, if—if, I should have to lay my hand on you——"

Here Walter laid a firm, strong arm on the young man's shoulder. With an irresistible grace, Ripley took the arm and wound it about his neck, saying, " I don't think I should fear you in the least."

" No," replied Walter, affectionately, drawing his handsome companion to himself, " no, you would have nothing to fear."

" David and Jonathan—ha! ha! " exclaimed Ripley, glancing into a looking-glass near them. When the laughter had subsided, Walter informed Ripley of his plans for the winter. Ripley was enthusiastic over it. " That is romantic, capital, splendid! Assistant-keeper of a lighthouse! Useful as well as ornamental! Money and the doing of good! Now look at me! I shall poke home—or what there is left of it—only my sister and I, living with an aunt—and it will be poke, poke, poke, all through the vacation. Really, I have thought seriously of taking a school——"

" No, you haven't! "

" You are right. I have not seriously thought of the matter, but—but it came into my mind, believe me. It would give me something to do."

"Wanted, a purpose!" said Walter, in the tone of a soliloquy.

"Who wants?"

"Oh! I was quoting something my uncle said. There are a good many of us who want a purpose. I have been puzzled myself, wondering what I would do. When I see some of the fellows of our class who say they are going to study medicine or law or for the ministry, I almost envy them. They know what they are going to do and life is a straight, clear path for them. You and I are bothered. We have not that definite purpose. I suppose though," added Walter, dropping his voice and speaking in a low, serious tone, as if to himself and for himself rather than because he had a listener, "I suppose we can do and ought to do this, attend to the present duty as well as we can, do what is right just now, knowing it will all bear on and help forward our final governing purpose when we do reach it——"

"Sermon!" cried Ripley, jestingly. "Not get into any scrapes, not go with any mischievous boys! Why, Logan, your chum, that steady old Rip Van Winkle, couldn't have done better. Why, you make me think of my sister Kate! I know she has a tender side and understands my weaknesses, and yet before I get through with her in talking, or she with me, she will break out into a sermon like that. Oh, there! you never saw my sister Kate! Don't you want to see her?"

He spoke with a tone of relief, as if thoroughly glad to have this opportunity of changing a disagreeable subject. He thrust his hand into a breast-pocket, pulled out a photograph and handed it to Walter.

"She is pretty!" said Walter, admiringly. "She does look like you and she does not."

"That's what people say."

"Glorious eyes, though!" commented Walter, gazing intently at eyes of the kind that have a very attractive way of directly, absorbingly giving themselves to you for the moment.

"What color, Rip?"

"Oh, black! No blue eyes in our family. Wish they were! I rather like sky-color."

"Well, blue, black, gray or hazel, there is no discount on those eyes, Rip. Yes, very pretty!"

And Walter continued to hold in his hand

the picture of the face whose eyes seemed to say, "I know you! Indeed, I have known you for some time. How do you do?"

At last, he handed the picture back to his companion.

"Yes, your sister has an excellent face."

"Thank you—I would like to have you see her. Well—I—must be going."

"I would stay in my room, if—if—you will let me advise you."

"Ha! ha! I don't doubt your sincerity, but——"

He closed the door after him, and it shut so promptly on the "but" that it seemed as if it must have been caught in that act of closing, and it was imprisoned, even jammed there in the door-crack.

Walter pulled his arm-chair in front of the fire, and sat down to think awhile. He had not spent many minutes there when he started up, exclaiming: "Why didn't I say it to him? What if he did call it a sermon? In this world, one must do his duty and not think of the fact whether another likes it or not. Wish I had!"

Walter's thoughts were going back to the subject of that needed purpose. He wished he had said something to Ripley on this one supreme subject, that of making God's will uppermost, seeking to know it and trying to do it every day. "Why didn't I put in a word? Didn't want to preach to him? We don't feel as ready to talk on that subject as we ought. Seems queer! Wish I had said something!" he murmured.

He did not feel at ease. Although he had seated himself again in his chair, he did not stay there long. He jumped up, seized his low-crowned black felt hat, and started for the door.

"I don't feel like leaving things this way," he murmured. "Some of the harum-scarum fellows will get hold of Ripley, perhaps influence him to drink, and get him to cutting up some absurd scrape to-night. I must go after him!"

He ran down the entry-stairs and then into the night.

"Black overhead!" he said, looking up. "Going to rain?"

The college windows, row after row, were bright with lights.

"Any light in Ripley Eaton's window?" he wondered, looking up at the illumined windows. "Don't see any—yes, there is one I think, but it shines faintly through some new, thick, red curtains he has had made for his windows. I'll go round there."

Along the narrow pavement of flagging-stone his footsteps were heard, echoing sharp in the damp night.

CHAPTER III.

BEFORE he turned into the entry leading to Ripley Eaton's room, he paused and glanced upward at the tall, dark chapel tower.

"Peaseley ought to be round if there's going to be mischief done to-night," thought Walter.

Nothing though seemed to be "round" unless it was the wind, which was vigorously blowing across the roof, trumpeting its notes about the belfry, moaning around the corners of the chapel.

"Music in the wind to-night to make up for any lack of it in the bell to-morrow morning! Wonder if this is the programme to-night, to take the tongue out of the bell, or, maybe, take the bell down from the tower, for that thing has been done and the bell thrown into the river! Ripley did not positively say the bell was to be troubled, to-night. Imagine those fellows climbing up that—tall tower, poking up into that windy belfry—my—I—I—

would like myself to see what I could do at climbing! I think—" He rubbed his hands and chuckled.

This voice came from one side of Walter's nature, the side that took an eager interest in anything adventurous. But there was another side and this had its turn and its say: "Pshaw! It doesn't seem a very manly thing squirming up there at midnight and then tug-ging at that old bell. Makes a lot of fuss for somebody. Peaseley will have a hard time, rushing around to wake the fellows up, and if the bell is carried off, or the tongue lost, why, there is a bill to be paid, and the fellows that cut up the mischief never pay for it. Catch them! Oh no, that is mean business. Then of course, their cutting-up-spirit gets to other fellows and provokes a kind of mischief-making all round—wonder how high that tower is! I believe there is a lightning-rod. I really believe I could climb it!"

A tall, heavy student went by and Walter thought he might be the bell-ringer, and he called out in an interrogative tone, "Peaseley?"

"No, Duncan!" was the reply.

"Humph!" thought Walter. "Duncan is a very different bird from Peaseley. Peaseley rings bells, and Duncan would be one to pitch them out of their tower. Wonder if I had better give Peaseley a hint of what is going on!"

In college, there existed two very different styles of studentship. It was the prevailing thought of one section that it was a crime almost to give any aid to the faculty in maintaining government and administering discipline. To furnish information to the faculty would stamp one with the brand, "faculty-dog." The brand was a black one. Neither by word or act, was the government to be assisted. The government was regarded as a contrivance for annoying students, for abridging their rights, and its methods were declared to be those of espionage and its spirit that of the despot. To mutilate the property of such a monster, to tear it down, bury it, burn it, was venial. To stay the process of tearing down, of burning up, of burying deep, was treason to the student family. Was a building on the college-grounds to be made a bonfire of? Terrible would be the disloyalty to a brother student if any one might throw a pail of water on the fire. If the bell in the high tower were to be deprived of its tongue, or if inverted it were to be filled with water on a winter night and then left to freeze up, sacrilegious was the act of one who would set the bell-ringer to watching for any invasion of his dominion. On the other hand, there was an element that regarded the faculty as friendly, and in college as their best friends, who did not believe in tale-bearing and yet did believe that the conservators of law and order at the head of the college ought to be sustained. They did not like to see property wantonly destroyed, or theft encouraged because it could be classified under the head of "a lot of fun," of roost-robbing and its after-part of a poultry supper in some room at midnight. They had no respect for lawlessness and believed it was a bad thing, not simply for the college in general but a worse thing for the lawless in particular.

"No sir!" said Walter, in low but firm tones. "I don't have any idea of encouraging Ripley or De Vere or any of that set—though—though—" here he tried in the dark, windy night to outline the high tower— "though I wouldn't object to climbing the thing myself, but I guess if I see Peaseley, I will drop him a hint to watch his belfry and ask me no questions why I dropped him that hint. If the bell is frozen up, 'twill make Peaseley an awful lot of work. It is not right. I will keep Rip out of this scrape if I can, for

the young fool will be sent home to rusticate
if—if——"

Walter now had turned into the entry of
the lower story of the hall where Ripley Eaton
and Peaseley roomed, and he hushed his
soliloquy.

Rap—rap—rap went Walter's knuckles upon
Peaseley's door.

No reply.

"Out! I'll try Rip's door."

Rap—rap—rap!

No answer.

"Out! Well—what is to be done?"

Walter did not wish to drop the matter
here, and learning at a neighboring room that
" Eaton had spoken about going down to the
railroad station," Walter hurriedly moved in
that direction.

"I will stop Rip, if I can," he resolved.
" How dark it is and this wind too is spiteful!"

He strode rapidly down the paths of the
college-yard, occasionally glancing at the different halls whose bright windows against the
night seemed like the sparkle of jewels set in
ebony. Passing out of the yard into a street
of the town, he was about to move to the left
in the direction of the railroad, when his eye
caught a sharp glitter to the right.

"Oh, that Simpson open? I thought the man was sick and his saloon shut up; no, a light is there. I believe there has been a change in the time of the arrival of the evening train, half an hour earlier, and if so, Simpson can tell me, and it will save me something of a walk. Too late to go down if the change to an earlier hour has been made," reasoned Walter. "Might have thought of that back at the college."

Simpson kept a restaurant. The law of the State and the sentiment of the community forbade all sales of liquor as a beverage; every thirsty student, though, knew that Simpson could and on the sly would tap a fountain of supply for their thirst. He had been sick and his saloon had been closed. Why then was that light suddenly, brilliantly breaking out of the one window of the little den? Walter curiously stepped forward to investigate. Nearing the window he saw two forms there in the light. Did one wear that broad brimmed, low-crowned hat which Ripley Eaton knew how to carry off so gracefully? Walter kept in the shadow of a tall fence adjoining the saloon and cautiously stole forward.

"Yes, it is Rip," he said. "Who is that with him?"

The second person's face was turned from Walter, but he could see the whole of the side of the face, and part of the neck also was exposed, and there Walter saw a scar.

The scar was very irregular.

"Looks like something open!" muttered Walter. "Why, isn't that the scar Uncle Boardman told about, a shark's mouth? Queer!"

The stranger now directly faced the light, and Walter saw the person's profile.

"Why, that is Rip Eaton's face over again!" he muttered. "Glad the wind makes such a racket or they would have heard me then," he added. "Oh, that eye! that is not Rip Eaton's eye!"

No indeed! The look of a tiger, a snake, a blood-hound, was in it.

"John De Vere!" said Walter.

He said it aloud in his astonishment. The two men heard the noise.

"What's that?" asked De Vere. "Any one speak to me?"

"Don't know! Wind, I guess," replied Ripley. "Don't be superstitious! Only the breeze!"

With an oath, De Vere told the wind to behave and not talk so much like a human being. Walter crouched close to the fence, prompted first to follow, and then moved to wait and watch events, knowing De Vere's dislike to him and thinking that any interference might madden De Vere, provoke Ripley, and so defeat Walter's purpose.

"I'll wait a bit and Rip may leave him. Anyway, if he don't, I can rush up any time and separate Rip from that fellow. What a bad pair of eyes he has got! He seems to be urging something on Rip. Let me see if I can catch anything. Won't the wind stop?"

Yes, the wind lulled, and he heard several clauses in an interesting conversation.

"Rip, Rip, don't be a fool! Come in with me!"

"No, John! It is not best. I will go to my room; I am not thirsty."

From this, Walter knew that De Vere was urging Ripley to go into the saloon and drink with him.

"If—if—" thought Walter, "he don't stop his coaxing, I'll—choke—him. I can, I know. I am strong enough. One glass, one mouthful of liquor, and Rip is gone. Hark!"

De Vere's voice had changed. It was now exceedingly pleasant, deep, musical. Walter saw De Vere's arm wound about Ripley's neck.

"It looks like a part of a snake's body," said Walter.

De Vere, for friendship's sake, the old friendship, asked Ripley to join him in a social glass. He smiled, coaxed, pleaded.

"That's the way the tempter looks!" thought Walter. "Like a basilisk, that evil glitter in his eyes! With that kind of voice, too, that soft way of pleading. I am just going to rush out and spoil his game. I'll try it if it does make Rip mad and spoil things. Yes, I'll rush!"

But somebody, even two somebodies, rushed before him. De Vere and Ripley slipped away into the dark somewhere and were gone.

"Why!" exclaimed the bewildered Walter, "didn't they go through a door into the saloon?" No! He went in the direction of their disappearance and came to the corner of the building. Then he remembered there was a passageway at one side of Simpson's den. He poked down this passageway, if such, for he could not tell by his sight what he had entered. Why did he not hear a door close if they had gone into the saloon? Was there a door? He felt with his hands along the wall, but could find no door-frame. He pounded on the wall the same as if he had found a door.

Only the wind answered him. He now went back to the front of the saloon. That was in darkness.

"Light gone? Well, a door is here. I'll find that, and bang on it," declared Walter.

He did bang savagely.

"Why, what is wanted?" said a smooth, slippery voice which Walter recognized as Simpson's, the fat, greasy, red-faced Simpson.

"Who is it?"

"Plympton."

Simpson's voice changed at once. It hardened. It became rasping, unwilling, unaccommodating. Simpson did not like the set to which Walter belonged. He put them all down as "stiff and pious," and they were hostile to his favorite practices.

"Well, what do you want?" growled Simpson.

"I want Eaton. He has just gone into your building."

"I wish you fellers would let us alone. If you think Eaton is here, come in and see."

"I can hardly see if you have blown out your light."

"You are at liberty to look in for yourself, sir," remarked Simpson, with a disagreeable suavity. At the same time he scratched a match and held up its small, twinkling light. Nothing could be seen save a dirty counter, a few benches, and a show-case thinly supplied with cake and candy.

"Eaton and De Vere are both in your house, and you know it," said Walter.

Simpson had lighted a dirty oil lamp. "Oh, if you know so much, then there is no use in my trying to tell you anything," said Simpson, sarcastically.

"Won't you tell Eaton I would like to see him, please?"

"I haven't seen Eaton."

"Eaton!" shouted Walter. "Rip!"

"Come, come!" cried Simpson, scowling and shaking his head. "This is my house."

But Walter was persistent in his search, and he called once more, "Eaton!"

Did he hear a scornful laugh behind a wall?

If he could have looked through lathes and plaster, he would have witnessed an interesting scene. Ripley, who had heard Walter's voice and at once guessed the object of the eager call, tried to reach a door into the outer saloon and meet Walter. De Vere threw one arm about Ripley, and coaxingly yet firmly detained him. With the other arm he lifted a glass of liquor and then pressed it to Ripley's lips. After that contact, Ripley's strength vanished. His will-power seemed to be withered as by the touch of death. In the dirty pen without, Walter stood obstinately waiting. Did he hear a mocking laugh behind that wall? He knew it was useless to stay longer, and he rushed out doors. As he crossed the street and hurried into the college-yard, he shook his head, and muttered "Didn't get him! Too bad!"

And the wind seemed to say it, "Too bad!" And the very night seemed to look it, "Too bad!"

The next morning no college-bell was rung.

CHAPTER IV.

A BELL WITHOUT A TONGUE.

THERE was much commotion the next morning simply because there was no commotion in the belfry of the chapel tower. Never did silence stir up so much noise of debate, of censure, of strife.

There was an upsetting of all the usual order of things about the college, in the homes of the quiet burghers, and in the shops of the traders. Good Aunt Dunham, who had kept boarders from the college ever since she could walk—so it seemed to her—and who generally waited until she heard the chapel bell fairly under way " afore startin' things for breakfast," made a " fearful mistake " this morning and everything did get into such a stew. Uncle Simon Toothaker, who did not generally open his store until Peaseley had rung the bell, was so very late this morn-ing that he found almost a mob about his store door, customers waiting here in wrath and wondering why he did not turn up.

Tombs, the milkman, coming up from the "meaders" with his milk-cans, would jog along through the extended stretch of pines beyond the colleges until he caught the tinkle of the chapel bell, and then he would stir up his dobbin into a business gait and arrive in season at the houses of his customers. This morning he jogged and poked, thinking he might hear the bell any moment, jogged and poked till he was seen at last whipping his innocent beast into an insane clatter only to arrive at his customers' doors in time to get—a first-class scolding. The most pathetic case of dis-location of arrangements, was that of Patty Dunham. She had told Peaseley's brother, who was also a college student and rooming with Peaseley, that she would be at the stile in her mother's fence to say good-bye to him on his way to the early train. This younger brother had asked that favor.

"I am going off to keep school, Patty, and perhaps you'll come to the stile to say good-bye."

"Yes," she said, demurely, "when the chapel bell rings I'll be at the stile."

And the bell did not ring! If it had rung and those two young hearts had met, the schoolmaster-elect would have said something interesting then, and in its effect reaching far into the future. As it was, Patty saw what he saw, an empty stile, and Patty stayed to be an old maid and helped her mother " take college boarders."

Inside of college walls, the disturbance was more immediate and emphatic. From door to door, Peaseley rushed frantically, banging away and shouting, " Prayers ! "

Walter heard him stormily invading his entry. Lying in bed and waiting for the drowsy clang of that herald in the belfry, yet knowing it might not be heard, he caught the sound of Peaseley's voice and sprang out of bed. He rushed to the door. He thrust his head out.

" What is the matter, Peaseley ? " he asked.

" Matter ! ask the bell ! " was the gruff answer, and the messenger stamped up-stairs to another row of rooms.

" There was a good deal going on last night," remarked a neighbor, opening a door and abruptly running a frowzy head out of the door of his room.

" I dare say," replied Walter.

" I know so," replied the neighbor. " Fearful yelling in the college-yard. That De Vere came up to your room."

"De Vere?" said Walter, in astonishment. "When was that?"

"Oh, you were out."

Walter had not gone directly to his room from Simpson's, but had haunted Ripley Eaton's quarters, hoping Ripley might soon be there.

"What did De Vere want?" asked Walter.

"I do not know. He said nothing to me. I only saw him coming out of your room. Had a paper in his hand."

Walter only remarked, "Don't understand that," and closed his door. He lighted a lamp and looked about his room.

"That fellow here last night? I wouldn't trust him with anything I owned. Anything missing?" wondered Walter. "What right had he to enter my room? I will lock it another time."

He was very confident that he had left upon his table a copy of a certain local sheet called the *Patriot*. Where had it gone?

"Can't find it! I will look that up," said Walter, "when I have come back from breakfast."

Before breakfast, in Walter's day, came prayers and recitation, also. Into the chapel now dropped the students, one by one, by twos, by threes, summoned by Peaseley's impatient

stentorian voice. There was an exchanging
of significant winks, of sly glances toward the
corner in which rose the tall, heavy tower.
Walter looked over to the seats usually occupied by Ripley and others whom Walter
guessed might have had a hand in silencing
the occupant of the belfry.

"Why, Ripley is there!" said Walter.

Not far away was De Vere.

"Those scamps in their places?"

Yes, Walter, and looking very fresh and
bright. Ripley's face was brilliant in its
beauty. He looked pale, but it was the ap-
pearance rather of one who had been bending over his books for two hours by the light
of an old-fashioned oil lamp.

Those who came in to prayers late, their hair
dishevelled, their coats hardly buttoned up,
were the "steady old men." Those credited
as "larks" and likely to be engaged in every
mean little scrape, were promptly on hand,
their toilettes carefully made, their locks
brushed, their faces studious and decorous.

"If this isn't funny!" concluded Walter.
"Why, I begin to feel as if I or Peaseley
must have been the ringleader in last night's
affair, as if Ripley had been laboring with me,
and as if De Vere, in Simpson's hole, tried to

keep me from the intoxicating cup. This is funny!"

To others, also, it seemed funny. Among the members of the faculty it was tacitly agreed that the perpetrators of this unmusical crime probably would be sleepy, would be late at everything and it was quite probable that in their classes their inability to recite would be conspicuous. Such cases were to be noticed and subsequently investigated. But the cases tardy in their arrival and deficient in their recitations were those of steady and usually studious men. Ripley Eaton and De Vere were both suspected by their instructors, and both of these ran the gauntlet of the classroom with special success. Things did seem to be going by contraries. But, "things" sometimes in this life even, will finally and strangely go straight. In this case, what was a snarled, and tangled, and knotted skein, was separated and straightened after this fashion.

Walter and the bell-ringer, at noon, were looking into the chapel tower.

"I tried," said Walter, looking up the tall, cold, stony shaft, "to give you a hint of this. It was a guess on my part, not knowing, of course, definitely, but I thought it was too bad you should be bothered. I did not really know, of course——"

" I hope not."

" But my hint did not get to you. Last time I was at your room, it was pretty late."

" Well, I was out with my brother at a party down town—a party made for him as he was going away—and I came home pretty near midnight. Tower was quiet enough then."

" Did they take all the ladders down ? " asked Walter, still looking up the gray stone tower.

" Took everything down, and the bell-rope and the tongue. They must have worked hard."

" Wonder where the things are ? "

" Don't know. We shall put up ladders after dinner and carry up something that will answer for a tongue and have a bell-rope in place. We are going to get some kind of music out of the bell for prayers to-night."

" But how did you get up to know about the tongue ? "

" Oh, there is a lightning-rod ! "

" And you climbed that ? You made good time to get up there and back and rouse us up for prayers."

"I had to make good time. No other way."

"Then you have no idea when it was done, or what they did with the things?"

"None at all."

They came to the chapel door and stood on the broad, massive steps of stone.

"What is that?" asked Peaseley, who had keen, penetrating eyes under bushy eyebrows, and he now directed that sharp vision toward the ground outside the walls of granite.

"Nothing, only the ground is somewhat disturbed there."

Peaseley was not satisfied with this answer. He stepped back to a closet in the tower, and taking out a heavy crow-bar, carried it outside to the base of the walls and rammed it down into this patch of disturbed earth.

"What are you up to, old man?" asked Walter.

Peaseley made no reply, but gave another lunge and this was a frantic one.

"What are you doing?" asked one of several students, who came up a broad path, leading to the chapel door.

"Going to dig for gold?" asked a second.

Peaseley's eagerness was now intense. He knitted his forehead, scowled, panted, set his

teeth, lifted high the bar, and with a tremendous effort rammed it into the earth.

"Hark!" he said, excitedly. "Hear that?"
He plunged and struck again.

"There! Hear it?" he asked, triumphantly.

"What does it sound like?"

He did not wait for an answer to his question, but rushed back to the closet and now
brought forward a spade.

"Say, Peaseley!" whispered Walter. "You
think you struck the tongue of the bell?"

Peaseley nodded his head.

He furiously worked that spade and pro-
duced the tongue of the bell! Amid the
shouts of all he held it up.

"There!" he exclaimed. "I suppose the
weasels who put this away thought nobody
would look for it under the very tower itself
and near the path where so many travel, but
they left the earth too ragged like."

"What have you got? Not the tongue of
the bell?" inquired Prof. Sampson, who happened along just then. "Indeed, indeed! But
what is that paper about it? Wrapped up
quite carefully! Experts did it. Oh, Mr. De
Vere! I beg your pardon!"

De Vere, seemingly ignorant of the nature

of the discovery, had come to the outskirts of the crowd, and taking a hasty squint at Peaseley and his booty, made some abrupt, angry, profane expression, and would have hurried off but Prof. Sampson had awkwardly bumped into him and checked him.

"I beg your pardon!" again said the professor. "We are all so glad to see that runaway tongue home again."

"I don't care anything about it," said De Vere impatiently. "I know nothing about it——"

He was interrupted by Peaseley's remark as the newspaper was removed from the tongue: "If here isn't a copy of the *Patriot!*"

"The *Patriot!* The *Patriot!*" cried the students. "The *Patriot* did it!"

"What?" asked Peaseley, in tones of surprise. "This newspaper has on it the name of W. Plympton!"

The crowd pressed up to the bell-ringer. The excitement was intensified. Prof. Sampson said, "Let's see the paper! Plympton, that your paper?"

"Ha! ha!" said an angrily sneering voice. "Plympton took the tongue down!"

De Vere made this bold charge, but it was then taken as banter and not anything serious,

"You don't mean it," said Prof. Sampson. "Plympton is not up to or down to such mean tricks."

"This was an up-trick, Professor," said a student, looking toward the belfry.

The laugh following this humor diverted the attention of the group from De Vere's charge, but Walter's loud tones now recalled all straying thoughts; "It is false, and you know it, sir."

As he spoke, he faced De Vere. As De Vere spoke, the latter disdained to notice Walter.

"I mean it, Professor Sampson. The paper wrapped about that tongue belongs to Plympton. He does not deny it. It has his name upon it as a subscriber. He is the high-minded patriot in this case. What more direct proof can there be than the finding of Plympton's property with the bell?"

"I can't think it is so, but it looks strange," remarked Prof. Sampson.

"If it were my paper, I should regard it as a hard case against *me*," said De Vere, looking contemptuously toward Walter.

Walter's face was red with indignation. He could not seem to reply to De Vere's bold, audacious, reckless, shameful charge. Walter was dumfounded.

"Look at his face!" cried De Vere. "Guilt is there."

Walter found his tongue at last. He stepped forward and faced De Vere. He was larger and taller than De Vere, and looked leonine as he confronted his evil-eyed adversary. He laid his strong hand on De Vere, and spoke under excitement but his voice did not break.

"De Vere, if I believed in fighting, I would thrash you for your impudence——"

"No, no!" cried Prof. Sampson, bustling forward. "Stop, stop!"

He was a little man—why were the big name and the meagre body thus allied? By the side of Walter he looked like a kid skipping up to a horse. "I—I command you both—de—de—SIST !"

"I shan't touch him, though he deserves a whipping. I say to his face his assertion is a mean, contemptible lie."

Here Walter stretched out his long, vigorous arm, and he shook his fore-finger emphatically. His voice became clear. His attitude was commanding. One of the students afterwards told him that he never spoke so effectively on any college platform as in his little speech at the foot of the chapel-tower.   He now continued: "I charge Mister De Vere——"

Sometimes the use of a title by raising a standard of comparison, makes any object named after it very small. The "Mister," when "De Vere" was brought close up to it, threw into a very damaging shadow the person owning that name.

Walter repeated his words, his voice rising and echoing, "I charge Mister De Vere with entering my room last evening when I was away, and carrying this paper out of it, and I can prove——'

De Vere was now looking up, both in anger and astonishment. Walter continued, "I can prove that he entered my room. I will produce the person who saw him coming out having a paper in his hand, and it was a *Patriot* I missed from my table, and I believe that is the one—and hold on!" Walter laid his hand on De Vere who was attempting some kind of a reply, and also turning away as if to go. "Hold on, you infamous slanderer, hold on! It was the paper published on the twelfth of the month, if you will look it up and if my charge be correct—ah, there is John Hastings now! John Hastings saw De Vere come out of my room! John!"

Walter was calling to a student hurrying toward this excited and rapidly-growing gathering. De Vere in the meantime was trying to squirm out of Walter's grasp, sputtering also and denying Walter's charge, saying again and again, "I should think it was enough when one finds his property near a thing like that bell-tongue, to show who had a hand in burying it."

Prof. Sampson was declaiming away in swelling, important tones to another professor who had arrived. Peaseley was saying, "It was published the twelfth." The crowd was murmuring, making its own eager comments. Walter's hurried appeal to Hastings, Peaseley's words about the twelfth, De Vere's sneering, wrathful gibber, the professor's learned proclamation, John Hastings' assent to Walter's assertion, the talk of the crowd—all were interrupted, dwarfed, set aside by Peaseley's abrupt exclamation, "Why, why, what is this in this paper? See here!" He repeated it, he shouted, "See here!" The talk ceased.

He held up an object that sparkled. It was a ring.

A diamond was embedded in it. It flashed brilliantly as a ray of sunshine stole down and touched it and laid bare its heart of fire. If any one had watched De Vere's face, the play of emotions across that sardonic countenance would have fascinated a spectator as much as the star-like sparkle of the diamond. But De Vere was not watched. His face swept by successive plays of the feeling of surprise, then anger, then perplexity, had a lessened interest for the crowd just then. Walter, honest-faced, noble in stature, had turned toward the ring.

"Where—how—whose—" Prof. Sampson was stammering forth.

"Whose?" answered Peaseley, turning up the ring so that he could see the inside of this band of beauty, and reading an inscription slowly. "It says J—Jo—John D—e V—ere!"

"And," said Walter, "as Mister De Vere himself has said, isn't property found that way proof——"

"Let me have it!" De Vere was shouting. "I don't know how it——"

"Hur-rah! Hur-rah for Plympton!" somebody was shouting.

It was never known who called for these cheers. It was asserted that the voice was Prof. Sampson's. No matter, the cheers were as heartily given as if it were known who had called for them.

"I believe you," the professor also said, shaking hands heartily with Walter Plympton. Others came up with like eagerness to proffer their assurance of confidence, and did anybody cry, "The trap set for Plympton caught the proof of the man who did trouble the bell"? That was not said.   It was the truth, however. De Vere meant to involve Walter in the affair and thus overshadow him with a cloud of suspicion.   He did not purpose to leave his ring in the newspaper.   That accidentally slipped off his finger while he was hurriedly digging a hole in the dark to receive the stolen tongue.   The ring fell into the trap he had carefully made ready for Walter, while the owner at night was fussing and fuming, panting and swearing, furiously digging.   De Vere's college course this time was peremptorily ended.   His connection with the college was absolutely severed.

Ripley's association also with the affair was discovered.   De Vere was the ringleader in the conspiracy against the bell.   He meant to rob it of its tongue the night of his return and thus signalize that return.   He did not anticipate detection though.   The ringleader having been discovered, it was like removing the keystone of an arch.   The other parts of the structure of this conspiracy dropped into a speedy and open disgrace. How, outsiders did not know. They were aware that somehow, the allies of De Vere were discovered. Of these, Ripley was the one first sentenced to suspension from college. He carried the load lightly among his college-mates. He mingled freely with them, jested and laughed about his fate, went to see Walter Plympton, and was prepared to joke over it in Walter's room. He did not find Walter there. In turn, Walter went to see him and Ripley was out. So the two did not meet before Ripley's exile home. This came speedily.

"Ha! I don't care!" was Ripley's thought. "Rather nice to be noticed." A set of reckless chaps whose admired centre had been De Vere, now transferred to Ripley their admiration and also their bills for treating. They followed him to the station when he took the train home. They surrounded him with a chorus of three cheers, gave him a handsome bouquet of flowers, said a little speech in which he was entitled the hero of the *bell* and the admiration of all *belles*. Ripley rather enjoyed it, or fancied that he did. He went off in a bewildering daze. It was pleasant to be noticed.

"Ah, the conductor smiles! Of course, that affair of the bell he regards as only a trifling escapade. Good joke, that's all," thought Ripley, sinking back comfortably in his seat.

As the cars rattled away from the college-town, it not only went down under the horizon's rim of trees and fields, but its life, its details of duty and pleasure, sank also. Another subject rose up in Ripley's thoughts and that was " Home," and next to it " Kate." One feature of college surroundings, though, remained, and there came up into the scenery of this new life, rising high above its horizon, just this object, a tower of stone with a belfry, and standing out sharp and distinct against the light beyond, a bell in the belfry!

"Nonsense!" thought Ripley, wincing in his seat. · "What have the people at home got to do with that subject? It's none of their business."

Notwithstanding his remonstrance the stone tower rose higher, the belfry swelled larger, the bell turned over and showed that the tongue was wanting.

"Next station is Perley!" shouted the brakeman.

"Why, that is home!" thought Ripley,

and he began to gather up his travelling bags and umbrella and college canes. "Where is my bell? Oh, nonsense! I don't mean that! Wish the old bell was further! Where is my handkerchief?"

When he alighted at the station, it seemed a very prosy place and the people very common-looking.

"Why, Ripley! You—you—home!" said a voice, pleasant, paternal and rather prim. "When I was in college, they did not let us out so soon. Nobody sick at home to bring you here, I trust? Indeed!"

A white neck-tie and a pair of blandly beam-ing spectacles went with the voice, and Ripley needed not to look twice or even once to know that it was Dr. Avery, the rector of the old parish in which he had been brought up.

"Oh—ah—you see—I—we are all very well, sir, I hope. Glad to see you! Thank—thank you!" and Ripley rushed off as fast as he courteously could. He did not rush far. He bumped against an obstacle that good-naturedly said, "Look out!" Ripley did not need to inquire the name of this obstruction, for he recognized the voice of the fat old hack-driver, David Simes, who laughed as he said:

"You—you home, Ripley? Wasn't looking

for ye, sure! Ha! ha! Some of them fellers down your way been trying to improve on the music of the old bell by taking its tongue out! Ha! ha! Now if they would try that on some old gossips here in Perley—ha! ha! Well, it would improve them, ha! ha!"

"There are my checks, David," Ripley replied with dignity. "I'll go home in your hack."

Looking neither to right or left, but darting straight on, like a needle in swift motion, Ripley went to the carriage. Something hard, crooked, was laid on his shoulder as he was about entering the carriage. He looked up. He saw the big crook of an umbrella-handle and behind the crook was the sharp featured face of "Miss Nabby Pelham," one of those Perley gossips that David thought could be improved.

"Naow! You runnin' off with David and forsakin' your best friend who knowed you when you was a leetle, tinty, tonty baby?"

Two young ladies were going by and "Miss Nabby" turned a moment to inspect them. Ripley heard them laughing and one said, "That's that Rip Eaton! Trouble at college, I believe."

He was halting on the carriage-step, blushing confusedly, coldly bowing, while warmly, enthusiastically wishing "Miss Nabby" was at the bottom of the Atlantic. But she was not in that retired locality. She was just there, on a Perley sidewalk, in time to hear this last piece of news. She pricked up her ears. She trembled with excitement to think she might grab a bigger piece of news through Ripley, who was now rushing into the carriage and slamming the door after him.

"Oh—oh—Ripley! she screamed, running her big-clawed umbrella-handle through the open window of the carriage-door. "What's that fuss down at the college? You was not in it, I know, and I shall say so—wherever I go. When I tell of it, now, you may depend on *me-ee*."

Ripley could stand it no longer: "Miss Nabby, you don't want me to have brain trouble, typhoid fever, say?"

"Why, no!"

"Well——"

David was here clucking to his horses and saying, "Git-git-up!"

Ripley with thankful fervor said, "Good-day," and Miss Nabby was left standing on the sidewalk, pointing the big-clawed handle at the retreating carriage and saying, "Massy! He's sick!"

She went away and reported everywhere that "Ripley Eaton had some kind of brain trouble at college and was acting real looney."

But Ripley's most dreaded trouble was yet in the future, not far off, but quite nigh, eight hundred feet away, seven, as the carriage rolled on, six, five, four, three, two, one—and when the carriage halted at the door of the old Eaton homestead, Ripley knew the trouble was just there, as a girl with large black eyes, and lustrous through crying, met him at the door, and said:

"Why—Ripley! The president has written us about it."

She held up a letter that carried the post-mark of the old college-town, and then burst into tears.

"Oh, sis, it is not so much of an affair——"

Somebody else just arriving, her head bound up in a camphor-saturated handkerchief, seemed to think "it" was something of an affair. This was Aunt Prissy, who laid her hand on his shoulder and then broke out into a wail, crying, "Why-y-y, Ripley!" Such a miserable being, this Ripley! It seemed to him as if everybody he met, when he went out doors, said in surprise and horror, "Why—Ripley!"

Strange, how unpleasant were all bell-notes now. Each bell said, perhaps in high treble, perhaps in deep bass, " This is the young man who took a tongue out of the mouth of one of our family! The wretch!"

He had a queer experience one Sunday afternoon at church. The rector's sermon was slowly but steadily going on. He was saying very soberly : " In this life we make mistakes, and quite often foolish ones. When we make one of these, we look back and wonder why we ever did it. If, before doing it, we had only looked *ahead* and considered the effect of our poor, foolish doings, the world would, quite likely, be saved much trouble and we be spared needless pain."

Just then the tower of the church took it into its lofty head to make a reply, and in deep, solemn, sepulchral notes, the big iron bell boomed, " Yes, yes, yes, yes!" It was four o'clock.

" Oh dear!" thought Ripley. " It is always that bell scrape."

Kate closely watched her brother. She was not sorry to see his moody discontent. She knew he was busily, seriously thinking.

" It will do him good," she said, one afternoon, as she looked out of the window. " Yes, thought will do him good. If I can only keep him under its influence! Ah, who is that?"

She saw a young man run up the steps leading to the front door. She heard him ask the servant, " Is Mr. Ripley Eaton in ?"

" No sir," was the answer.

The stranger went slowly, hesitatingly down the steps.

" Ah! I don't like his face! Bad!" thought Kate. " Who is it ? "

She felt like one who is walking in the fields. Suddenly, an ugly snake twists its way out of the grass and writhes along before her. Kate was impulsive.

" Margaret!" she said to the servant, " If that man ever comes again and you see who it is, don't open the door! "

" Yes, mum."

That evening the rector's bible-class met at the church. In announcing it, he had said from the chancel: " Some one may want to stop after it and they will allow me to say a word to them on the subject of personal religion, on the question of their entire duty to the Church of God. Confirmation soon will be here."

Kate saw Ripley's earnest look as these words were uttered.

" Puss," he exclaimed, when at home, calling her by a pet name, " I—I—heard what
was said about the bible-class. Think Doctor
Avery would let the ' prodigal son ' attend ? "

" Oh ! ' Prodigal son,' who—who——? "

" This one, that all the town is staring at ? "

" Oh, Rip ! You need not call him that
way——"

" Yes, that is his name. Will Doctor Avery
let him come ? "

" Rip, do you want to go, really ? "

" Why, yes, I rather felt like it."

" Then, Rip, do go ; yes, do ! Now, **won't**
you ? "

" Yes, I rather think I will."

He had not been out of the house five minutes, when the door-bell was rung, and its
sharp tinkle echoed in the long, old-fashioned
hall.

" That man ! " whispered Margaret, rushing
into the parlor.

" What man ? " said Kate.

" One you told me not to let in."

" Then, *don't* you ! "

The bell was rung peremptorily the next
time, violently and impudently the third time.
Then the snake crawled off, slowly twisting
down the steps.

The next minute Kate was regretful.

"What if he should find Ripley out on the street, undecided about the church, and he should influence Ripley not to go in? Oh dear!"

He found Ripley, and in this way. Ripley stood at a corner, not far from the church and not far from a saloon.

"There goes the bell, and hark!" he said.

He heard the discordant thump of piano music in the saloon. At first, the invitation from the saloon repelled him.

"No, I have been fool long enough. That makes me think of Simpson's old hole at college. I am going to church, to-night!" said Ripley, resolutely.

He turned and advanced two steps toward the church door.

A hand suddenly was laid on his shoulder.

A voice said with a peculiar, powerful effect:

"Rip, come back! This way!"

Ripley turned.

"You here?"

"Yes, come!"

It was De Vere, and with De Vere he went.

CHAPTER V.

AT SEAL'S HEAD.

"WONDER where Tom Walker is?" soliloquized Walter Plympton on a November afternoon, as he sat on a fragment of a mast, that had drifted ashore, and looked off toward the lighthouse at Seal's Head. "He wrote he would meet me here at the old fishhouse on Perkins' Point and take me to the light. He is not here though."

Tom Walker certainly was not there. Behind Walter, who was sitting on that mast, thrown up by the wrecking ocean, was the black fishhouse with its nominally one door in a southern wall, but really half a dozen "cracks" would have made good door frames and through these the wind whistled dolefully.

Before Walter was a slope of dark gray sand, that the receding tide had exposed. Beyond this beach was a sweep of chilling, uneasy November water. On the outer edge of this cold, lustreless sea, rose the lighthouse. It was a tall, symmetrical, heavy shaft of granite. At its side, in very positive contrast, was a red fog-signal tower, round and squatty. Two tall pipes projected from its roof. Out there in the cold, restless sea, it was good to catch sight of this lighthouse tower. It suggested human life there, vigilant, on the watch against the vicissitudes of night and storm.

At the left of the lighthouse was a knoll in the sea, its brown base whitened by the ceaseless play of the surf. In summer there was a fringe of green along the top of this knoll. This was a crown of the wild, stout, coarse beach-grass. The people on shore knew it as "T'other Seal." It was the companion of the ledge on which the lighthouse stood. This ledge at low water, in the old days, when unoccupied, resembled the head of a seal thrust above the surface and looking across the wide, cold waste of water. "T'other Seal" had never been occupied by any structure. Its merits as a lighthouse foundation had often been discussed, and among some of the older fishermen it had its champions, who by the hour would stormily discuss the good points of "T'other Seal," insisting that the lighthouse ought to "have gone thar." It never went "thar." Only a humble patch of green beach-grass made its abode on "T'other Seal."

It was out over this watery waste, which the house of stone at Seal's Head was supposed at night to light up, that Walter Plympton was looking, wondering how he could get to Seal's Head if Tom Walker, the assistant-keeper at the light, should not appear and his boat appear with him.   Walter sat on the old mast, kicking up the sand with the toe of his boot, and wondering If he could not borrow a boat somewhere and go alone to the light. "Only a mile to row!" he thought. Suddenly a "Hul-lo!" echoed in his ears.

A heavy hand came down on Walter's shoulder.

Walter turned and there was Tom, the same rough, good-natured, hearty Tom Walker as of old.

"Walter, how *are* you?"

"First rate, Tom; how are *you?* Shake hands!"

The two men shook with an energy that seemed great enough to crack a nut getting between their clinching hands.

"I was looking round for your boat, Tom."

"It is on t'other side of the Pint."

"Is it? Then I see why I didn't see it."

"Zackly! Step over this way."

The two men crossed to the other side of

the point, where a small sailboat was waiting by the shore, uneasily pulling at its rope as if anxious to lift its one white wing and be away. It was off very soon.

"They're 'spectin' you over at the light, Walter. Your aunt is a gittin' up a special supper for you. Your Uncle Boardman and me say we don't 'spect any sich attentions to us. My! she's kept us a-fishin' for cunners off the rocks, I don't know how long to-day."

"Well, here is somebody that will appreciate it all."

"Oh! your Uncle Boardman and me will appreciate it, too. We're comin' in for our share. Well, young man, I give up my place to you, to-morrow. Jest stay over to-night, to help you start things. Fact is, Walter, I have a trouble, not ser'ous, you know, not ser'ous, but needs a leetle lookin' after, and I can do it by takin' a good long squar' furlough on shore. That's the long and short of it."

To prove this need, Tom gave a little cough.

"You're wise, Tom," said Walter, in an approving tone.

"Now, Walter," resumed Tom, "I like your uncle's sperrit. Folks wonder what a man at his time of life wants to keep a light for. All

are interested, you know, and all give an opinion.　Couldn't live unless t'other folks gave an
opinion on every breath we draw.　He takes
their remarks all in good part, and tells 'em he
wanted suthin' to do——"

"Yes, it does show a good spirit.　Fact is,
in this world, we all need to have something
definite and decided to do.　We all need a
purpose.　That would bring a lot of bewildered people out of their troubles if they had
one strong, overmastering purpose to do something.　That would make the weak strong,
drive the devil out of the hearts of the idle,
keep old age off and help sick folks get
well."

"Hoo-rah, hoo-rah!" shouted Tom.　"The
minister couldn't do better.　Now I told you
what I was thinkin' about.　Winter is comin'
on and the weather will be rough and I know
I can't do duty at the light, so I'm goin' to
put into port for repairs.　Now what your
uncle did, has set me to thinkin' whether I
hadn't better do something, some light kind of
indoors work.　And I have got a chance to
make brooms—learned a leetle of the trade
once—and instead of mopin' over the fire, my
marm says she will fix up a place for me, and
I am goin' to be at work.　Couldn't do it

always, you know. 'Twould be like tyin' up a sea-gull in a cheese-box. But, while I am in-doors, I'm goin' to have suthin' to do."

"That's it, that's it, Tom, you are right. But whew! How that lighthouse looms up! Do you know I was never inside it? That's a beautiful piece of work."

"Lovely for the kind, Walter. We'll be there soon. Topsy is a-flyin'."

"The name of your boat?"

"Yes, Topsy. She's small, but she's got the go in her. A reg'lar leetle witch, I call her."

"That outside red tower is for the fog-signal. isn't it?"

"Yes, you go from one to t'other, from the signal-tower to the lighthouse by a covered way. You will see how it is."

"We land at the signal-tower?"

"Yes."

The boat flew on. At last Tom cried, "See there! There are two in the door, ain't there?"

"Yes, Uncle Boardman and Aunt Lydia?"

"Sartin! No others. They're waitin' for us."

"I have a good appetite for that supper."

"Ha! ha! Your Aunt Lyddy will look arter that. Smart old lady! Smart as a steel trap!"

"She has got a purpose."

"I tell ye! She often speaks about it. Says she needed suthin' well as Boardman to stir her up. No sleepy bones there!"

The Topsy was spinning over the waters. Had not Topsy a purpose? The little waves rose up as if to stop her. She went over them as if round rollers, laid specially for her convenience. The lighthouse and its companion tower rose higher and higher. Every detail came out into more and more distinct outline, the lantern of the great tower, the long fog trumpets, the doorway.

And in the doorway, who were there?

"Your Uncle Boardman, see?"

"Yes, he's a-waving his hand!"

"And if your Aunt Lyddy isn't a-wavin' suthin' in her hand! It's the fryin' pan! Hoorah!"

The young men gave three ringing cheers while Uncle Boardman looked down, and his face beamed as he shouted, "Welcome!"

"Welcome!" screamed Aunt Lydia. Again she waved that magical frying pan.

She could not have waved a sceptre more significant of woman's power when confronted by a hungry man's appetite.

The sail of that witch, the Topsy, was

dropped and the boat laid alongside the signal-tower. It was high tide. The water swept all about the two towers. By a ladder closely secured to the wall, one climbed to the signal-tower door. This door was on the landward side of the tower. A door on the opposite side would have been exposed in an easterly storm to the full sweep of the heavy Atlantic billows.

"Going to tie your boat down here?" asked Walter.

"Yes, I think so. It's a mild night. Won't be much of a sea to trouble the boat."

The two young men climbed to the door of the signal-tower.

"Welcome to our ocean-home!" cried Aunt Lydia. "Yes, a thousand times welcome!" And the frying pan was cordially flourished.

"Glad to see you, Walter, yes, I be," said Uncle Boardman.

The honest light-keeper and his sprightly wife gave the college-student a reception that he declared was worth the taking of his journey. They went through the signal-tower and reached a narrow covered way under which Walter could hear the strong restless swash of the sea. This passage may have been ten or twelve feet in length. It led to the first room

in the lighthouse, the tank and store-room.
Here was a large tank under an iron lid in the
floor, holding a supply of fresh water. In this
room were accumulated various stores for the
comfort of those keeping the light. Walter
noticed with interest a pile of glass flasks filled
with a chemical preparation.

"Want to know what those are?" asked
Uncle Boardman, taking up a flask. "That is a
hand-grenade in case of fire. You just smash
it into a fire; the chemical escapes and puts
out the flames."

" Pretty solid walls you have here to keep
the sea out, uncle."

"Amazin'! A foot and a half of brick and
a solid four foot of stone. Some heft and se-
curity there!"

They went up over an iron staircase whose
only fault was its color, a cheerless black.

"Do you have this style of staircase in the
light, uncle?"

"Sartin! That is underneath. Don't want
anything that will burn. You will see what I
mean."

They were at the top of the first staircase.

"And here is my kingdom!" triumphantly
exclaimed Aunt Lydia, introducing the party
to the second room or kitchen.

"Yes, your aunt's kingdom. She is Queen Lyddy here," said Uncle Boardman.

"This is homelike!" said Walter, in his enthusiastic way.

"*I* think so, too!" remarked Uncle Boardman.

Aunt Lydia said nothing, but her bright, black eyes kept snapping, snapping, and she showed that she was silently enjoying Walter's enthusiastic praise.

Walter stopped after crossing the threshold. He caught a familiar, sober, dignified "tick-k! tick-k."

"You don't mean to say you have got your old eight-day clock that stood in the kitchen, out here in this lighthouse?" asked Walter.

"She speaks for herself," replied Uncle Boardman, pointing at the tall, old home-relic now standing opposite the stove in this light-house kitchen. "Your Aunt Lyddy would have it. I told her it would be risky a-histin' it up, and where she would stand it, I couldn't see. However, the old clock is here, and going to stay!"

Aunt Lydia did not say anything. Walter spoke for her: "Well, seems to me I would give up the very chairs, and sit on the floor, rather than give up the clock. Out here, you don't want things to seem just like a lighthouse, and if the old kitchen clock doesn't upset the usual order of things and make it seem like home, then what would do it?   Now, you say, this is not a lighthouse kitchen.   This is Aunt Lydia Blake's home."

Aunt Lydia's eyes snapped sharper and brighter, and she now spoke: "That is my idee, ezackly.   I had the idee, but I couldn't express it.   You want things that are so-so not to be something else."

"That is it!   You've got it!" replied Uncle Boardman.   "Lyddy hits the nail on the head."

Aunt Lydia shot a triumphant beam out of her spectacles.

"And you haven't got the old kitchen pictures here, uncle, have you?" said Walter.

"Yes, that is Lyddy's work."

"There used to be," explained Tom, "under the last keeper, two or three sea-pictures, the 'Wreck of the Polyphemus,' the 'Outer Light in a Storm,' the 'Sally Ann at the Banks.'"

Aunt Lydia silently shook her head.

"You didn't want those, Aunt Lydia," said Walter.   "I don't blame you.   You wanted these walls to say 'Home! home!'   That's it!   I recognize them."

Yes, Walter recognized the old friends,

"Morning in the Farm-Yard," "Getting in the Hay," "Bob-o'-links in the Meadow," "Husking in the Old Barn."

"Yes, Aunt Lydia, you are right."

Aunt Lydia shot more triumphant light out of her spectacles. Then in silence she pointed behind the stove.

"Ha! ha!" cried Walter. "If there isn't Uncle Boardman's arm-chair and his red handkerchief across the back."

Uncle Boardman when a land-lubber used to take an after-dinner nap. He took it in an old arm-chair. This stood behind the stove. Invariably, he would throw over his face an old red bandana, tip his head back, and forget this world and its occupants. Maybe, the handkerchief was first used by him as a fly screen. However, it was used, and here it was, in the lighthouse kitchen. It occupied its old place, on the back of the arm-chair.

"Skipper Jim Bailey took to criticising things when he was here to dinner, one day," remarked Uncle Boardman. "He said it wasn't lighthouse like. He wanted—— "

"Yes," said Aunt Lydia, interrupting him, "he wanted sich things as 'Storm at Sea,' and a 'Wreck on the Rocks.' I told him I didn't. I wanted it 'hum,' and I've got it."

She here pointed at the floor. The last keeper had done nothing to disturb the oilcloth on the floor. Neither had Aunt Lydia removed it, but she had almost completely covered its rather sombre green and black checkered-work with the most cheery green and white, scarlet and gold, azure and saffron home-made rag mats.

"Skipper Jim said his heels were a-gittin' on fire. I told him that was because his heels were so big and presented so much surface to the flames. He didn't say nothin' arter that leetle remark upon the size of his feet," said Aunt Lydia.

"Well, I think it is the most cosey, the brightest, pleasantest, most home-like place I have seen for many a day," said Walter, throwing himself down in Uncle Boardman's arm-chair.

"Fust-rate!" declared Tom Walker.

Uncle Boardman was here looking out of the western window. "What!" he exclaimed, "sun so near goin' down? Walter, you want to see me light up?"

"Certainly, uncle! If you will permit me. I want to get my hand in."

"Then come up this way."

As he spoke, Uncle Boardman beckoned up another staircase.

Like the first, this was of iron and painted black in the days of the former light-keeper. It still was of iron. It still was painted black. The iron though and the color were hidden under a soft warm carpet and one of lively color.

"Got a carpet down, uncle?"

"This is one of your Aunt Lyddy's idees. I I told her Silas Manent would never know it, and she didn't care if he didn't, she said. Skipper Jim kept stumbling as he came up the stairs and said to Aunt Lyddy that he kept hitting his toes and a-tripping. She told him he mustn't have so big toes or he must take them in, and he did better after that. Well, Lyddy must have her way, and it's a good one. She says she wanted a home. She's a-going to have something on the kitchen stairs, she says."

"And whose is this room?" asked Walter, when they left behind them this second staircase.

Uncle Boardman chuckled away, and said, "It *was* the light-keeper's room, but Miss Lyddy Boardman lives here now, I tell her. Oh, she's the one that has been at work."

The carpet on the floor, the long curtains falling gracefully at the windows, the bed curtained off at one side, the little work-table, the sewing machine, said very plainly as if written on the wall, "Lyddy Boardman."

"She hasn't any wrecks, you see, on the walls, Walter."

"I should think not, uncle. Let me see what she has got, 'Lovers' Walk,' 'A May Brook,' 'Sunset in the Mountains'——"

"My, Walter! excuse me, but that sun is a-skipping down the western hills lively. We had better look after our sunset."

The keeper and his assistant hurried up into the next room, which was appropriated to the "assistant," and then by another staircase into the watchroom, and finally into the lantern. It had a circular wall of iron three feet high and was lined with wood. Above this was a succession of big panes of glass. In the centre of the lantern was a polished lens of glass covering the lamp.

"All ready to light!" exclaimed Uncle Boardman. "Sun is right on the horizon. I generally let her give a good, square dip and then touch off the lamp."

"I will go outside, uncle," said Walter, stepping out upon a shelf of stone surrounding the lantern and furnished with an iron railing. "I'll give the word to you."

The disk of the sun had touched the horizon. That disk contracted. It shrank to a semi-circle and rested like a dome on a distant hill, then dwindled, narrowed, sank, and for a moment was only a red blazing coal that had an incendiary attitude toward the pine-trees it had invaded.

"Out!" said Walter, the next moment.

"Up, it is here!" cried Uncle Boardman, touching a lighted match to the wick that promptly sent up an answering flame.

There was something of peculiar interest in the stand of that solitary watcher without the high lighthouse, looking across the darkening waters to that sinking sun, and then giving the word of its disappearance to the stout light-keeper crouching in the lantern, match in hand, waiting to touch off that little combustible within the glass lens. Walter lingered without and glanced up and down the coast-line. Miles away to the east, he quickly saw a little silvery star beyond a jutting point, while out at sea there was a distant twinkle on an island, and landward, a lighthouse in the harbor lifted its faithful torch. He thought of other stars, other twinkles, flashing here and there on the coast-line as the sun went down, and he felt that he never appreciated before, how impressive lighting-up time might be in a lighthouse.

When they came down to the cosey kitchen, Aunt Lydia met them with an announcement that the frying pan was doing its best and supper would soon be heard from.

That supper was unanimously voted to be "remarkable." The fish so nicely browned, the biscuit tender and flaky, the coffee of a delicate flavor and aromatic and warranted by Aunt Lydia "not to keep folks awake," were all appreciated. The wind might be "risin' and the stars a-gittin' hazy," as Tom reported, but those in the snug little kitchen did not care. Beneath them was the solid rock and around them were walls that no waves could shatter. There was a deeper sense of protection visiting them when Uncle Boardman said, "We will have prayers now."

He read one of his favorite psalms. How often Walter had heard him repeat in earnest tones the words:

"They that go down to the sea in ships, that do business in great waters, these see the works of the Lord, and His wonders in the deep. For He commandeth and raiseth the stormy wind, which lifteth up the waves thereof. They mount up to the heaven, they go down again to the depths. Their soul melteth away because of trouble."

Through a slightly lowered window, came the occasional sound of a heavy swash of the sea, but there was the strong, sure foundation to give confidence.

"We'll try to pray," reverently said Uncle Boardman, folding up his spectacles and laying them away. His words at first were hesitating, but they were free and confident at last, like a flock of sea-birds flying up from the rocks, unsteady at first, but then soaring into the blue sky or sweeping landward toward some refuge in the wide marshes or shadowy pines.

"That prayer put a new foundation under the lighthouse," thought Walter, as he rose from his knees.

He went up into the lantern and then stepped without. The sky was black. Every star was hooded in deep, dark shadow. The wind had sprung up out of its hiding-place and was racing across the sea. A hoarse, noisy breaking, as of surf on the cold rocks, came to Walter's ear. That noise of the surf seemed to sweep from the east to the west. It was a long wire heavily, hoarsely vibrating in the night.

The wind swept round the eastern wall of the lantern, and Walter passed over to the western side. Clinging with one hand to the high rail, holding on to his fluttering hat, he looked across this dark, great, uneasy Something far below his feet. He caught the brilliant flash from the lanterns of other lighthouses. He felt the inspiration of this common purpose in one lonely light after another to illumine the sea, to make a safe track for the perplexed ships, to lead out of stormy waters into safe harbors, and he murmured, "Good to have a purpose! Better to make some definite resolve to do good and to stick to it! Good, better, best, is the resolve, the purpose, to help those in trouble, who don't know what to do, who don't know where to go. Yes, good to have such a purpose!"

Walter insisted upon beginning his duties that night. A lantern must not only be lighted up, but the lamp must be "watched," and in these watches Walter took part.

CHAPTER VI.

ALMOST A LOSS.

THE next morning, Tom Walker went down the signal-tower ladder to his boat. Walter watched him from the door above.

"Good-bye, Tom!"

"Good-bye, Walter! A first-class time!"

There was a mutual waving of hands and then Tom untied his boat. He had rowed but a few feet when he called out, "There! Came nigh forgittin' it! Don't you want this?"

"Yes, if it belongs to me."

"And it does. I took it out of the post-office, yesterday, for you——"

"Sent to me?"

"Yes, waitin' in the office."

Tom held up a letter.

"Your marm probably sent it. Female handwriting."

"I'll come down after it, Tom."

Walter descended the ladder and held out his

hand to receive the letter. Tom's boat was struck by an unexpected wave and gave a sudden lurch. He was standing up at the time, and the toss of the boat threw him off his feet. He fell back upon a seat, and the letter fell into the water.

"Too bad! Hurt you, Tom?"

"N-n-o! Where's that letter?"

There came a second throw of the sea. It swept the letter beyond Tom's reach with his arm.

"No, you don't!" cried Tom, gripping a paddle and dipping it into the water speedily. "I'll chase ye!"

"That letter seems possessed!" said Walter.

"'Twill be when I get hold of it, Walter."

The letter though was whirled away a third time, Tom energetically pursuing it and at last overtaking it.

"I sometimes think, Walter, that things that git lost and will stay lost, ought to have vitality long enough to take a whippin', and that is the way I feel toward this thing. Here it is and you may pound it for me. Good-bye!"

"Thank you! Good-bye."

Walter climbed the ladder again. Tom lifted his sail to the sweep of the wind and sped home rapidly.

"Shall I pound this letter?" thought Walter. "Let me see whom it is from? I may feel more like it then. Not from mother, that is certain. Let me look at the signature! What! Kate Eaton! Ripley's sister! What is up now? No, I won't pound this letter."

He thought it would be pleasant to read this arrival by mail in the kitchen, for the outside air was chilly and it made its way into the signal-tower. Aunt Lydia was in the kitchen making mince pies.

"She will have too many questions to ask me and I will go into the engine-room and read it there," wisely concluded Walter.

Perched upon a heap of wood by the side of the engine, he began to read this valuable document. As he read, he felt that the eyes which he had seen in the picture shown him by Ripley Eaton, were now fastened on him. The solitary reading became a kind of conversation.

"MR. PLYMPTON, DEAR SIR:

"You will pardon this note from an entire stranger, and yet as I have often heard my brother speak of you, you do not seem like a total stranger and will allow me to address you."——

"Certainly, madame!" replied Walter. "Proceed!"

"—It is about my brother Ripley. He is in a discouraged state of mind, and has written to you——"

"I never received his letter."

"—and why he does not receive an answer, he can not conjecture. I tell him the letter may have been miscarried, which he says is quite probable, and yet he is afraid you are tired of him, and having received his letter do not wish to answer him."——

"No such thing! I do wish to answer anything he may send me."

"—I urge him to write once more, but he is afraid of intruding his personal matters upon you. I have not told him of my intention to write, knowing he would not permit it, and yet I feel that I must get a message to you and ask you to write a few encouraging words to him and assure him that you have not given him up."——

"Given him up! I rather think not. Hul-lo is it getting foggy?" said Walter, looking out of a window toward the open sea. "I really believe it is. Uncle Boardman will be up soon, and be starting up this engine. I must finish this letter quickly as possible. No, I will shift my retreat. I will go up into the watchroom."

On his way into the lighthouse, he passed Uncle Boardman.

"Walter, there's a fog coming in, I do believe, and I must be starting up that engine."

"Let me help you!"

"Oh, no! Nothing to do. Wood is in the furnace, all ready to light. 'Twill be no trouble to touch a match to it. That is all."

"I will come down again. I have a letter I want to finish reading."

"From your marm? She well?"

Walter felt that two big lustrous eyes were still fastened upon him, and he blushed.

"Oh—oh—no!" he hastily replied, and hurried away.

"Guess his Aunt Lyddy must be looking after that young man," reflected Uncle Boardman, as he went up into the engine-room and proceeded to light the engine fire.

Walter went up into the watchroom and resumed the reading of the letter.

"You know as well as I do, without any doubt, that my brother came under the spell of a bad man. I cannot explain it, but know

that such is the fact. Ripley has a very sensitive temperament, an imagination that is very
strong. Because this De Vere saved Ripley's
life, or says he saved it—I doubt it——"

" So do I, and a lot of others."

"—Ripley therefore has thought he must
cling to the fellow, try to see his good points, try
to forget his bad ones, believe in him, uphold
him—and—but you know the rest. A change
though has taken place since Ripley came
home. He has been thinking seriously, profoundly. His mood was a religious one, and
in it he was deeply moved. He was on his
way to church one night, when, alas, he met
De Vere! This De Vere came to the house
previously. If I had known who it was, I
might have kept him away from my brother.
Such a character ought to be put under lock
and key, if—but let it go."——

" I would have done it for you, if I had
been there."

"—That my brother's religious interest was
not entirely empty, is proved by the fact that
he and De Vere had a serious disagreement
that night. For the first time, Ripley did re-
fuse to listen to the solicitations of this evil
one. He did throw him off, and then came a
scene of almost violence, De Vere roughly press-

ing and my brother resisting firmly. Oh, I thank God for that resistance! Then De Vere made cruel charges. He said my brother owed him, whereas De Vere owed my brother. That night, he tried to obtain money from Ripley. Now, I cannot go into the details of other accusations. The seeming end of the interview was an abrupt breaking away of Ripley from De Vere, but not the end. This De Vere went into various vile places and sowed people's minds with various accusations against Ripley. Consequently, they have been scattered through the town and have borne fruit in great anxiety on Ripley's part——"

" Abominable!" exclaimed Walter.

"—and fearful lest friends away might get hold of the matter, he thought it might reach you, but oh, sir, don't believe the accusa-tions——" ·

" I won't——"

"—remembering the source from which they come——"

" I will——"

"—and pardon it, but could you write to him and say a word of encouragement?"——

" Certainly!"

"—Just now is a special period in his life. My brother has a noble nature really, but he came under a wrong influence and is trying now to break away from it. I feel if friends will bear with him——"

"Here is one."

"—and write to him an encouraging word, perhaps suggest something of help, it will put him, his aunt and sister under great obligation. Excuse me for troubling you, but you can understand your friend's situation.

"With much respect, yours,

"KATE EATON."

"Well, that is interesting, very! I can write to him, that will be easy, but she says, 'suggest something,' and what can I suggest?"

Toot-t-t-t!

This response was a hoarse, nasal, nigh deafening blast outside, on a level with the western window of the watchroom.

"That the fog signal? It must be!" cried Walter, springing to the window. The mouths of the two long red trumpets were inconveniently near, but this fog-signal aimed at faithfulness and did not consult the convenience of any listener.

Toot—toot—toot-t-t! "That will wake them up all about here. But what a fog! And it came so quick!"

Walter could see neither the water below nor the sky above. He was in the centre of a great gray cloud up into which ran the two red trumpets.

" I'll go down where there is some humanity," concluded Walter. "Lonely up here! I get an idea of the possible loneliness of a light-keeper's position, and how many of these lonely stations there must be! I did not think about it before. No, I don't want to stay up here. If obliged to do so, I don't know but what I should welcome the society even of De Vere. No, I wouldn't! Give me a lonely rock, leagues out to sea, but not that reptile on it."

When he reached the kitchen, he expected to find Aunt Lydia there, but she had quit her kingdom. Walter found her in the kingdom of her husband, out in the signal-tower, talking with him and watching, also, the air engine. Walter wanted to speak of Ripley, but the keeper and his wife were too busy with the fog-signal and the fog.

" That was a buster! Could hear that at Land's End," declared Aunt Lydia, after a blast.

" Hope so! The folks out on the water that can't see but can hear, are the safer for this. Good little engine as ever I see!" exclaimed Uncle Boardman. " Ho, Walter! that you?   Just look out and tell me if the fog is thickening or if thinning out, or how she is! I start this signal when I can't see across to Solomon's Pint."

" It is not quite so thick, I believe," said Walter, looking out of the window.

"That is good! I don't admire this ere screamin'," said Aunt Lydia. " Guess I must go in and be a-lookin' up suthin' for dinner."

" Ah ! " thought Walter, " that will be a good time to tell about Ripley, at dinner-time."

The dinner-hour came. The weather had brightened. The fog had lifted its damp, chilling wings off from the sea, and slowly, dismally flown away. The sun was doing his best to cheer up the lonely lighthouse, and poured into the kitchen window just as golden a stream as ever enlivened Aunt Lydia's domain on the land. An inshore breeze brought the sound of a bell ringing out cheerily the hour of twelve. A steamboat splashed vigorously by. Fishermen putting off from land steered their lively craft so near the light they could sing out to the keeper in the tower door :

" Hul—lo, Boardman ! "

Aunt Lydia in lively fashion tripped down to the door and said :

"Dinner's ready, Boardman!"

Then she tripped off in the other direction and cried, at the head of two flights of stairs:

"Come, Walter! Dinner!"

"Guess it would be a good time to speak of Ripley at the table," thought Walter, and at the table he opened the subject. Only the click-click of the tall, stately clock, and the clatter of the knives and forks interrupted his words.

"I had a letter this forenoon which Tom handed me, that brings up an interesting subject. Do you remember, Uncle Boardman, in a letter you wrote to me, that you spoke about picking a man out of the water, you and Aunt Lydia, that had a strange scar on his cheek, a shark's mouth, and I wrote you that I had found him out at last?"

"Oh! that crittur turned up agin and been writin' to you?" asked Aunt Lydia.

"Yes, I remember," said Uncle Boardman. "What does he want now?"

"He has not been writing to me, but he has been troubling some people I know——"

"He has? Then I say, pizen him!" advised Aunt Lydia. "Nothin' but evil can come from that crittur. His face keeps a-hauntin' me, and that shark's mouth I see in my dreams. Wall, why should he turn away from us and act as if he wanted to avoid us, the moment your name was spoken?"

"That I don't understand, unless he didn't want me to know he was here, but that is a mystery, if so, for at that time I did not know him. I knew of him, it is true. He had under his influence one of my friends, a Ripley Eaton, a college-student, a splendid fellow——"

"What did he want to do to Ripley?" asked Aunt Lydia, impatiently.

"Your Aunt Lyddy has a strange interest in that shark's-mouth-kind-of-man she calls him," explained Uncle Boardman.

"What did he want to do to my friend, Aunt Lydia? Oh, this letter——"

"He write it, that Ripley?" asked Aunt Lydia, who had a disposition to investigate a subject thoroughly when once she began it. She was something like a gimlet that needs but a slight pressure to keep boring and boring until it has gone through an obstacle.

Walter colored and held his tea-cup between his face and Aunt Lydia's scrutinizing spectacles, replying:

"He did, I mean—he did not write it—but—but it was about him. And he is breaking away from the influence of that man and I am asked—I want to encourage him and suggest—or am asked to suggest something, this Ripley—and——"

"Well," said Uncle Boardman, promptly, "if he don't want another snake-bite, don't let him go near the snake again."

"That's my mind zackly," said Aunt Lydia with emphasis, satisfied with, and admiring this prompt disposition of the subject.

"But the snake has gone, it seems. This De Vere has left Eaton, but he has been circulating various slanders and these stay to annoy and discourage my friend."

"Oh, he mustn't mind 'em," said Aunt Lydia. "Live 'em down!"

"Such things, Aunt Lydia, sometimes live you down."

"Not if there is true character in the man that is slandered," remarked Uncle Boardman.

"He needn't stay where the stories are," suggested Aunt Lydia. "If he has money, he might travel."

"Or. he might take a lighthouse," remarked Uncle Boardman, laughing. "He will get away from people then. Lonely enough then."

"Unless the light-keeper have an 'Aunt Lydia' to go with him, and in that case he will be well off," said Walter, directing a complimentary look toward Aunt Lydia.

Uncle Boardman nodded his head, chuckled and said: "Couldn't get along without Aunt Lyddy."

The bright spectacles out of which looked a true woman and a noble soul, gleamed with an intense satisfaction. Such acknowledgments did her good. For a few moments, there was an uninterrupted clatter of dishes. Then Aunt Lydia spoke;

"If a lighthouse would be a good thing for your friend, why couldn't he come here?"

"What, Aunt Lydia?"

"You mean, Lyddy, have him make a visit?"

"Why yes, father."

Aunt Lydia sometimes called her husband "father," though they were a childless couple now. All their children had been gathered to a safer home than any of earth.

"That's a good idea, Walter. Have your friend make us a visit while you are here. He might see some things to interest him, and we would warrant that that snake wouldn't get at him," declared Uncle Boardman.

"Not if I am in the kitchen," said Aunt Lydia.

"That is very kind in you, Uncle Boardman and Aunt Lydia, to invite my friend here, and it strikes me as a capital idea. I will do so at once—invite him—if you say the word."

"We do, Walter!"

"Yes, we do!"

That very day, Walter sang out to a fishing-craft passing the light, "Ship ahoy!"

The mulatto cook, waiting while his fire was heating up the oven of the galley-stove, was leaning over the starboard rail, and heard this hail of the assistant-keeper, and put his hand to his ear to catch the next word.

"Going up to the village, up to the Harbor?"

The houses at the port were called the "Harbor."

"Aye! aye!"

"Can you drop a letter for me in the post-office?"

"Aye! aye!"

Walter ran down the tower ladder, quickly put off in the light-keeper's dory, and threw his letter upon the deck of the fishing-schooner.

The cook picked up the letter and slowly

read the address, "Ripley Eaton—What? Wh-wh-wh-ew!"

His look and his tones were those of surprise.

"Ah! He send money fur de job. I'll do it."

CHAPTER VII.

WAS IT DRIFT-WOOD?

SCHOOL-HOUSE "No. 5" stood in a corner made by the intersection of two roads, one of the latter dwindling to a lane, and coming down to the shore about a mile from Seal's Head. If this lane could have been stretched across the water, it would have struck the ladder climbing up the signal-tower. The school-house was not more than three hundred feet from the water. It met the intellectual wants of the scattered population on the right hand side of the port, whose entrance the light at Seal's Head indicated. On the other side of the port was the village known as the "Harbor." This village had a so-called graded school, but that one school-house at the crossing of the roads received all that might desire to climb from the A B C round of the ladder to the round proudly occupied by any student in Latin, provided the teacher could manage such a high-round pupil. The school was now in session. It had a "mistress," young, but packed with energy, her face expressive of decision, while her blue eyes searched her scholars in a direct, fearless way that rogues disliked, but promptly respected. She was now approached by a colored boy, once living with Boardman Blake. He was known as Dom Pedro in full, but Dom in the ordinary school vocabulary. Dom now lived with a farmer in the neighborhood.

"Miss Selliott!"

The teacher's name was May Elliott. Her scholars generally made a pudding of her name and prefixed "miss" when they addressed her.

"What is it, Dom?"

He lowered his head before the eyes that saw so far into him.

"Don't you want some more wood fur de stove? A-gittin' shilly!"

"I do want some wood, but thought we might get through the afternoon, and then one of the boys said to me that our wood-pile was used up."

"I could pick ye up a heap of fus'-class drif'-wood down on de beach. Be handy fur to-morrer."

She smiled. She knew that Dom had a greater desire for liberty than to bring drift-wood. The room, though, was uncomfortably cool, and she gave him permission to search the sands for any fuel dry enough for the stove. "Anyway," she said, "we want it to-morrow."

It was a bright day in December. For the twelfth month, the sun was warm. No clouds were in the sky. There was no snow in the fields. The air was crisp. It acted like an elixir on Dom's spirits. It specially affected his heels. He began to throw them up briskly and ran down the lane to the beach.

"Now fur drif'-wood!" he murmured. "Ole spar! Too big! Ben dar dese years, I spec. Chips! Too small! Nuffin here!"

Nothing that he cared to pick up, though he could have got an armful of small stuff. This would have started up the exhausted fire in the stove and brought up the temperature to a point near that outside, for to-day the air with-out was warmer than that within the school-house. Spurning as too small the wood that he saw, he raced jubilantly down the sands. The sun in the heavens was good enough stove for Dom Pedro. He forgot all about that at the school-house. Suddenly he stopped.

"Who dat?" he wondered.

His eyes grew.

He whistled one low note of perplexity.

"Man on dat ole log! Nice lookin' man!
Like a genlumman! A heap ob fine clothes,
all nice an' new, fus'-class! What he want?"

Yes, what did this elegantly dressed stranger
want, seated on that log, looking off intently
upon the water? He carried an umbrella.
Once, he rose. He waved it energetically in
the direction of the—lighthouse or a fish-
ing-boat or—what?

"He don' 'pear to see a t'ing dis yer way.
Don' know I'm here. A right smart lookin'
genlumman. I'll jes' ax him what fur he
down dis yer way."

The stranger though had now noticed Dom
and eagerly approached him.

"Say, sonny!"

"What, sah?"

"Do you know of any way of getting over
to that lighthouse?"

"Swim, sah!"

This amused the young man.

"You might as well say 'walk.' No boat
round here?"

Dom shook his head.

"Might make a raf', jes' hab some wood."

"Do you know of any wood for a raft?"

Dom shook his head.

"Well, do you know of any people round

here, people that could help me get across somehow ? "

" Miss Selliott."

" Where does she live ? "

" She don' lib ; she keep school."

This tickled the young man. His handsome face was illumined immediately.

" Where does she keep school ? "

" I'll show ye."

Off started Dom, having an unquestioning faith that the stranger would follow. Dom was one of the kind eagerly interested in new projects, and this office of pilot so engaged his thoughts that he did not slacken his eager pace until he reached the school-house door. He then turned a moment, as if to make sure that he was still towing that beautiful vessel, the strange young man.

" Dar he is ! " he said to himself, with satisfaction. " I see him." Then he hurried into the entry, closely followed by the stranger who liked an adventure as well as Dom, and was curious to see the person who did not live, but taught school.

" Miss Selliott ! " said Dom, bursting into the room where May Elliott presided, his eyes excitedly glistening.

" Well, Dom, where is your drift-wood ? "

replied the teacher, who had folded a shawl about her shoulders.

"Oh—I—here he is!" exclaimed the pilot of the craft picked up on the shore.

The next moment, the young man had stepped into the room. He was smiling, for he had caught the teacher's words and Dom's reply.

"Oh—oh!" said the embarrassed teacher.

The scholars were giggling, but Dom looked on in triumph, well-assured in his own mind that if he had not secured any drift-wood, he had brought a much more interesting object to the school-house.

"I beg your pardon. I—I am Mr. Eaton," said the object. "I wanted some information or help which my guide here kindly suggested that I might find at the school-house."

Ripley Eaton with his graceful manners and sparkling face made a very interesting picture there in the old school-house.

"Won't you be seated?" said the school-mistress, recovering her self-possession. "I shall soon dismiss my school, and earlier, to-day, because my fire is out and I have no wood to start it up again."

"Burn me, as your messenger brought me," Ripley was inclined to say, but he merely re-

"THE NEXT MOMENT THE YOUNG MAN HAD STEPPED INTO THE ROOM."

Page 139.

plied, "Thank you," and then Dom's driftwood disposed of itself in the companion to the teacher's chair on the platform.

"Am I driftwood?" he asked himself. "Afraid I come very near it."

He was disposed to do a quantity of serious thinking, but he was aroused out of his reverie by the teacher's decided command, "Attention!"

"That little thing ordering me?" he asked.

No, she was speaking to her school. They promptly obeyed, packed their books away in their desks, folded their hands properly and primly on the lids of the desks, and then, sitting back in their seats, gave their eyes and their thoughts to the teacher. Not all, however. Some of the scholars looked slyly at Ripley, who was the most distinguished looking person that had been in the school-house for many days, if not years. Ripley, himself, had eyes only for the teacher.

"That little thing magnetizes me," he kept saying to himself.

He found that he was making a study of her ; of the figure, which was rather light, but trim and compact ; of the dress, which had a blue background over which tiny white vines were gracefully running ; of the smooth, brown hair ;

of those blue eyes which had a direct, positive, but very friendly way of looking into as well as at people ; of the voice, round and musical and with just a bit of imperativeness to it. This imperativeness could be effectively emphasized, as her scholars well knew. Better than any-thing else about her was a certain expression to the face which said you could trust her, and if you knew her, you would love her.

" Before we go we will sing something," she said, quietly.

Giving the key-note, beating time without any flourish, but decidedly and exactly with her small yet well-shaped hand, she led the school in the singing of a twilight composition. It was a Church hymn. Happily, the senti-ment of the neighborhood permitted it. The voices of teacher and scholars blended into a pleasant harmony, rising like some flame kindled on an altar top :

> " The sun is sinking fast,
> The daylight dies ;
> Let love awake, and pay
> Her evening sacrifice. "

The altar flame gathered volume and rose higher in the next stanza :

> "As Christ upon the Cross
>   His head inclined,
> And to His Father's hands
>   His parting soul resigned;"

Still higher, yet ever sweet:

> "So now herself my soul
>   Would wholly give
> Into His sacred charge,
>   In whom all spirits live."

Ripley had only ears for the beautiful hymn, only eyes for the singer who led in the chorus. She was a revelation to him. He seemed to know her already, or rather, she had looked into his soul and knew him, and yet they had never met before.

"I am sure, too, that I never have heard of her anywhere," he thought; "no, not even heard of her."

In a moment, he added, but still to himself:

"This is a very interesting school."

Out from that central figure of interest, the young school-mistress, with her steadily beating hand, her rich, triumphant voice, went an influence that changed all the place and transformed those who sat there. The walls were no longer scarred, but smooth and richly-tinted, the rough corner-posts turning to fluted columns. The windows, with dented and marred sashes, with panes often cracked and always in stiff, homely squares, were glorified into those famous chapel-windows at college, that to Ripley's sensitive imagination seemed to have stolen from the sun its richest rays and imprisoned them. The scholars took on strange grace and dignity. The big boys became St. Gregorys, while the girls were, by a curious process of alchemy, passing into beautiful St. Cecilias. Among the benches was Dom? No, he had gone. In his place sat a swarthy young seraph singing. Ripley's imagination, so rich in its resources, so sensitive to the touch of the outer world, had swept him away into a new existence. He forgot why he came to the school-house. He lost all thought of the place where he wished to go. He only heard singing and at last saw only the school-mistress. The singing stopped. He was hardly conscious of it. In thought, the music of these voices went on. His rapt mood extended itself. He was in an exalted sphere. Suddenly, he heard a voice saying:

" Excuse me, sir, I did not say, I fear, that I should be glad to have you say something to my school, but we would be pleased to hear you."

Ripley's mood went at once, as when a sunset cloud is blown away by a sudden wind. He was conscious that he was in a rough, country school-house, struggling to get on to his feet, blushing, stammering, while before him were several rows of giggling scholars, and in their centre was a swarthy face grinning at him. It was that of Dom, the dusky enchanter, who had found Ripley on the sea-shore, and under the guise of African-boyhood had charmed him into this place of Circean power, the school-room. The disposition of Circe, however, was not here, though a suggestion had been made by her that must be obeyed. What could Rip ley say? A dimness was coming over his eyes. The faces before him were all running together; all the faces—save one! That encouraged while it commanded. He must make a harder effort, and he did.

"Well, I must say this is the most interesting school I was ever in. Thank you!"

Down he sat.

A cold sweat stood in beads upon his forehead. He was so glad that he owned a handkerchief and that he had it that moment in his pocket.

"Just made a fool of myself!" was his inward exclamation.

The teacher, though, looked gratified, and the scholars all smiled approbation.

" He showed his sense in making a short speech," Ripley heard one of the older girls say, when she was passing out. That brightened his clouded spirits.

The teacher came forward to thank him. Dom stepped up, looking as if he wished to say something if he only knew how. Then other scholars clustered about the teacher's desk, all throwing a friendly smile toward this orator with few, but very weighty words. He was so fine-looking, they were contented only to gaze at him.

Ripley was at ease, for it was only conversation that was now expected of him, and he was a charming talker.

" I am afraid, Miss Elliott, I should never make a success if I tried to do your work. Now, I think you turn it off very successfully."

" Yeth, thee doth," said a lisping pupil, in low tones.

" I don't know," May Elliott said, dreamily. Then she collected herself. " Yes, I do know. My work is not a success that at all satisfies me. As for yourself, Mr.——"

She could not recall the name he had given her.

"Eaton," he said, once more.

"Mr.—Eaton! As for you, I think you would have more success than ever you anticipated. Come! Let me make a suggestion. I close by Christmas, as I go away to study. How would you like to take this school then?"

"What?" he asked, in astonishment. "I—I—teach this school?"

"Why, yes, sir! Somebody must teach it."

"Oh! never—that is, not I."

"Yes, yes, yes," said several girls, who had already given their hearts to this splendid being, dropping so suddenly from a superior sphere down into this their humble school-world.

"Ha! ha!" laughed Ripley, in his hearty, musical way. "It would never do. School-master, ha! ha! Why, how would I do?"

"Fus yate!" said Dom, encouragingly.

"Then Dom thinks his driftwood amounts to something after all, ha! ha!" said Ripley, rising from his seat.

All left the room with him and went to the door. As Ripley lingered upon the threshold, he looked down the lane stretching to the shore. Beyond the shore, out in the sea, towered the lighthouse.

"Oh, there!" exclaimed Ripley, coming back suddenly to the errand that started him in his walk to the school-house. "I was going to ask you if you knew of any possible way of getting to the lighthouse, or if your scholars knew. I am aware that school-houses are reservoirs of information, that through the scholars, possibly, one may find out anything——"

The brow of the school-mistress showed a wrinkle of perplexity, but at a remark by one of her flock, the wrinkle was smoothed down.

"I know, teacher, where there is a boat."

"You do?" asked Ripley. "Where? A boat is a long step toward getting out there. What a nice thing if this lane were only continued out to the lighthouse!"

"Yes," replied May Elliott, as she walked down the lane, a small flock of eager, curious scholars attending her and her grand visitor, Dom going ahead, every few moments looking back proudly.

"It would be a good thing for the people at the light, if this road were continued out there, but I don't know how long it would last. We have fearful storms that rage between the lighthouse and the land."

"That is good."

"Good?"

She looked at him in perplexity.

"Oh, I mean it will be interesting. I expect to be awhile at the lighthouse——"

The children all edged closer to hear about the purposes and plans of the stranger. Dom came nearer to catch all he could.

"Not quite so close, children!" cautioned the teacher.

"Children!" That word spoken just there, spoken just then, fell on Ripley's ear with a pleasant sound.

He smiled.

It seemed like a family walk, as if through some enchantment of that young, colored wizard met on the beach, he had been changed into a patriarch, and this was the family-flock he was leading to the shore. He smiled again.

"Oh, there is the boat!" said the scholar, who had told of a craft she knew about.

It was at the right of the lane. It was almost hidden by a projection of the shore.

"Whose boat is it?" asked the patriarch, eagerly turning aside to examine the treasure.

"Father's," said the scholar, who had led to it.

"Do you think he will let me take it?"

"He—he don't like to let the boys take it—they—they—bang it, but I know he will let *you*."

"Oh, thank you! I am sure I won't bang it. But——"

He was wondering how he could get in this boat to the lighthouse. He thought he could row—could he? But how was the boat to be brought back?

"Which of you young people can row?"

"I can," said Dom, proudly and immediately.

There was no other response.

"Ye can't row cross-handed, Dom?" said a girl.

Well, no; Africa could only pull a single oar.

"I see. You could not then take me over and bring the boat back?"

"No, sah."

"We may hunt up somebody," said Ripley.

"Somebody," though, did not come. The scholars one by one all left save Dom. He had a special interest in this drift-wood he had picked up and he was reluctant to quit the spot. The teacher felt that she must go, sorry that she could suggest no boatman to this perplexed stranger. He had asked, "Any hotel in the neighborhood?"

"On the other side of the harbor, there is a village where one can find lodgings, sir."

"Thank you, but how do you get across to that village?"

"Oh, there are people going and coming."

"Do you know of anybody?"

"I have a brother that comes for me——"

"Excuse me—could I go in his boat if I can't get to the light?"

"Certainly, he would be glad to take you."

"I believe——" he was looking off to sea and he spoke slowly as if while speaking he was looking at something—"I believe—what is that at the left of the lighthouse—a black object?"

"Oh, that is not a boat, if you mean that. It looks like a rock, and is a rock. They call it 'T'other Seal.' The lighthouse is on 'Seal's Head.' Over on the farther shore, can you see a farmhouse on a point of land, off to the west?"

"I think I do."

"I have heard my grandfather say that a line running from that house and continued to the lighthouse and beyond it, would fall across 'T'other Seal.' On a dark night, if that farmhouse be lighted up, he would say, he could just take his bearings, and go at once from 'Seal's Head' to 'T'other Seal.'"

"That may be worth remembering."

"Oh—oh—oh!" Dom was exclaiming. At the same time he pointed toward the lighthouse.

"What is it, Dom?" asked the teacher.

"A boat comin', teacher!"

"So there is. Don't you see it, sir? It is just in the line of the lighthouse. I can make out its body. It is black, and then above it is the white sail."

"I think you are right."

"They are coming for you."

"How could they tell?"

"They have a glass. They have seen us on the beach."

"I told them when I would get here, and they said they would be on the watch. Oh, I understand! I mentioned the hour of my arrival, and I got here before the time I said. Yes, they are coming."

"I will bid you good-night, sir."

He thanked her and bade her good-night. Dom trotted off with his teacher.

"I didn't want to say good-night," thought Ripley, turning to watch the teacher's figure retreating up the lane. "This is a queer chapter in my life! There's the boy turning to look back. Wonder if she will look back!"

No, she resolutely kept her face turned toward the school-house. Dom, though, reported what was going on behind them, guessing any information might be acceptable.

"He hain't gone yet. He a-looking dis yer way!"

Another report: "Dar's de boat, teacher! Somebody's gittin' out ob it, an' *he's* a-gittin' in."

Still, she did not turn.

Beyond the school-house, as if she had passed beyond the sphere of the school-teacher and as a private person she could do what she pleased, she turned and saw a white sail receding from the shore.

She was alone now and she lingered there, thinking awhile how human life is like the great sea. We meet like the ships that approach one another on the sea, lie to awhile, and call out friendly greetings. We part. We watch one another's dwindling sails that sink and go out of sight below the dim, distant horizon. Will we ever meet again?

Would May Elliott ever see again this fascinating young stranger, this ship coming up so suddenly above the horizon of her uneventful life ?

" They know about him at the lighthouse. They can tell me who he is," she thought. "Oh, I must mention him in my letter to-night ! Yes, I will."

She purposed to write a letter that very evening to an old friend, a room-mate at an academy. She anticipated its writing with new pleasure. She was glad when at home she could go to her chamber, light the lamp there, drop the curtains, start the whirring flames in their flight up the little fireplace, and then, while the wind murmured without and lent to her thoughts the accompaniment of its music, she wrote to her old school-friend.

She pictured the country school-room, the withdrawal of Dom ostensibly to hunt up and bring in drift-wood. When he finally appeared, his arms were empty, but with him was this fine-looking young stranger who made such a nervous, funny little speech ! She also told how he won the hearts of all the scholars, how they wanted him to be her successor, but he said his present occupation was not that of school-keeping but lighthouse tending at Seal's Head, and there were her friends, the Blakes and Walter Plympton.

"There, that will do," she murmured, having added a brief account of her personal plans. Then she folded it up and addressed it.

"She will be glad to know about things happening in my little life," thought May.

She went to sleep dreaming about lighthouses. She saw a row of them. She went from one to another, trying to light them up. That at Seal's Head was malicious. It was a wayward candle. It was a kind of locomotive. It would approach, then recede. She was about crowning this candlestick with flame when she awoke, and it was morning.

At the lighthouse, Ripley's dreams were about drift-wood. He saw Dom Pedro on the shore. Dom picked up several pieces and made a pile of them. Then he came to Ripley standing on the beach and looking off anxiously at the lighthouse. Dom laid his hands on Ripley. "Horrors! Am I going to turn into drift-wood to be lugged off to the school-house fire?" thought Ripley.

In spite of any remonstrance, he began to turn into something vague, indefinite. Then he felt a hardening outside. He turned a dark brown. Then indefiniteness became definiteness. He was conscious and yet he was a log, long and round. He was dented. He was slimy. One end was pointed.

"What's a feller gwine to do wid dis!" Dom muttered. "Kent lif' dis! Shub him out to sea agen!"

This interesting drift-wood was on its hopeless way to the surf, to float far out to sea in a useless existence, to be pelted by the great rains, and mocked by the roaring winds and contemptuously thrown about by the huge waves, when somebody interfered!

"This shall *not* be drift-wood. This winter he shall teach school. There!"

The rest of this prophecy was inaudible, but it was a prediction made by a prophetess. She had a voice firm but very pleasant. It was May Elliott. Then there came to Ripley the charm he had felt in the school-house. He was at ease. He was strong. A restful confidence in her presence, and a consciousness of power came to him and blessed him with a new happiness. A destiny of usefulness was before him. He was about to become a human being when suddenly he was aroused out of this state. A rough hand was laid upon this log. Had May made a mistake? Must Ripley go out to sea again? Was he only driftwood after all? To the heavy hand was added a voice, a man's. "Come, Ripley, come!" Was this De Vere's interference? The voice was urgent just like De Vere's, and Ripley awoke.

There stood Walter laughing, saying, rather imperatively, " Come, wake up! Breakfast is ready! Aunt Lydia has made some corn-cake, which she says can't be beat by all the college cooks between here and Kamchatka. Can't you smell the coffee?"

CHAPTER VIII.

"LYDIA," said Uncle Boardman to his wife, on a mild winter day, " Walter and I must go ashore to see about some iron-work that is to be done here at the light. You and Ripley can take charge——"

" Leave it all with me. I'll take care of everything and everybody," was Ripley's offer.

" You be light-keeper?"

" Yes, sir, certainly! I can light up at night and blow it out in the morning."

" That is good. Walter and I have got to go back into the country, perhaps two miles, and we may possibly not get to Seal's Head till after lighting time, but we will arrive some-time. Don't worry. It is a quiet sea and won't upset anything. We shall get back."

" All right, sir," replied Keeper Ripley, " I'll take charge of the light."

" And I'll take charge of *him*," added Aunt Lydia.

They all laughed, and separated. Walter and his uncle went out to take their boat, Aunt Lydia and Ripley remained in the kitchen. She was knitting an immense stocking. Ripley was examining a book he had found in the lighthouse library up in the watch-room. Now and then he took up a pencil and wrote a few words on a sheet of paper. If he had looked up, he would have noticed that Aunt Lydia shot occasional glances in the direction of his chair.

"Sakes alive!" she said to herself. "What makes me interested in that man! Can't help likin' him! He is jest one of the perlitest fellers I ever did see. I must say I take a great fancy to him."

It was not difficult to account for this interest. Ripley was a fascinating picture, simply to look at. Then he had rare tact in meeting the prejudices of people and in shaping his methods to the style of their ways. He had, too, such a chivalrous attitude toward Aunt Lydia, like a knight in the presence of his queen, that he was irresistible.

Ripley captured Uncle Boardman by showing from the first such a profound interest in the lighthouse and all the work pertaining to it.

Walter was amused. He was frequently smiling.

"Why," he thought, "that Ripley is always hunting up something of interest about this place, telling of some discovery, seeing some new thing every moment. He is the greatest fellow out."

Ripley acted as if he had suddenly, out here in the sea, come upon a toy. The toy was his lighthouse. He talked about it, asked questions, praised its merits, suggested changes where it was deficient.

"Can't help likin' that boy!" said Aunt Lydia, on her side of the household.

It pleased her to see the interest that he took in this place whither she and her husband had come with a purpose.

If he saw much of interest within the walls, he was continually making discoveries without and finding features of interest. The white surf rushing about a ledge of rocks farther out to sea, he spoke of as a charge of horses of snow, forever trying to mount the slippery rocks and forever falling off and falling back. The bell in a buoy near the channel, tolling gently when the sea ran low, and ringing violently when the sea ran high, affected strongly his imagination. He was frequently speaking of this sad, this monotonously echoing bell, doomed to an eternal unrest night and day, moaning, moaning.

Aunt Lydia had heard about his unsatisfactory course at college and his desire and purpose to do better. She therefore took a pitying interest in this mortal, who having fallen, was trying to stand upright. Was he one of the handsome angels turned out of heaven and now trying to get back? She now continued to watch him as he sat at the table, one moment energetically writing, and the next intently searching inside his book.

"There's a lot to him," she was thinking. "Smart? That word don't begin to fill the bill."

"Aunt Lydia!" he said.

He had learned the household title for her and used it, never intrusively but with a certain reverent air as to a mother or a superior friend. It was very taking.

"What is it, Ripley?" she said, returning his tribute by recognizing him as one well-known, close at hand, beloved, counsellor, friend—best of all, her son.

"I have been reading about lighthouses and have written down some things about them. I must say we have a great institution, in these lighthouses, and I wonder if people know about them. I am going to—if you will kindly let me—read what I have written."

"I should be very much pleased."

He began at once, his sympathetic voice taking up and expressing every turn of thought. Aunt Lydia responded, occasionally, like a wire struck by a master-hand.

"'I wonder who built the first lighthouse! To go farther back, I wonder who kindled on the land the first beacon-flame that should be a guide to the poor souls at sea! Of course, it all began in a simple, natural way. A wife anxious for her husband,—he might be a fisherman delayed at night or a sailor from afar,—might light on a hill near the water, a hill not far from the route home, that fire which would be a sign of the love of those on land as well as a guide for the imperiled souls at sea.'"

"Yes, yes, jes' so! Poor critters! Lots of 'em to-day!" said a voice.

It was Aunt Lydia, and she turned her head away and secretly wiped her eyes.

"'Of course, as a people grew in numbers and wealth, and their trading with other nations became commerce, these shore-lights were of greater importance. There was need of system in their management. I can think of people employed definitely to fire the gathered heaps of wood when the night blackened, when not even a star might kindle its taper, when the rains beat heavily and the huge billows like the roll of chariot-wheels without number, thundered on the shore.'"

"Awful!" murmured Aunt Lydia.

"'Then they raised pillars, some day, of stone; they were very rude at first, but were beautiful and strong as the people learned how to build, and the light-keeper became a personage of recognized importance.

"'The light may have been only that of wood-fires on these pillars of stone, fires kept through the night and flashing across the sea, dark and cold and wild, their cheerful radiance. The most famous lighthouse of olden times was one built on the island of Pharos off the coast of Egypt. This was in the year two hundred and eighty before the birth of our Saviour, and lighted up the path over the sea to the city of Alexandria in Egypt. It was so prominent that it gave a name to lighthouses. In the French language to-day, we find a trace of this custom, for *phare* means lighthouse in that graceful language.'"

"Yes, lovely!" murmured Aunt Lydia, who

knew French about as well as she did San-scrit.

" ' In our day, we have had instances of the erection of fine lighthouses. In the English Channel, off the port of Plymouth, are very ugly rocks that have tripped up many an unlucky vessel. Their very name suggests what an awful whirlpool these rocks in a storm must be the centre of, Eddystone. Lighthouses of wood with a base of stone were built here. One a storm swept away, and it carried the architect with his tower—— "

" Poor man ! "

" ' Another wooden building that stood over forty years was burned——' "

" Oh, dear ! Massy ! "

" ' And then Mr. Smeaton built a tower of stone which became famous. Its blocks were very heavy, from one to two tons. The stone was dovetailed into the foundation. The light was about seventy feet above the water and could be seen thirteen miles. Finished in 1759, this stood over one hundred years. England has other noted lighthouses. One at Bell Rock has a tower a hundred feet high, and that at the Skerryvore Rocks, rises to the height of one hundred and thirty-eight feet. This coun-try has a splendid system of lighthouses——' "

" Beat all the world ! "

" 'And among its superior structures may be mentioned Minot's Ledge, Mass. This is off in the sea, on the Outer Minot, a rock off the town of Cohasset. The shipping bound for Boston Harbor must pass this light. I have heard about the lighthouse once standing there. Long iron piles screwed down into the rock bore up the lighthouse, but before the gale, it was like a little martin-house before a tornado——' "

" There never was a truer figger than that," broke in Aunt Lydia forcibly, while admiringly. " I can remember that gale that took away them long iron pipes, and the poor keepers went with them, yes, they did. It was an awful gale all along the shore. The billers were awful. They jest took ashore big blocks of stone weighin' one or two tons. So they said."

" Thank you," said the essayist. " It must have been terrible. 'Well, when they built again, in 1855, they profited by their sad experience. They built of stone. They carefully prepared the foundation. At the end of the third season, they had laid only four stones but they were laid to stay—yes, to stay.' "

" That is the best way."

" 'At the base, the tower is thirty feet in

diameter. It is circular, gradually tapering, and from the base of the tower to the centre of the lantern there is a height of one hundred feet. Its entire height is given as one hundred and fifteen feet. Off Cape Ann, in Massachusetts, are two handsome symmetrical gray-stone towers. They are less than a thousand feet apart. These candles by the sea, over a hundred feet high, are planted on Thatcher's Island, and they rise stately and grand as the night comes on and the sailor on the great deep thinks of home and the perplexing way to it.'"

"Yes, yes!"

"'I think our lighthouses though, are all noble. This in form and construction is a magnificent one on Seal's Head, but if a lighthouse may be low and its material be only wood, still I think the purpose of a building glorifies it. The intention is to light up the highways along our coast, to make navigation safe, to guide to their homes those who go down to the sea in ships, to make less wearisome the anxious nights of the sailor's wife and to give hope to the sailor's child. Yes, it is a glorious service.'"

"Glorious, yes, glorious!"

The obedient wire had promptly responded

to the touch of the master-hand, and then there was silence in the lighthouse kitchen. The clock ticked, the fire purred in the stove, the sunshine lay on the floor, nestling among the warm, bright patterns of the home-made rugs.

Aunt Lydia now spoke with such abruptness and energy that Ripley gave a startled look as she said, "What are you goin' to do in this world?"

He quickly smiled and replied, "Oh, I don't know. That is a hard question to answer, one in the higher mathematics, as we say in college."

"There's a good deal to you," said Aunt Lydia, with intense directness.

"Oh, thank you, thank you! It does me good to be here."

Yes, there was diffused about him an atmosphere of confidence, of trust, of respect, of love. His sensitive nature was cognizant of this at once. And, as we are very likely to come up to the level of an outside opinion that is favoring and helpful, going down also to the grade of any public estimate that will not believe we have intellectual merit or good morals, so Ripley adjusted himself to the opinion reigning in the lighthouse.

"He has merit, he is trustworthy, he will be of great use," said public opinion at Seal's Head. Ripley lifted his head accordingly. He now said again:

"It does me good to be here."

"Well, *I* am glad," said Aunt Lydia, positively. "And I think there is suthin' to you."

Ripley's face beamed.

"—And I don't believe those stories about you."

Ripley's face was clouded.

"S—stories?" he said, falteringly.

Aunt Lydia did not falter. When she saw his embarrassment, she wished she had made no allusion to the subject, but she was not one to make a mistake worse by any equivocation. She went straight to the point and spoke in plainest English:

"What that De Vere said about you when you were a yachtin' with him and that you owed him money. Jest to think it, that that ere scamp should have been in this very neighborhood and that your Uncle Boardman——"

"My uncle? Oh, thank you! He is a good man."

"Wall, you do seem like one of the family, for we do take a lot of interest in you and mean to stand by you."

That braced Ripley at once. His face flashed with a spirit that defied De Vere and all the kingdom of evil.

"Yes, your Uncle Boardman—there it is agin, but 'tis true—to think we two should have picked up that scamp! Why, I would have let him take a longer salt-water bath if it would have done any good. But never mind!"

"There is one person who was with us on board De Vere's yacht who went on shore with us and he can tell whether De Vere's stories about me are true or not. De Vere says the conduct he charges upon me was a matter on shore. Martin could tell——"

"That the man?"

"Yes, that is the one. He is a colored man. He helped De Vere about his little boat and followed us on shore. Then De Vere says I owe him money, and he has my note and it is for a large amount and I am defrauding him——"

"Why don't he show it?"

"That is where he is cunning. He says it is in a tin box in his boat, and his boat is at the bottom of the sea. He can only hold over me a threat which he cannot prove, but on the other hand I can't disprove. If I could get hold of Martin, I could disprove the stories, and if I could get hold of the box, I could disprove the debt unless he has a forged document there, and he would not dare to forge."

"I don't know, I don't know. The day we took him out of the water, he looked as if he would do most anything. But where was Martin the day we picked up *him?*"

"Oh, he had left, about the time I did. De Vere was sailing round alone. It was a little craft. Nobody knows where it is now."

"Wall, let it go. I am glad you are here. Now, you haven't answered my question, what you are going to do by and by."

"I can't. I don't know myself."

"You ought to be thinkin' of it. You ought to be makin' up your mind. It is good to have a purpose, reel wholesome. Now it has made a new man of my husband, havin' this lighthouse, a sure, definite thing. I can see it plain as a pair of specs on a man's nose. And I feel better, too. Folks say it is lonely. I know it is lonely here, but I have too much to do to think about it. If you keep reel busy, you won't be troubled. Now, if I do say it, I have got a lot of knittin' on hand for spare moments, and I mean to make a pile of stockings and mittens. I can sell 'em. I know I can, and they'll beat any of your knit-goods. They'll keep some poor fel- ler warm, another winter. But I am spendin' too much time on that pint. I only wanted to say a purpose warms you up and keeps you a-goin', and then you do more, of course. Now, you scuse me. I feel as if I were a kind of mother to you, and say what is in my heart."

That touched Ripley profoundly and his appreciative nature responded at once and cordially.

" Oh, thank you ! Yes, talk like a mother to me. I haven't any, you know. Yes, I do mean to have a purpose in life. I hope I have got one for this winter——"

" Goin' to keep that school ?"

" Do you think I had better ?"

" Sartin, sartin, why not ?"

" I didn't mean that when I spoke. How- ever, I want to have a purpose for life and give myself to it. I know it will be better, oh, infi- nitely better! I am thinking about it, be assured."

" And, Ripley——"

The old lady paused. She looked at this adopted son, directly, intently.

" What is coming now ? " he asked himself.

Aunt Lydia hesitated, but she was saying silently all the time, " Guess I must do it, I am the one, I feel. Now is a good time." She asked, aloud, "Ripley, why don't you be a Christian?"

He started, turned in his chair, looked at her inquiringly, then dropped his head.

"I mean by that, why don't you give your heart, yourself, fully to the Saviour? Why don't you have that purpose to serve Him and love Him? You needn't wait to have the other purpose for life, and this will help you form the other one for life. Yes, why don't you become a Christian?"

"Well, Aunt Lydia, I have been thinking about doing something. I knew, of course, I ought to be better. People, though, did not seem to have confidence in me——"

"Some people, say. 'Twasn't so with 'em all, Ripley."

This again brought him to the surface and at once, like a man who sinking in the water feels the touch of a life-preserver and clings to it.

"I suppose I ought," he murmured.

"And God wants you to," she added.

"You think so?" he asked, almost fiercely.

"I know so. Isn't He sayin' 'come' all the time in the Bible?"

"Yes, yes."

"What does it say in that prayer? 'Who wouldest not the death of a sinner, but rather that he should turn from his sin, and be saved.' Then again—but you know well as I. What is——?"

She rose and went to Uncle Boardman's big, worn, leather-covered prayer-book lying on the table. She took it up.

"There! This is one big 'come,' ain't it?"

She laid the book down.

"Now, Ripley, you do your duty to-day. I must go down-stairs now."

She descended to the store-room. He went up-stairs to the watch-room. He looked out of the western window. It was very quiet on the water. The sea was rapidly stilling. All its water-wrinkles Nature seemed to be smoothing down like the skilful hand that is taking out of a rich layer of silk all its creases and stretching it out in one shining surface of sleek silver-gray. The sun was floating amid the island-like clouds, giving them glory while taking honor from them, like a noble character among one's good neighbors. The hour, the scenery, invited to meditation, and Ripley fell on his knees.

"She said 'God wanted me,'" he murmured.

Yes, God had confidence in him, believed in

him, thought him of use, wanted him. He began to pray. Into the outpourings of his soul, came fragments of the profoundly penitential prayers of Ash Wednesday. In the midst of disturbance, there was satisfaction. It was like the rich, green pasture-ground succeeding the brown, parched herbage of the drought. New desires were aroused within him and his soul was satisfying itself with new food. A stream of water ran across this green pasture. He drank as well as ate. How many minutes he stayed there he could not say. He was partly conscious at one time that he heard a step. It was a light footfall and made little impression on his mood. He still knelt. Something was going out of his hands, his will. Something was coming into his heart, the Divine Blessing, and the Divine Presence and the Divine Will. Something was passing away, the old indefiniteness and the old purposelessness, like a fog rolling away from the morning sea. Something positive, definite, was stirring within his soul, a purpose to be God's, a resolution coming up into shape and declaring itself, like the sun rising above the waters, shaking off the mist and shining.

When he raised his head, his first look was

out of the window. The sun had gone out of sight.

"What, set so soon?"

His second thought was, "Why, I ought to have looked after the lantern. Sorry I forgot. Somebody will complain of Uncle Boardman that he did not light up promptly."

He hurried up the stairway leading from the watch-room to the lantern. The lamp had been lighted. It was burning with a clear radiance, strengthening as the shadows deepened.

"Why, who has been here?" he said. Then he recalled the light step that he had heard.

"Aunt Lydia has been here, faithful soul!"

He stepped outside the lantern. He looked down upon the sea. The silver-gray was changing to a cold, dark blue. He looked off toward the clouded eastern horizon. He saw the dim fading sails. In a southerly direction, a fore and aft schooner lifted a large tower of canvas toward the evening sky.

"That vessel certainly will see this light," he said, "and steer more confidently." He thought of other vessels that would surely see the light at Seal's Head and be faithfully guided.

"What a good thing is a lighthouse, and what a useful work is that of a light-keeper! To give light and guide others!" he reflected.

And then his soul seemed to become a cradle for the holding of a newly-born purpose, that his life in some way should be for the lighting and guiding of other men.

"God being my helper!" he said emphatically, reverently.

Looking up from that lonely station, far above the sea murmuring about the black rocks, he took inspiration, hope and courage from One Mightier, who was looking down in blessing.

CHAPTER IX.

LIGHT IN THE HOLLOW.

"GOIN' to be a cold day but a busy one," exclaimed the light-keeper one December morning, as he rose from the breakfast-table. "The inspector will be here soon."

"I'm ready for him," declared Aunt Lydia, looking with pride upon her stove, which she had blacked and rubbed till it shone like polished marble.

"Yes, we're all ready from lantern down to the store-room and out in the signal-tower," said Walter. "Ripley and I did nothing, yesterday, but scrub and clean."

"I mean," said Uncle Boardman, "to be ready every day, and any day to be inspected, but I wasn't quite prepared without the scrubbin' by you two boys."

Walter and Ripley went to the door of the lighthouse to see if the tender might be approaching.

"I am impressed," said Ripley, "with the

size of this institution, our lighthouses.   I have been looking at some documents your uncle has.   I find there are sixteen lighthouse districts in the whole country, all marked off, each with its inspector and engineer.   Once every three months the inspector is required to look in upon each light and examine details.   Then the lighthouses are all catalogued, location given, details as to structure, height and other items, kind of light, kind of fog-signal, and so on.   The lighthouse world is quite a world, and a very distinct, definite one."

" Much more so and much larger than people imagine.   I am proud of it and the way it is managed.   Hullo! There comes the light-tender!"

"Never saw one before.   A steamer, isn't it? I see."

"Yes, a screw, and over a hundred feet long."

The steamer was painted black, save that its deck-houses were white.   It had that trim, tidy look characterizing our navy vessels.   Besides its big, black smoke-stack projecting above the deck, were two masts rigged with small fore and aft sails.   A derrick was attached to the fore-mast, and behind this mast was a steam-engine or winch, for hoisting.

"Got a derrick on board?" Ripley had asked.

"They couldn't get along without that," replied Walter. "You see those spar-buoys lashed to the starboard side of the steamer, red ones there and black ones on the port side. Some of them are pretty long, sixty feet. Well, an old buoy may need to be taken up and a new one set. That derrick then comes in handy."

"Yes, I see. She has supplies on board, hasn't she? Barrels of something."

"Yes, supplies going to some of the light-houses. Maybe flour or potatoes, coal, and so on. That tender has a lot to do. Ah, there comes her boat, and the inspector's in it too?"

"Yes, he is there doubtless."

The boat was soon moored at the foot of the red signal-tower, and up the ladder came the inspector. He was delighted with what he saw. He praised Aunt Lydia's stove, which delighted Aunt Lydia. He had a good word for the bright lens up in the lantern, for the windows free from dust and spot, and at various points down to Aunt Lydia's kitchen, he halted to say a commendatory word. Then he went through the signal-tower, and approved as he passed along.

"Wish you would stop to dinner. I like to entertain sich folks as you are," declared Aunt Lydia, frankly.

" Ha, madame, thank you, but I have quite a run to make to-day and must be off soon as possible," replied the officer, bowing gallantly.

He had a wise, profound, official talk with Uncle Boardman about the fog-signal, how well it continued to shriek, whether the lantern leaked any now-a-days, and if the foundation of the tower showed that any of the stones had started in rough weather.

The tenants of the lighthouse watched him as he took his boat.

"Come agin !" said Aunt Lydia, hospitably.

" Thank you, madame !" replied the officer, touching his navy cap.

" He'll come fast enough, Lyddy," said her husband.

" 'Spect he will, but I want to let him know he is welcome and we ain't feared of him if he is an inspector."

" He is a navy officer, is he ?" said Walter.

" Yes, and the engineer of the district is an army officer. So we have the army and navy to back us," said Uncle Boardman.

They watched the tender steam away, churning the water energetically with its screw, its long wake widening and subsiding, the hull of the steamer dwindling, dwindling, till off in the east was only a dot at last, while the sea resumed its long, monotonous swell, and the old bell-buoy that had had an undignified, spasmodic shaking, tolled out once more its methodical, plaintive moan above imaginary treasures lost and buried in the sea.

"There!" exclaimed Uncle Boardman. "The inspector has gone, and if I didn't forget to ask him about a blacksmith on shore who is going to do some work here. Now I shall have to go off and hunt him up. Might have sent a letter by the inspector, who will get to a post-office before night and the letter would have got to the blacksmith to-morrow morning. And he comes to-morrow afternoon and wanted to know about some stock he must bring. I must go and find him."

"Won't the morning do?" asked Aunt Lydia.

"I have so much to do in the morning, I had better go to-day, at once. Walter will go with me, I guess, and if—if I don't get back in time for lightin' up, you and Ripley can do that for me. Yes, I had better go. I thought it would be cold, but the weather has softened very much, contrary to my expectation and 'twill be a good day for the trip."

At the lighthouse the day, until twilight, was uneventful. Two fishermen called. A call from such generally meant a halt in their boats off the foot of the tower-ladder. Then they shouted up, "Any cod, hake or haddick to-day?"

After several such loud bellows, someone within would hear them, run to the door and shout down an answer to the upturned, expectant faces. Two seamen in a boat, from a coaster, also called to learn about the channel ahead.

Twilight came. The lantern raised high its golden torch. Other lighthouses gave back a bright, friendly wink. The stars picked the wicks of their lamps and lighted up. The sea around the lighthouse stilled as for a quiet night and a sleepy rest.

"The folks don't come yet and we will have supper," said Aunt Lydia.

Supper passed. Still Uncle Boardman and Walter did not appear. Aunt Lydia and Ripley were up in the watch-room.

"What's that light over there?" asked Ripley, standing at an eastern window.

Aunt Lydia's sharp eyes had already detected it.

It was not like the flame of a fire, but a glow twelve feet above the water.

"Where is 'T'other Seal'?" she asked. "I have been a-wonderin' what that lightish place was."

"'T'other Seal,' 'T'other Seal'! Well, I remember what the teacher told me, May Elliott. She pointed out a farm-house over at the right and she said, a light there and our light and 'T'other Seal' would be in a line with one another. Now let me see! Let us get the range of the two lights. Well, why isn't that 'T'other Seal'? A ray from the farm-house would come through that western window, go out this eastern and fall across 'T'other Seal,' and that is where that light place is."

"Oh, I know now! Boardman and I were over there one day in autumn weather, and the top of 'T'other Seal' is covered with beach-grass. Jest in the centre is a holler place. The day we were there, we found a man who had been in a sand-barge, and the thing had upset off there and he swum ashore to 'T'other' Seal.' It was in the night and we didn't know nothin' about it. He had found some dry chips round 'T'other Seal' and had made a pile in that holler place. Then he was tryin' to light some matches he had brought with him, but they were wet, of course, and he couldn't do anything. We took him into the light-house and warmed him up."

They watched the strange lustre crowning the head of " T'other Seal."

"Yes," yes said Aunt Lydia, confidently. " Must be castaways. It is a still sea, but their vessel may have sprung aleak."

" Why don't they come here ? "

" If they come on a spar, or anything like that, they couldn't, maybe, get any further. We shall see them in the mornin'."

" Perhaps we may hear them now. I'll raise the window. Hark ! "

Ripley had raised the window. Both anxiously listened. A wild cry rent the glow above the rocky knoll and reached the watchers at the window.

" There it is ! " said Aunt Lydia, pityingly. " We must get to 'em somehow."

" How ? The boat has gone."

Aunt Lydia was ready for any emergency. Her brain was good soil for expedients, and crops were raised quickly.

" One boat has gone, Ripley, but another is on the davits above the lighthouse door."

" Oh, I forgot that one, but it will take two to lower——"

" I am good for it. Come."

"But you must not go with me to that island. I shan't really need you—it is so short a distance—and then someone ought to stay in the lighthouse."

"Oh, yes! I forgot."

"If you think you are strong enough, and can help lower——"

"Strong enough! Think! Jest try me."

Aunt Lydia in the lighthouse seemed to be receiving the gift of her youth again, its quick step, its strength, its courage.

Together, they seized the fastened ropes reaching down from the davits, and the suspended boat soon was lowered into the sea. Then Ripley descended to the boat and pushed off.

"Now I must fly round !" said Aunt Lydia bustling back through the signal-tower into the lighthouse. "I must have some hot coffee and mince pie and some ham sandwiches and dry clothes for them poor fellers to eat—and—and—to put on, I mean, and have a hearty welcome jest the same as if I was their wife or mother givin' them a good welcome home."

In the enjoyment of such an imagined relationship, she went nimbly from the storeroom to the kitchen, and then from the kitchen to the store-room, now humming, then singing softly, "Hum agin, hum agin, from a foreign shore." Dropping this, she caught up and spun out the air, "What is Hum without a mother?"

The stove seemed to kindle anew at the enthusiasm of the hour and began to roar away, while the tea-kettle sang its most cheerful tune.

"I do enjoy this!" said Aunt Lydia. "I wonder how the poor fellers live, where they were when they got upset, if they have any children! Poor men! I pity 'em. I'll do my best for 'em."

She almost wished she had gone with Ripley, remembering one Grace Darling who had covered herself with fame, also Ida Lewis. She did have a secret desire to secure and enjoy the reputation of these heroines of the sea, but she said to herself, "There has got to be a Grace Darlin' in the kitchen when the folks get back to the lighthouse. They may be snatched from the horrors of the deep, but they'll die without suthin' to eat afterwards."

Urged by this wise reflection, this good kitchen-heroine went about her humble, happy task.

Meanwhile Ripley was making his way to " T'other Seal " which was quite near. The night was mild for the winter. The ocean was quiet and only the long ocean-swell rolled lazily between the lighthouse and that knoll in the sea. The stars low down shone through a veil of mist that swathed the horizon, but up above, they twinkled and flashed with all the brilliancy of diamonds from whose face every bit of earth has been rubbed off. If Ripley had turned to the right, he would have seen the North-star proudly stretching its bright, immovable sceptre among the heavenly lights, while around it Big Bear and Little Bear were slowly sweeping, like the golden hands on the dial of a clock. " Seven ! " said this clock.

" Most time," thought Ripley, " for Uncle Boardman and Walter to be here. I would like to get those castaways safely stowed in the lighthouse before their return. They must be hungry. Hope their fire is burning well ! "

He turned to look toward " T'other Seal." Its crown was not so bright now.

" Drift-wood is giving out perhaps. I don't know why it would not be a good idea to keep a supply of drift-wood there for such cases.   If I had known anybody would be cast away there, I would have had a good supply on hand.   And Aunt Lydia, I expect, would have had a table set there with all kinds of good things on it.   Men of the sea have a rough time of it."

Ripley was now near "T'other Seal," so short was the distance.   He could look up and see the lantern of the granite tower, its noble light towering in the air.

" Must be a great comfort to sailors to see that light.   Strange I never thought about lighthouses specially before, what noble institutions they are," reflected Ripley.   " It must be a great comfort to those castaways to have a good fire near them and then look up and see that lighthouse and feel that there is a keeper, who in the morning will be on the lookout for them!   Guess they don't know I am so near them.   Wish I had brought them some more wood!   I would like to have a hand in warming them up.   However, I will do that kind job for them at the light, or Aunt Lydia will, with her hot coffee.   Ah, here we are!   Close up to ' T'other Seal '!   How quiet the sea is ! "

He allowed his boat to rub gently up a sandy tongue in a cleft of the stubborn sea-

ledge, and then feeling for a stout rocky projection, he slipped the boat's painter about it.

"'Don't forget to tie your boat,' Uncle
Boardman said only yesterday," thought
Ripley.

Climbing up the ledge, he soon reached the
soil that the beach-grass peopled in summer.
Then he looked over the edge of the hollow down into the isolated sea-camp of the
castaways. The fire was now burning low.

"Where are the men? Oh, I see!" said
Ripley.

Two forms were coiled up on opposite sides
of the hollow. The sides of this sandy bowl
that hid the flame of the camp-fire from the
two pairs of keen eyes up in the watch-room of
the lighthouse, served also as fences to keep
off the cold air blowing in from the sea.

"They seem to have overcoats on," observed Ripley. "They look comfortable down
in there.—How still they are! Must be fast
asleep. Guess I will step down and speak to
them. Of course, the sooner they get to the
lighthouse, the better. Soaked through,
probably, getting ashore from their wreck.
I'll slide down and touch this one near me.
Ah, good! that fire is waking up a little.
Shines quite bright now! It is burning up

some drift-wood it had not reached before. I'll touch—this one."

He touched "this one."

The sleeper stirred drowsily.

"He does not feel wet as if he had been in water," thought Ripley. "Very dry!"

He shook the castaway harder.

The man now sleepily mumbled the words, "Go 'way, Martin! Tired!"

"Come, get up!" persisted Ripley. "Get under cover! Come to the lighthouse!"

The castaway turned over and then sat up mumbling incoherently something about "Martin a foolin'," and rubbing drowsily his eyes. When he took his hand away from his face, by the light of the reviving fire, Ripley saw—De Vere!

Ripley started back.

He had as soon expected to see the Witch of Endor. He was so surprised he could only say, "*You*—you—are—not—De Vere?"

If Ripley's astonishment almost paralyzed his tongue, De Vere admirably concealed his surprise. If he had any other feeling in his heart than hatred, this, too, was covered up. In the readiest, most easy and cordial way, he greeted Ripley.

"Why, bless me, if this isn't my old friend,

Rip! If I am not glad to see you! Sit down, old boy, sit down on the warmest side of the fire! Where in the wide world did you come from? How did you get to this barbarous place?"

In the sweetest tones, in the most unhesitating, voluble language, De Vere welcomed Ripley.

"Funny quarters to make a feller welcome in, Rip! Seems like magic! But sit down, Rip, sit down!"

So hearty, so natural was De Vere's manner, so sincere his tones, so forgetful was he, apparently, of any interruption of kindly feeling in the past, that Ripley's surprise at this was greater than his astonishment at finding De Vere in the hollow. If Ripley could have seen clearly De Vere's eyes, these would have declared the true state of the "castaway's" feelings. They gleamed with all the hatred and murder of the old fabled basilisk. But any ugly tales, De Vere did not permit his eyes to tell. He instinctively hid them. He only kept the sweet poison-tongue below them in active employ.

Ripley felt the old fascinating power of De Vere, who had thrown one arm about him now and was drawing him down to the ground.

Ripley wanted to ask him why it was De Vere had circulated those awful slanders about him, but somehow his tongue would not work easily. He began to say, "Why did you talk so about me? You know it all is false."

He only succeeded in saying, "Why—why —why——?"

"Why—didn't I come before? Rip, you want to say that? You—you sit down."

He forced Ripley down before the fire. Then he felt in a huge pocket of his overcoat, pulled out a flask and drinking-cup, and quickly filled it and proffered it.

"There!" he said, holding it up to Ripley's nose that he might catch the odor of it. "There, you take that! It will make life worth living."

Ripley now realized that the situation was full of peril. Besides, looking across the little hollow, he saw Martin, the colored seaman, formerly on board De Vere's yacht. Martin was awake, and sitting on the opposite side of the hollow. He malevolently grinned at the actors in what was a comedy to him. That malicious, sardonic smile more fully aroused Ripley.

"No, no! I can't take that. You know I ought not, De Vere," expostulated Ripley.

"Oh yes, yes!" said De Vere, soothingly.

Ripley saw him beckon to Martin, and Martin leaped like a black dog to the help of a master whose heart was much blacker than Martin's face.

"No, no!" said Ripley, decidedly, and he shook off De Vere.

"Yes, yes!" said De Vere, soothingly. "Just open his mouth, that's a good boy!"

Was this said to Ripley, or to Martin? Was it a summons?

Ripley felt Martin's heavy hand laid upon his shoulder. De Vere pressed closer. Then Ripley raised his arm and knocked the drinking cup into the fire, shouting, "Away with it!"

De Vere's manner changed at once. "Open his mouth, Martin—open it," he shouted, "and I'll pour the whole flask down the rascal's throat!"

No smoothness, no sweetness now, but a savage brutishness to De Vere's voice, while his lifted eyes, so black, were fiercely glittering with a demoniac malignity. Looking higher up, though, Ripley saw the noble light of the tower on Seal's Head. Its rays touched him. He felt their power, as of a magician's wand. It represented the influences ennobling and life-saving. It summoned him to an effort for which it also gave him strength. In college, there lingered stories of what "Rip Eaton" had done some previous "season" in the old gymnasium under the college-pines, an institution only worked in good out-door weather. He had made some marvellous jumps, and with pride the points he had reached were shown to new students. His agility in running, his nimbleness in swinging, his cat-like activity in climbing, all were emphasized.

"Not so very stout and not tall, but he has got the muscle and the spring, I tell ye!" was the boast made by old college-men to wondering freshmen.

Ripley now felt the influence of one of those warm spring days which made him such a marvel in the gymnasium. His muscles began to swell. "The jump," "the spring," stirred and grew within him, and in a moment, it broke loose and dashed out in a fearful energy. De Vere's arm was tightening about Ripley, while Martin's coarse grip was contracting on the other side. In an instant, though, Ripley slipping down, wrenched himself out from under De Vere's embrace and then tore away from Martin, while striking out with all his power, he planted such a blow in the side of each assailant, that De Vere, with an oath, went sprawling one way, and Martin the other.

"Hold him!" wrathfully shrieked De Vere.

"Aye, aye!" Martin was roaring.

They would have thrown themselves upon Ripley again, but just then there was a din of voices on the outside of the hollow.

"Hullo, hullo!" shouted Uncle Boardman.

"Away with ye!" Walter was roaring.

Ripley thought that Aunt Lydia was there also, screaming, "Help, help! murder!

He was mistaken.

She was shrieking, but her piercing tones issued from the watch-room window from which she was trying to look into the heart of the strange, mysterious hubbub at "T'other Seal," wondering what was going on.

The next moment Uncle Boardman and Walter were tumbling over the margin of the hollow, Walter trying to hold up a lantern he had brought with him. In the furiousness of their charge, they went headlong and took Ripley with them, the three making a confused heap at the bottom of the hollow.

"Well, well!" said Uncle Boardman. "Pick yourself up!"

"That's what I am going to do if you'll let me," said Walter, laughing.

Rescuing his lantern promptly and holding it up, he asked, "Where's Ripley?"

"Alive still!" said that survivor of this charge. "I can stand what *you* have done."

They all were laughing now, as they disentangled themselves and faced one another. They saw by the lantern's light that the hollow was occupied only by friends and that there would be no further war inside.

"Well, Ripley, what have you been doing?" asked Walter. "We heard a great racket."

"Doing? Fighting the devil, two of them, Walter."

"Indeed!" exclaimed Uncle Boardman. "Well, where are they now, those—those castaways—ha! ha!—Aunt Lydia told us about, and said she thought they were murdering you. We came in a hurry."

The castaways?

Gone, gone!

They had wriggled up out of the hollow, and then writhed over its edge. If Ripley could have seen them, he would have thought two crawling, repulsive monsters of the deep were twisting back to their dark, slimy home at the bottom of the sea, such as once murdered Laocoön and his sons, and such as men now fancy may be in deep ocean dens.

"Let's chase them!" proposed Walter.

"Oh—oh!" now gasped Uncle Boardman. "What if they have gone off in one of our boats!"

Search was made, but the lantern did not prove any theft. In whatever kind of a craft the two men had arrived, they departed in the same.

"Let us chase them!" said Walter.

"Which way shall we go?" asked Uncle Boardman. "Can you hear them rowing?"

The only sound audible was the mild washing of the sea against the base of "T'other Seal."

"It is my opinion that we had better go home," said Uncle Boardman. "We might row one way and they be going exactly in the opposite. Then, what shall we chase them for? If they had taken anything of ours, we might go after them. As it is, I think we had better go——"

"Home!" answered Walter.

"Home!" said Ripley.

The two boats were launched and their crews pulled them quickly to the base of the signal-tower. The sea was placid and made little opposition.

"All safe and sound?" shrieked a voice from the platform above.

" All here ! " replied Uncle Boardman. " We thought, though, we wouldn't bring you any castaways."

" Thieves, villains, murderers—" cried Aunt Lydia, discharging a succession of uncomplimentary titles.

If it had been hot water, instead of indignant breath she was pouring forth, the impetuous outflow would have scalded Uncle Boardman and his assistants, who were now climbing up the ladder.

" To think," said Aunt Lydia, " I should be wasting my sympathy, calling them castaways and they should turn into thieves and robbers——"

"Oh, I hope not that," charitably said Uncle Boardman.

" I don't know, Boardman. The disposition is there, all ready to come out, you don't know in what. I went to the watch-room winder, when Ripley did not come back, and I heard enough to convince me that trouble was a-brewin' and—brewed, too. You came jest in time to git the warnin' and go out there."

They told her who were found by Ripley on " T'other Seal."

" Sakes alive ! " she cried in horror. " That De Vere there ?   That explains everything."

"I don't know but that Ripley would have escaped without us. It seems he routed them," said Walter, applaudingly.

"Hard work, I fear," said Ripley.

When Aunt Lydia heard about his efforts, she said, "It's allers so. One shall chase a thousand."

Uncle Boardman lingered at the signal-tower door and said, "I don't know about leaving both of the boats down there. Those scamps——"

"Then you think they may be thieves and robbers after all?" said Aunt Lydia, quizzically. "I'd hist both boats, one on top of the other, pull the rope in, shut the door, lock it, bolt it, bar it, and then we would be safe."

It was decided just to hoist Ripley's boat back to its old place and then there was an acceptance of Aunt Lydia's invitation to "Come to supper."

"It is a late one," said Aunt Lydia, "but I 'specially prepared it and it is still hot, Boardman——"

"And will be appreciated by us castaways, Lyddy, ha! ha!"

The kitchen of the lighthouse never seemed cosier than it did that evening. There was such an air of peace and protection to the place. The clock ticked serenely. The deep-set windows showed the massiveness of the walls. The stove diffused its warmth through Aunt Lydia's small, but securely sheltering domain.

"To me," whispered Ripley to Walter, "it seems like heaven after being in hell. It was an awful time out there."

Up in the watch-room, Uncle Boardman discussed with Walter the meaning of this episode.

"What do you think it all means, Walter?" inquired Uncle Boardman. "It is very queer for a man like De Vere and that Martin to be off on 'T'other Seal' on a winter night. I don't wonder your Aunt Lyddy thought they were castaways, for what else would people want to be on 'T'other Seal' for, unless they were after a place of refuge from the sea? Now if there was a wreck off here——"

"Which there is not, uncle."

"Not at all likely in this quiet sea. Well, if they didn't come for that, what did they come out this way for? They couldn't be a-huntin' up the lighthouse, for they didn't come near it. They could see its light plain enough."

"I think, uncle, that De Vere wanted to see Ripley."

"Why didn't he come in the daytime? Why didn't he call at the light? Out there on 'T'other Seal' at this time of the year, without any protection, going there not because there is a wreck—well, it is a mystery."

Walter nodded his head. It was all he could do. He could give no explanation in words. He signified that it was a mystery.

"It will be interestin', Walter, to follow up that De Vere's case."

"Follow it up?"

"I mean, see how it will turn out, what he will do. We have had some talk, your Aunt Lyddy and me, about having 'a purpose.' That De Vere has got one, only it is of the bad kind, and there is no telling how it will develop. When a man hands his soul over to that kind of a thing, look out for volcanoes and earthquakes. Now your Aunt Lyddy tells me she had a talk with Ripley and urged him to form a good purpose."

"And I think he has."

"Do you? That's good."

"I have seen him praying and reading his Bible, and all his attitude toward religion is very different, and I can see he is trying in various ways to do better."

"Oh, you can tell 'em, always know 'em, I

say to your Aunt Lyddy. Now we will go down and have prayers."

Perhaps to Ripley's mind there was no plainer proof of his changed front toward spiritual things than his interest in Uncle Boardman's family prayers. First he endured them. When he began himself to pray, then he took a singular interest in Uncle Boardman's devotional appointments for the family. He felt their appropriateness. He appreciated his personal need of them. He enjoyed them.

This night of the adventure with De Vere and Martin, Ripley noticed with peculiar interest Uncle Boardman's selection of a psalm.

" Lord, how are mine adversaries increased ?
Many are they that rise up against me.
Many there be which say of my soul,
There is no help for him in God.
But Thou, O Lord, art a shield about me ;
My glory, and the lifter up of mine head.
I cry unto the Lord with my voice,
And he answereth me out of his holy hill.
I laid me down and slept ;
I awaked ; for the Lord sustaineth me,
I will not be afraid of the thousands of the
    people,

That have set themselves against me round
    about.
Arise, O Lord! Save me, O my God!
For Thou hast smitten all mine enemies upon
    the cheek-bone.
Thou hast broken the teeth of the wicked.
Salvation belongeth unto the Lord:
Thy blessing be upon thy people."

After prayers, Uncle Boardman was up in
the lantern, inspecting the lamp, and then
he stepped outside the lantern and watched
the sky, and lifting his hand he caught the
drift of the wind, and prognosticated the
weather for another day.

He heard a step and looking back into the
lantern, saw Ripley.

" That you, Ripley? "

" Yes, sir.   Shall I come out ? "

" Sartin !   Glad to have ye."

Ripley went outside and looked over the
parapet-rail down upon the dark, chilling,
lonely sea.

" I liked, sir, your selection that you read
to-night."

" Did you ? "

" Yes, sir."

" That's good."

"I never appreciated it before. I wondered why David said so much about his enemies, or rather, why it should be thought that people generally can find any particular value in those passages. After my experience to-night on 'T'other Seal,' and realizing how unscrupulous an enemy might be, I seemed to feel the force of the psalm."

"Oh, those psalms will fay in somewhere, sooner or later, we may be assured. That is the beauty of them, they are so practical."

"I see it, more and more."

"I am glad you see it, Ripley, and I am glad you use the psalms. We can't get along without our Bibles. They are food and water. When a man has a good purpose, the Bible is awful strengthenin' to the roots. The Bible feeds our roots if we have got any. I would be particular about reading it, every day, Ripley. Just let me say that your Aunt Lyddy takes an interest in you and wants to help you, and you will excuse anything——"

"Oh, certainly! I like to have you speak of things. I mean to follow up my Bible."

"Well, Ripley, be assured then that it will follow you up and help support you."

"I will try to do my duty."

"That's right! You will take solid satisfaction in doing it."

The two men lingered still outside the lantern. Finally Uncle Boardman said, "Wonder where those two castaways are?"

"I don't know, I am sure."

"Well that we didn't try to follow them. We had nothing for which we could well follow them, though it is true they acted roughly enough toward you to deserve a whippin'. Ha! ha!—don't know which way we could have gone and yet overhauled them."

Ripley thought of various places where the two adventurers might have gone. He thought of them as rowing off to some possible vessel anchored late in the mouth of the harbor. He imagined them pulling hard for the shore, and then tramping along some lonely, dark country-road.

"Ha! ha!—" he exclaimed, laughing loud and looking down toward 'T'other Seal,' or its supposed place in the dark. "Glad they are not there now!"

But there they were, that very instant. Rowing off in their boat a short distance, they then pulled back and occupied the hollow once more.

"You see, Martin, they will never think of

looking for us in the same place where they found us before."

" Jes' so!"

" The safest place in the world, when you come to think of it. They might pull to land to find us, or off to the next island, but they won't look here. "

" Der—zackly!"

" Then let us turn in."

Rubber blankets they now spread under them, and they drew heavy shawls over them. They wore also inside very thick overcoats. They coiled up into a small compass, trying to keep warm. Fortunately, it was mild weather.

"Hark, what is that?" at last asked De Vere.

" Sound jes' like one a-laffin' somewhere. "

" Well, let 'em laff."

It was Ripley outside the lantern laughing and saying, as he looked in the direction of ' T'other Seal,' "Glad they are not there now ! "

CHAPTER X.

THAT FOG ALARM.

"IT is a quiet day, Uncle Boardman," Walter remarked the next morning, when the usual work at the lighthouse was over, "and if you have nothing further for us, Ripley and I thought we would go off to Cod Rock fishing."

"Very well. Now is your chance. We have been looking for a big winter storm, but it does not seem to arrive. It will get here and 'twill be rough and cold, and you had better improve your chance for fine weather while you have it."

The two young men pushed off from the lighthouse and pulled for Cod Rock. It was overcast and on the edge of the sea were huge, irregular folds of mist like stranded vessels, that the tide might lift and set at liberty any moment and they bear down upon the coast and overwhelm it with their vapory masses.

"Any chance for fog?" inquired Walter, as his oars splashed into the water. "Do you think there is, Ripley?"

"Oh, I guess not! Hope not, anyway. I hate the blast of that old fog-trumpet," said Ripley, glancing at the bulky signal-tower. "Now, I suppose it would make a great difference in our feelings if we had ever been on the water in a fog, and that trumpet's blast had helped us."

" Oh, yes, of course ! "

The young men pulled out in the direction of the bell-buoy, which was plaintively tolling.

" This sounds quite mournful, though I suppose it tries hard enough to be cheerful, but that old fog-signal is a nuisance," affirmed Ripley.

Walter changed the subject: " Now we are going to Cod Rock, and I think it is just south of this bell-buoy. Let me see! Let us take our bearings. Due south from this point, and we fish on the side toward this bell-buoy. Ought to have taken a compass. That is very handy in case of a fog."

" I dare say it is, but I can't say, for I never had any experience."

" Oh yes, fog is a bad thing! Why, I have heard of fishermen out in a fog who knew the coast well enough, but they would be utterly puzzled. I heard of one that the fog surprised at evening, and the poor fellow pulled this way and that, and when morning came he was three miles from home. He ought to have had a compass."

"And we haven't any, Walter? That is cheering."

"Oh, I hope everything will be satisfactory."

At Cod Rock the fishing was very tempting. It almost seemed as if the fish knew the work of the forenoon might be interrupted and very self-sacrificingly bit as often and promptly as possible. Now and then Walter interjected some comforting remark about helpless mariners in a sudden irruption of fog. He had the reputation of being something of a tease, but he justified himself on this occasion with the thought, "I am not going to have this young man run down that fog-trumpet. He doesn't know how useful it is."

The fishing was continued. The young men laughed and jested, pulled in their fish, talked about the sea, about college, and, at last, about school-keeping.

"Say, Walter, would you advise me to keep school this winter?"

"I would if I were you; that is if I had a chance. It is a good thing for the teacher, and if it be under a good teacher, it is well for

the school.   I shrank from it myself, but discipline we don't like ourselves, we don't *hesitate*
to recommend to others."

"And this school up here, where May
Elliott has taught, you would apply for, would
you?   The scholars up there seemed to take a
fancy to me."

"Certainly!   That is one sure sign of success, when your school wants you rather than
you want the school."

"I don't specially want it, but it might be
good medicine as you suggest, but——"

He paused.

"Those ugly stories!   And De Vere's in the
neighborhood."

"Well, let him be, though that is to be
proved.   To-day he may be off in some vessel
from which he and Martin came ashore.   Let
the stories go.   They are false, you know."

"Yes, absolutely untrue.   If I could get
that Martin to tell what he knows, or get hold
of De Vere's boat at the bottom of the sea
and find that little box in which he said was
the paper proving my big debt to him, everything would be seen to be in my favor."

"Oh, well!   You yourself are better than
any tin box.   Your character is an answer.
De Vere himself is an answer.   People look

at the hole from which those slanders crawl out."

The young men had ceased fishing, and their lines unemployed hung over the gunwale of the boat.

"There is nothing like a decision, you know," Walter remarked, and casually looked abroad upon the sea. "Say 'yes,' that you'll apply for it!"

"Apply for the school? I know that is what you mean——"

"Say quick! Settle it now. Say 'yes'! Might as well. Quick!"

"Yes!" answered Ripley, smiling. "But what is your hurry? Why are you rushing me in this thing?"

"You might as well decide it one time as another, and then it is well to get one thing out of the way before we attend to the next thing, for look there, young man!"

"What is it, Walter?"

"See!"

Walter pointed back toward the eastern horizon where so many of those fog-ships had been stranded. They were all afloat now, and advancing rapidly. There was something spectral in their shape, so loose of outline and irregular. There was a menace, too, a threat, in those huge, towering, lowering and gloomy masses.

"It is upon us, Ripley! Wind up your line and let us be off!"

"Which way?"

"North, of course. We'll aim at the bell-buoy."

"Well, where is north? Why not at the lighthouse?"

"Where is it?"

Had that granite structure melted, evaporated, turned into an ally of the fog-fleet and gone off with it?

The lighthouse had disappeared!

"Whew!" Ripley murmured. "Well, we can see the tip of the bell-buoy and ought to hear it."

"'Twould be nice to hear a blast from that old fog-trumpet, wouldn't it?"

Ripley smiled, and nodded his head. They now pulled stoutly for the bell-buoy.

"I can see it still," said Ripley, twisting his neck to get a near look. "Boat is heading exactly for it."

Walter said nothing. He was watching that fog-fleet where never a rope was pulled, where anchor was never weighed or heaved, where never a pulley creaked, and whose crew never sang one jolly song of the sea, but abode in one continual dumbness. There was something grand, portentous, awful in this silent, steady, shadowy foe, coming nearer and nearer.

" A penny for your thoughts! " said Ripley, who disliked long-continued silence and solitude.

" I was watching that fog. Can you see the bell-buoy, Ripley ? "

" N–o–o ! Why don't we hear it ? "

The young men lay on their oars and looked off to the supposed north.

" The sea is very quiet, so that there is little disturbance of the bell. Then the wind, too, is carrying away all the sound."

" Why doesn't that fog-trumpet give a blast ? "

" Then you do want to hear it ? Well, I should enjoy it also, but you see while the fog is thick out here, Uncle Boardman doesn't start up the fog-signal until it is so thick he can't see across to Rocky Point. Then he lets it scream ! Well, we know the bell-buoy is over that way somewhere. Pull away ! "

The fog was dense about them very soon.

" Hark, Ripley ! "

They listened.

"Ting—ting—ting!"

"That is it, Walter! That is the bell-buoy, but it ought not to be over there."

"But it is, ha! ha! We shifted our course and did not know that we had done so. It is easy to lose your bearings."

They pulled toward the sound and were glad to welcome the bell-buoy.

"It looks home-like, Walter, doesn't it?"

Walter nodded assent.

The young men rowed up to it and halted.

"We can stay here at any rate, Walter," said Ripley, laughing, "Tie up to the thing until we can see the lighthouse, ha! ha!"

"Ah, young man," said Walter, teasingly, "what if the fog shouldn't lift and we couldn't *see* the lighthouse, and night set in and hunger and thirst, and then another foggy day begin and go on, and there come more hunger and more thirst and another night of mist, and so on and so on until at last men come here and see in a boat two skeletons! A serious matter, young man! No laughing occasion, I tell ye! Say, which way should we go to get to the lighthouse? Tell me! Which side of this old thing would you call north or south?"

"Where is that old fog-trumpet, that beau-

"WHICH SIDE OF THIS OLD THING WOULD YOU CALL NORTH OR SOUTH.?"
Page 204.

tiful, useful, superior, grand invention? We ought to hear that by this time," said Ripley.

"Don't be impatient, young man. Did you see Uncle Boardman before you left, and say in his ear, 'Start up this music for my benefit out on the sea'? As it is, you can't expect him to start it up until it is so thick about his post of duty that he can't see Rocky Pint—not Point, but Pint—and then won't there be music! Just beautiful, yes, but not now, young man!"

"Well, we can hold on to this."

"Yes, no objection to that. Can stay until we are skeletons if we wish to do so."

The young men here examined the bell-buoy.

"Made of iron and painted red," observed Ripley.

"Yes, a sort of bowl or boat and from it rises a conical frame, and the bell is hung at the top. You might say it is a cradle and the bell is the baby that gets the rocking. It is chained down to the dangerous ledges hidden beneath. Did you know what a dangerous place this is? Just awful!"

"Get out! Might call this a belfry. You could get up a very interesting story under the name of the 'Lone Belfry of the Sea.'"

"Begin it! You will probably have time

enough in this foggy spell to finish the story that this fascinating spot seems to inspire. Now I hope you see how useful buoys may be. They not only guide the navigator but inspire the novelist."

The conversation soon became a sober one, and Ripley inquired:

"How many kinds of buoys are there, Walter?"

"I can tell some of them, anyway. There is this kind, the bell-buoy. Then there are what are called spar-buoys which are very common, can-buoys, and nun-buoys. There are what they call whistling-buoys. I can think of one off Portland, Maine. It is described as a mammoth nun about twelve feet out of the water and about ten feet in diameter at water-line. This is topped with a whistle. The action of the sea forcing the air through the whistle produces a blast. It will give from twenty to thirty blasts a minute. That is no mean sound-engine. I have heard it. If you want to see the list, Uncle Boardman has in the lighthouse a record of all the buoys, beacons, stakes and other day-marks in his district. This is issued by the Lighthouse Board, at Washington. We will take that spar-buoy one can see at the left going into the

the harbor here. You will find it in that government list, its locality, color, number, the important points near it and the distance, the depth in feet of lowest tides there, and other matters of interest, on what side of the channel it is to be found, and so on."

"I must get hold of that list. Well, I remember our spar-buoy—the one you spoke of—is black, and yet some buoys are red. What is the idea in that? Just fanciful?"

"No, there is a purpose in it. Take that black spar-buoy. You will find an odd number on it. The rule I saw in the printed list is that black buoys with odd numbers will be found on the port side of the channel and must be left on the port hand in passing in. The pilot, bringing a vessel in, can read that buoy as if it were a book, and knows what its advice is. Looking ahead, supposing he sees a red buoy. This has even numbers on it, and the direction is, that it will be found on the starboard side of the channel and must be left on the starboard hand when coming into harbor. Now let us suppose we find a buoy with red and black horizontal strips. That means it is located on obstructions, that a channel-way is on either side, and may be left on either hand when coming in from sea. If those had been white and black *perpendicular* strips, that would have meant that the buoy was in mid-channel, and a vessel must pass close to it or it will run into trouble. A buoy then is a guideboard in the sea, and it indicates the road to the mariner. If he find a buoy peculiarly marked, he must consult the printed list given by the Lighthouse Board. Then supposing there are various channels to a harbor, and all to be marked. Just a spar-buoy will be placed in the smallest or least important channel, while a can-buoy shows one of more consequence, and a nun-buoy would mark the principal channel. If you find a day-beacon, or stake, or spindle on the side of a channel, it will be colored like a buoy. I noticed quite a number of 'spindles' in Uncle Boardman's list. This was one way they were recorded: 'Iron spindle, thirty feet; cage on top.' Beacons that I noticed might be of wood or stone. But one can see it is a department of much interest, when you think of the sea-coast and river-banks and lake-shores that are covered."

"Western navigation must demand many helps of one sort or another, that you have been mentioning, Walter."

"Western? I guess it does. Why, in the

last report I saw, one thousand two hundred and thirty-two beacon-lights on Western rivers were mentioned. The government task of lighting up these great water-ways of our country is no small one, and is, comparatively, a recent one. A beacon-light on one of these rivers is described as 'simply an inland lighthouse of modest proportions. A short wooden post, braced to withstand wind, and bearing a small hooded platform at its top, eight or twelve feet from the ground, forms the support of a lantern of superior construction.' These beacon-lights are visited occasionally by special steamers that repair damaged lights, reset them, if necessary, leave supplies of oil and give the lightkeepers their wages. One recent estimate gives over thirty-five hundred miles, sparkling with about thirteen hundred lights. But oh, what long, lonely, unlighted stretches of water there are!"

All this time the bell-buoy was gently rocking, for the sea was quite pacific in its mood, but the fog was as unconquerable as ever. It surrounded the young men with a very thin, yet to the sight, a very impenetrable wall. Just mist, mist, everywhere, folding down on the water. A contracted sea, in whose centre was a bell-buoy, slightly rocking, and near it the boat, in which were two young men wondering which way they ought to go to find the light-house.

"Getting tiresome!" exclaimed Walter.

"And chilly!" said Ripley, shrugging his shoulders in the wintry air.

"I am hungry and long for a hot dinner at Seal's Head Hotel, kept by one Lydia Board-man, Ripley."

"And I am thirsty and there is nothing to drink but this ocean of salt-water."

"The bell music is sounding mournful. Sort of dirge-like now!"

"How would it do to row off a little way, not getting out of sight of this buoy and not losing its sound?   Might see the lighthouse."

"All right!   We will try it."

There was trial and there was failure.   The boat came back to the bell-buoy.

"Wretchedly tiresome!" said Ripley.

"You know what I said about two skeletons found in this boat!".

"Don't want to know anything about it."

Suddenly, over the sea, from a quarter at the right of the young men, came a loud, vigorous, nasal, but cheery, "Toot-t-t-t-t!"

"Hoo-ror!" shouted Ripley, jumping up

from his seat and flourishing his cap. "Most cheerful, the sweetest, grandest music I ever heard!"

Walter laughed and waved his cap also.

Once more Ripley cheered and pronounced it the sweetest sound ever made.

"When I hear it again, I shall think of our experience out here, and imagine, Walter, the poor, perplexed fellows off at sea, wondering where they are and then hearing this sound which tells them the world of humankind is nigh at hand. But how could you tell this from the whistle of a steamer at a distance? The sound might not be peculiar enough."

"I think it is peculiar, but one clew to its character is its length, Rip. Uncle Boardman tells me each blast is ten seconds long and there are intervals of thirty seconds. You could take your watch, having looked at your list of fog-signals given by the government, and you would soon conclude it was no steamer, blowing with such regularity and giving blasts of such definite length."

"Well, let us go where they make those heavenly noises."

They rowed away.

Up out of the great mist-world, loomed, ere long, the granite lighthouse, and the most interesting feature of the view, in Ripley's opinion, was that of the long, red fog-trumpets. The young men quickly climbed the ladder to the signal-tower door and went up into the engine-room.

"Welcome home!" said Uncle Boardman. "Your Aunt Lyddy has been a-worryin' about ye. I told her it was all right and you would report in due season."

"Undue season, this time," said Walter. "I will report to her and relieve her mind."

He found her in the kitchen.

"There, if I ain't glad to see ye!" exclaimed Aunt Lydia. "Been a-worryin' myself most to death. Now tell me all about it!"

In the engine-room of the signal-tower, Ripley was asked to do the same thing for Uncle Boardman. When he had finished, he said:

"Now tell me all about this machinery. I want to be able to run it. I think it is one of the nicest things invented."

Smiling at the young man's enthusiasm, Uncle Boardman began:

"This is a Daboll trumpet, as we call it, a third-class one, and it is operated by this hot-air engine. Now I will give you the details. I build my fire in here, where this door is. See?"

"But you have two engines."

"I know it. In case of disaster to the one, the other can be used. We have to be ready for emergencies, you know, and if accidents happen, we can't get to land and have repairs made at once. We must help ourselves. In some foggy spells of weather, we use this signal hour after hour. I heard of a down East light where it is said a fog-signal was going twenty-one days when a visitor left. No wonder something may break down, and we must be ready for the emergency. Now to return, I build my fire in this little furnace. The motive power is hot air. When the air is heated, that expands and drives the piston of this engine. Then the work of the piston is to compress the air in these air-tanks. This piston goes with vigor, and you can imagine how powerfully it can work an air-pump and so press the air into these tanks. The air is forced then into a reed-box, as we call it, and that makes the music."

"I see, I see! But here is something that is a mystery; how is the length of the blast regulated? Why does it not last twenty, or thirty, or forty seconds?"

"It depends on this cam, as we call it, and that you know is this projecting part of the circumference of this wheel. Resting on this cam or projection is an arm of that lever you see there, which moves the rod, opening a valve for the escape of the compressed air. We will suppose the wheel is revolving. As it turns over, the cam is reached and that at once affects the lever raising it and that opens the valve which affects the valve-rod. This will stay so the air rushing into the reed-box and making that scream until the projection or cam has slid round, and then the lever drops back where it was before, *the air* is shut off from the reed-box and the music stops."

"I see now. Instead of a blast of ten seconds, you might have a blast of a different length by making a difference in the size of the cam."

" That is it. The reed-box you may know, has just a strip of metal or reed which vibrates and makes the blast."

" Toot—toot—toot !" went the trumpet, as if emphasizing the explanation that had been made and declaring it a success.

"I suppose there are other kinds of fog-signals."

"Oh, yes ! It may be just a hand-bell that is rung, or a bell is struck by machinery. Once at Minot's Light, one of the keepers went with me up to the parapet. There a big bell was attached to the wall. He struck this with a big hammer or something of the kind that he seized, and it made a stunning noise. In a fog that may have been once a keeper's occupation to keep dinging that bell, but I see it says in the list that it is struck by machinery. Once, I was in a steamer passing Seguin Light, at the mouth of the Kennebec in Maine. The fog was so thick you could only see a blotch of yellow up in the sky and I knew it was the Seguin Light. All the time, a sharp-toned bell went tolling, tolling mournfully. It was a dismal spot to be in. Steam is also employed to sound a warning blast in a fog, but I am contented with this one."

"Toot—toot—toot," went the self-satisfied red trumpet, overhead.

"Walter has been giving me some particulars about buoys and other helps to navigation. I never knew the work was so systematized and superintended, that it was so extensive."

"Very, very, and all with one end in view, to make life more secure, to help people to be more comfortable, more safe and happy."

And the fog-trumpet assented, letting out a big, jolly "Toot—toot—toot," to echo across the sea.

Not all movements in life are to make people safer and happier, more comfortable and
secure, and Ripley had an illustration of it
that day.

Aunt Lydia had something to tell Walter,
and Walter handed it over to Ripley. Aunt
Lydia's black eyes flashed and snapped as she
told this interesting fact to Walter.

"Your Uncle Boardman was in the signal-
tower a-firin' up his engine, for he saw the fog
a-comin' and knew he must be ready. Wall,
the fog kept hangin' off and on, nearin' Rocky
Pint and then fallin' back, botherin' your
Uncle Boardman to know what to do. Wall,
he was there by his engine like a faithful sol-
dier at his post, a-watchin' and a-lookin'. 'One
way or t'other' is my motter. A good thick
fog well sot in, or a clear sky. None of this
backin' and fillin'! However, there it was. I
happened to be down at the door, a-lookin'
out to see what I could see, if I couldn't hurry
up that fog, for I thought of you boys on the
water and I knew that to hear a good 'toot'
might help you. I heard suthin' else, a man
shoutin' away down at the foot of the ladder.
I looked over the railin' and saw a colored
man in a boat a-lookin' up. 'Is Rip there?'
he asked familiar like. 'You mean Mister

Eaton?' I says, wantin' to show him what was respectful. He was sulky and says, 'I spose so.' 'There is no other one here,' I sez. 'Wall, is he in?' 'No sir,' I sez, wishin' to teach him manners, 'he is not in.' 'When will he be hum?' 'I can't say. It looks now as if he wouldn't be here till the fog let him, *sir*.' I jest sounded the *sir*. I heard him a-mutterin' down in his boat. At last, he sez, 'Tell him De Vere wants him to pay what he owes him.' Sez I, 'Who is it?' I thought he said suthin' that sounded like 'dev—' and the rest you can imagine. But he made me no answer. Off he rowed looking sullen and sulky enough. Now ain't that pro-vokin' to have him a-follerin' that young man up, a-keepin' him uneasy, a-worryin' of him, a-tormentin' him?"

"Of course it is, Aunt Lydia. I don't believe a word of it. If we could only get hold of De Vere's boat at the bottom of the sea, and find that tin box which he said had a paper proving the debt, we might get some light on this subject. How can we, though, get hold of it?"

"The Lord can raise it up from the depths of the sea, Walter. He does raise things mightily sometimes. If you were out here all the time, you would see how things could be shaken."

"Yes, He can do it, but only He. Seems too bad that Ripley should be bothered this way."

"What do you suppose that dev——?"

"De Vere?"

"That's the one. What is he doin' round here?"

"That is what I don't know absolutely, but I have my suspicions. Ripley's sister has written to him that De Vere is in trouble, that it was said he was hiding somewhere lest they might arrest him."

"You don't say!"

"Then the people on the shore have got hold of it. They say the police are after him, and were about making inquiries concerning him the night of the day when you heard De Vere on 'T'other Seal.' Looks to me as if De Vere came off to the little island to get rid of the uncomfortable people wanting to overhaul and visit him. He must go somewhere, of course."

"Yes, and he'll git where he belongs some-time."

Ripley was deeply agitated when he heard of Martin's call.

"I feel disgraced, Walter."

"Oh, no! you needn't."

"But what will the people here think?"

"Oh, they look at the source of the charges. Don't you?"

"Do they?"

Ripley spoke eagerly.

"Certainly they do."

"Then I will."

CHAPTER XI.

ONE SUNDAY.

A SUNDAY may be a very lonely and uncomfortable day to one in a light-house, especially if it be a bit of time that tries to shut out a happy eternity with God, a day when He is forgotten, and the soul sinks down into sloth and sleep. That was not Uncle Boardman's Sunday.

"Happiest day in the week has come!" he would say. "Now we will get our mornin' duties out of the way, soon as possible, have the lamp cleaned and trimmed, prism rubbed, lantern-windows wiped, and then have services. Mebbe we can 'practice' a little our music."

Aunt Lydia with pride had accumulated in her youth a little stock of music. It had not been increased, but on the other hand, it had been kept from wasting. It was represented in a small melodeon, very old-fashioned, and in the volume of its sound modest, but its voice was exceedingly sweet.

"Now, Boardman, I don't know where we

can keep that ere melodeon, but I can't spare it. We must take it to the lighthouse."

"Don't know, as you say, where we can keep the melodeon. That is the only puzzle."

"Must take it, Boardman, if I have to keep it on our bed in the daytime, and take it off and set it on the floor by night. It must go! There! I've got it! We can take it off its legs, can clap it under the bed when we don't need it. It must go."

"It shall go if you say so," said the accommodating Boardman.

So to the lighthouse went the big old-fashioned clock and the little old-fashioned melodeon. Room was finally found for the latter up in the watch-room. This became the chapel of the lighthouse. Here the little congregation would assemble Sunday morning, warned, perhaps, by Aunt Lydia's voice, "Church-time, folks! I have been to the door and I can hear a bell ringin' on land."

Then Uncle Boardman in his best Sunday-suit, would stand up in the watch-room and begin morning prayer. Aunt Lydia at the melodeon would be ready to strike up the *Venite*, Walter's and Ripley's rich, resonant voices filling up the scant measure of her now worn, deficient tones. Uncle Boardman always tried to " help Aunt Lyddy out," but the *Te Deum* had been above the level of the efforts of these two humble performers.

"Glad you've come, Walter and Ripley! We will have the *Te Deum* now," Aunt Lydia said, one Sunday morning.

Oftentimes, has that grand, inspiring, uplifting chorus ascended from the earth, and under circumstances the most impressive and stately. How many have looked up and cried in song, "We praise Thee, O God ; we acknowledge Thee to be the Lord"! It had, though, its own rich and peculiar significance when, out amid the rough waves, the watch-room of the lighthouse became a chapel in which the *Te Deum* was sung. The tall, gray granite shaft seemed to be lifting before the Maker of sea and land this humble offering of Aunt Lydia's old melodeon up in the watch-room, her worn voice, Uncle Boardman's tremulous bass, and the young men's richness and fulness of tone. It was all acceptable ; that which was worn and tremulous through the usage of many years, and that which had the freshness and strength of youth. So the forenoon passed at the lighthouse.

When the dinner-hour came, Aunt Lydia

would bring out some nicety treasured up for the Sunday table.

"This is a peculiar day, one of joy," she would say, "and I want its mark to be seen everywhere."

After dinner, Uncle Boardman would say, "We would have a walk if on shore, mebbe, but as there is no chance for anything extended here, I will do the best I can."

He would go outside the lantern and there his stubby figure could be seen from the deck of any passing vessel, stopping awhile to lean over the railing and look down to learn how the sea was behaving itself. Then he would turn away and go to the other side of the lantern to gaze into the mysterious recesses of the northeast, and wonder if from that storm-vexing quarter would issue shadows and cloud, chilliness and mist, rattling rain and roaring wind to make the coming night a dismal one for the mariner.

"Now I will go," Uncle Boardman would say, "and hear my Sunday-school class. Aunt Lyddy and I have the same lesson they have at St. John's, at home. We find it pays and seems home-like to keep up the lesson."

Uncle Boardman would mount his spectacles upon his nose, open his big family Bible, and begin to question his class about the lesson. This class had consisted of Aunt Lydia and Tom Walker. The place of the latter was more than filled by Walter and Ripley. Especially to Ripley, who was so sensitively alive to every novelty, was the Sunday-school in the lighthouse attractive. He and Aunt Lydia were rather inclined to get into a discussion, but it would be promptly terminated when Uncle Boardman, looking blandly but decidedly over his spectacles would say, "Guess now we will take up the next question."

"Very well, fether," would be Aunt Lydia's prompt, submissive reply.

She had great respect for her husband's practical judgment in the management of his class, or any other department of duty.

The winter-hour for lighting-up came early, the sun setting red and flaming in the west, or going down to his sleep, a nightcap of cloud already on his head.

After tea, Uncle Boardman had a shortened form of evening prayer, but this service was in the kitchen. A good-night hymn would be sung and peace would fold its wings over the souls of those in the lighthouse. Outwardly, there might be anything but peace. A stormy night might keep Uncle Boardman long in the watch-room. Aunt Lydia would lie awake hearing the wind roar and the rain crash down. Peace, though, was within, for the happiest day in the week seemed to bring angels to give their benediction at night, to those in the lighthouse.

While the programme of Sunday, as here detailed, was generally carried out, it was not observed one day in its completeness. Uncle Boardman had seated himself in the afternoon, Bible in hand. Of his Sunday-school class, Aunt Lydia was there, prim and expectant. Ripley sat next to her, prepared to open a discussion with her at the earliest moment. Walter was absent. He was up in the watch-room, detained there by his interest in the course of a fore and aft schooner making for the harbor.

"She—she—must look out!" he thought, eying the schooner through a spy-glass. He muttered aloud, " That bell-buoy, seems to me, says plain enough where to go. If the skipper doesn't look out, he will be aground on——"

The next moment he was rushing down through the bedroom of the assistant-keepers, then through Uncle Boardman's apartment, bursting into the kitchen and provoking

Aunt Lydia to the startled exclamation, " Massy ! "

" Uncle Boardman, there is a fore and aft schooner aground ! " cried this herald from the watch-room.

" Where, where ? " asked Uncle Boardman, his spectacles slipping off his nose and his Bible going to the floor as he hastily, excitedly rose.

" Near the bell-buoy."

" Not surprised, not one bit of it !   They are very careless.   Lyddy, where's my overcoat ? "

" You goin', Boardman ? "

" I must."

" But it is growin' cold."

" Lyddy ! "

That was all Uncle Boardman said, but what he did not say was this, " What are we here for ? "

She understood him and brought his coat immediately.

Walter and Ripley were both slipping on their coats.

" I guess, Ripley, if you will be so kind as to stay with your Aunt Lyddy——"

Ripley gave a disappointed look which Uncle Boardman noticed ; and Walter answered, " Rip, if I find you're wanted, I'll raise a signal on one of my oars."

"Take this towel," was Aunt Lydia's offer.

"Can I see it plain enough?" asked Ripley.

"With the spy-glass in the watch-room. You can see with that. I saw that schooner strike when I had the glass. The vessel fluttered, fairly fluttered, and shook all her sails," replied Walter.

"Wall, fether, if you must go, do mind and look after yourself."

"I will, Lyddy," said Uncle Boardman, hurrying out of the kitchen and followed by the others. "You see, I may be able to tell the skipper about his chances to get off before night. And, Ripley, I hope we shall get back in an hour or two, but if detained, you will light up, please."

Uncle Boardman and Walter descended the ladder, took their boat and quickly rowed away.

"I hate to have 'em go off this cold weather and at this time of day," said Aunt Lydia, watching solicitously the departure.

"Oh, they will come back all right and do a lot of good, Aunt Lydia."

"I 'spose so, but things do happen so sudden in this world! There we quietly were a-settin', and in a moment like a bomb-shell, this thing was exploded. In a lighthouse, there is no tellin' what may happen to scare ye."

"And where there are two such willing souls as yours and Uncle Boardman's, what a lot of good you may do!"

"Oh, I thank ye!" said the blushing Aunt Lydia. "And I suppose one man's danger is another man's opportunity."

"Good! A lot of sensible, cheerful philosophy to that."

Aunt Lydia's face fairly glowed with pleasure. They went back into the fog-signal tower. Aunt Lydia started and held up her hands, exclaiming : "Oh I hope not!"

"What is it?"

"Oh, that a fog won't set in."

"Why, any chance for it?"

"Not the least that I know of."

'The fire all ready to be started in the engine-room?"

"I guess so."

"Let's go up and see."

The wood was not in the furnace waiting to be kindled, but it was there on the floor beside the engine.

"Now I may be the foolishest person in the

world, but I seem to feel as if fog might be comin', Ripley."

"Fog? I will go up to the lantern and look off."

He came back hastily, and excitedly said he thought he could, through the glass, see the sign that he was wanted at the bell-buoy.

"And the fog, Ripley?"

"I think it does look suspicious."

"I will be ready," declared Aunt Lydia.

"How will you get along without me, if I must go, and I think I ought?"

"Don't you worry! Women can run light-houses. I shall have to help you lower the other boat. What we have done before, can be done agin."

The "other boat" was suspended from the davits above the signal-tower door. It was now lowered, and Ripley quickly rowed away.

"All alone!" thought Aunt Lydia, as she returned to the engine-room in the signal-tower. Looking round she solemnly declared, "Nobody in this tower, nobody in the light-house."

It seemed all the lonelier because no one could say what might happen to her husband and the young men, and the thought of possible accident made any present solitude seem all the more oppressive.

Aunt Lydia had a reputation for "pluck." An emergency would always arouse a spirit of courage and self-reliance. She would rally her resources at once. It was so, this Sunday afternoon.

"Lonely?" she queried. "Nobody here? *Somebody is* here, Lyddy Boardman. And what did I come here for? Came to be a help, yes, came to do suthin, and—we will do it. Here," she called aloud, addressing the wood at her feet, "you go in there!"

Into the furnace went the wood, and it was kindled at once into a ruddy blaze.

"When that fog comes, we will be ready," said Aunt Lydia.

It is wonderful how resoluteness, daring act. ivity will spread around an earnest soul an atmosphere of hope, cheerfulness, companionship even. Through some subtile law of association, you seem to communicate to the inanimate objects about you your spirit, and wake up a vitality within them which becomes responsive and helpful. The flames in the furnace in that solitary engine-room, seemed to be saying, "Ha! ha! ha! You can rely on *us!* Here we are!"

Aunt Lydia hurried into the kitchen of the lighthouse to look after the fire there.

"Don't want that to droop," she said.

Its spirits were good, and it purred and mildly declared its hopefulness, while the clock patiently, cheerily ticking away, seemed to call out, "Count on *me*," and the little tea-kettle on the stove responded, "Me too!"

"It does look real cheerful and home-like and cosey here. Now I must go back!"

The mistress of the lighthouse did not appreciate that it was her own brave, indefatigable self that was getting outside of her, stimulating with its own spirit, coloring all things with its own sanguine hopes.

"Now let me see!" she added, looking at the engine. "How is it you start this ere thing up! I believe Boardman does—so. All right when the time comes. We will be ready."

Out at the bell-buoy, Uncle Boardman had held a conference with the skipper of the schooner.

"Cap'n, I advise ye to get out both your boats, pack all your crew in and then—we will help, and we have just signalled to the light for another boat—and see if we can't pull your vessel off. You see, Cap'n, the tide is risin' and that may be in your favor and may not be. This is a peculiar ledge and the tide may lift her forrard and wedge her in where the rock splits and she'll have to stay some time. I have seen that done. Now, jest hitch a cable astern here, and we will all pull on it with a will, and, as the tide lifts on her, we may draw her back. What say?"

"That sounds reasonable," said the weather-beaten old skipper. "We will try it. I have five in my crew. I can spare one man for your other boat that is coming."

"All right! The sooner the better!"

When Ripley arrived the four crews took their places in the four boats. The skipper cried, "All together! Hearty, boys, hearty!" and at their task went sixteen muscular arms.

The tide gently lifted. The boats stoutly drew.

"Something must give!" declared Uncle Boardman to Walter.

"And we don't mean to give here. No sir!"

"Hun—now!" cried Uncle Boardman.

The muscles in sixteen stalwart arms strained harder. The rope on which they drew was stretched tight and firm as a wire. The rising tide pressed gently.

A loud, exciting cry broke from the skipper in the rear boat; "She gives! She gives! Hun — now! All together! Thar! Thar! Hun—now! Hoo—ror!"

Back into deep water fell the schooner, easily and gracefully, bowing as if in gentle courtesy, to make up for rude stubbornness in rushing into such a vise.

There was a scramble now made for the vessel to see if the hull showed any sign of leaking.

"Jest a scrapin' of her skin, I guess!" declared her skipper, after the investigation.

"Lucky!" said Uncle Boardman.

"And thanks to ye for bringin' good luck!" exclaimed the skipper.

"Set it down to the lighthouse," modestly answered Uncle Boardman, "and these two young men."

"Obleeged to ye all! Lighthouses, we may well be proud of."

"And of young men," said Uncle Boardman, pointing proudly toward Walter and Ripley.

"And of sailors," added Walter, thoughtfully, nodding toward the schooner's crew.

"And of their skipper," was the last compliment in this circle of mutually admiring members, and given by Ripley.

A hearty laugh all round followed the compliments, and the light-keeper and his assistants prepared to return to the lighthouse.

"What!" exclaimed Uncle Boardman, turning seaward. "Fog comin'!"

"Sartin, major!" said the skipper, who had found a title for the light-keeper. "Glad enough am I to have this chance to git into harbor if I can."

He turned to Walter, who still lingered on the schooner's deck where he had climbed, Uncle Boardman staying down in his boat.

"Say," remarked the skipper, turning to Walter, "do you know that feller? Hold on there!"

"That feller" was at the door of the cook's galley, sulking; and seemed anxious to avoid Walter. The skipper's words arrested the man's attention.

"N-n-o! Some colored man," replied Walter.

"I picked him and a white man up—they seemed to be wanderin' round in their boat— and I have half a mind to set 'em adrift."

"Where is the other man?" asked Walter.

"Complained of feelin' sick and got into a berth. I believe he lied, so as to shirk a pull on the oars, and this colored feller, he escaped me, too. They seem to want to go ashore with us, spoke of bein' tired. Bummers!"

"Don't I know you?" asked Walter, addressing the stranger. "Didn't I get you to take a letter ashore for me, one day?"

It was the letter addressed to Ripley and given to a colored man on board a passing schooner. In the letter, Walter had invited Ripley to the lighthouse.

"Yes, sah."

"Well, it got to its destination. One good turn deserves another—Oh, if they've been drifting about and are used up, guess I would let them go with me, skipper, if I were you."

The colored man gave Walter a grateful look, and slipped into the caboose.

"Wall!" said the skipper, "I don't like the looks of. things, but I'll take your advice. You've helped us amazin'ly."

"You're welcome, sir, and I guess that colored man will come out all right."

Here a dark face showed itself again at the caboose door, and gave a gleam of thanks from its dark eyes.

Walter now dropped over the vessel's side into his boat, and thought no more about this episode. The schooner raised its wings and rapidly moved toward the harbor.

"Where is Ripley?" asked Walter. "We thought we might hitch boats together, and get into one boat, and he and I row while you steered."

"Ripley has gone. You can see that his boat is some way ahead. That fog is close upon us. Hope the schooner will get far as the light before it is thick about her. And my! What will Lyddy do?"

"I think aunt will be the one for the emergency."

"She is one, if any woman can be. I ought to have looked after the fog-signal, and told her how to manage it."

"I have faith to believe she will come out all right."

Occasionally, the men, as they rowed, swung their heads about to glance at the light. They could see the mist skirmishing with it, sending toward it detached masses, then vigorously rushing upon it with great, wide-spread wings, like some big bird of prey clutching at this poor, helpless victim out in the sea. Finally, the victim disappeared under the dismal wings covering it, and hiding it, and threatening to bear it away. Yes, it was borne away!

"Gone!" said Walter.

No!

Suddenly, piercing, echoing, defiant, triumphant, came over the water a blast from the fog-trumpet!

"Three cheers for your Aunt Lyddy!" cried Uncle Boardman, springing to his feet. "Hoo-ror! Hoo-ror! Hoo-ror!"

Walter joined.

"There!" exclaimed Uncle Boardman. "If I didn't forget it was Sunday!"

The skipper of the schooner going out of sight in the fog, heard the cheers and said:

"That is for us, a good-bye! We must return it!"

Uncle Boardman heard it.

"They're about passin' the light, and they must be cheerin' your Aunt Lyddy," was Uncle Boardman's interpretation of the huzzahs.

"This has been quite an eventful day, uncle."

"Yes, yes!"

But they did not appreciate all its significance. When the schooner reached its wharf, there crept over its rail and stole away in the rear of a fishhouse, as if anxious to avoid observation, Martin and De Vere.

CHAPTER XII.

AN ANGEL ARRIVES.

"THERE is the lighthouse, but where is the boat?" a young woman was wondering, as she stood on the shore, one December afternoon, and looked away toward Seal's Head. "I said I would be here at three o'clock. Soon it will be growing dark! Not the least sign of a boat. Here I have been waiting for ten minutes! What a Ripley! Here he writes to me that they want me to be their guest and spend Christmas with them, and he will meet me if I will take a five minutes' walk from the school-house where the stage leaves me, to the seashore opposite the school-house. That Ripley! I expect in his enthusiasm he has forgotten all about me—I don't mean enthusiasm about me, but about keeping the lighthouse. Nothing like it in his estimation, unless it is the keeping of that school back there, for I expect it is that one. Well, no boat! What shall I do? I think I will go back to some house and inquire how folks get to that lighthouse—if there is any boat round —or what they do? How cold that water looks! And that lighthouse—just the loneliest place in the world! Ugh! going to snow for Christmas, too, I believe!"

The young woman fastened her large, lustrous, black eyes on the sea a few moments longer, and then turned away. The first house she saw, was an unpretentious building at the right of the road. It was humble and low, old and black. At first, she thought it showed no sign of life. Nothing can be more indicative of life than a chimney-top in the wood-burning, open country. No folds of smoke curled up from this battered top toward the clouded, wintry sky.

"Don't believe anybody lives there! I don't know though. There is a curtain at the lower half of that window, and it is partly drawn. That looks as if the house had an occupant. Curtains don't hang themselves, and curtains don't draw themselves. Guess I'll knock." After this soliloquy, she tapped on the door.

"Hark! Don't get any answer! Nobody there. I will rap once more."

She rapped, and then listened.

"Come in!" was the faint response.

The young woman entered and found herself in a poor, mean room, and before a big,
open, ashy, fireless fireplace, sat an old colored
woman, in a rocking-chair that had a dis-
jointed, rickety look.

"Oh, I beg pardon!" said the stranger.
"I don't mean to trouble you, but I wanted to
know about going to the lighthouse—how one
could get there. Is there anybody about here
who would row me over? Of course, I would
pay them."

"Set down, honey! Scuse my gittin' up.
Ain't berry smart. Jes' hab to keep my settin'
mos' all de time, mos' all de time!"

Sometimes the old woman would give her
words additional emphasis by shaking a bright
yellow turban made by the tying of a handkerchief about her head, and the ends projected
directly on top. It looked very much as if the
upper part of the old lady had budded into
wings, and this much of her was going to fly
away. When she shook her head, these wings
flapped with an energy that made an immediate
flight quite probable.

One other chair, the stranger found. It
had no back, but luckily had legs. She was
glad to occupy it.

"Now, honey, ef Don Pedro were here, I

spec' he'd row ye 'cross. Mos' looks as ef ye could paddle yoursef, but it's longer dan ye tink."

"If you will let me, I would like to sit and wait till he comes."

"Jes' as well as not!"

The yellow wings began to flap heavenward. The caller now inspected the room.

"It is dreadful poverty-stricken!" she reported to herself. "Only this chair—and it is not a whole one—besides the old lady's! Two windows, and half a curtain, and that topsy-turvy! An old table and the things on it all awry! A poor piece of carpet before the fire-place, and that in disorder! And no fire in the fireplace, this cold day! Too bad! See how she tries to pull that ragged old shawl over her shoulders!"

The young woman sprang up impulsively and asked:

"Couldn't you, while I am waiting, just let me make you more comfortable? Couldn't I start your fire up?"

"You're drefful good, honey! Afraid you won't find nuffin—no, nuffin to make de fire wid—no nuffin!"

The wings flapped, but not up, this time; down, rather, as if broken and helpless.

"Don Pedro had to go ober de ferry to what dey call de Harbor, an' he ain't got back, honey. He didn't spec to be gone so long, 'an——"

"Oh, well, I'll look round and get some wood."

"Drefful 'fraid de wood-pile is on de beach, an' de wabes are what pile it."

"You mean drift-wood? Oh, well, don't you worry!"

She was gone in another minute, and was flying down the lane to the beach. Here she picked up hastily any pieces of drift-wood she might find. She did not notice a boat coming from the lighthouse, and that the head of the young man rowing it chanced to turn while she was on the sands, and conclude that he must have seen this nimble, female faggot-gatherer. She sprang away, burdened with drift-wood, and was soon before the fire-place, scratching matches.

"There!" she exclaimed, as the kindling of paper she had taken from her showy travel-ling-bag flamed up among the dry wood. "Isn't that better?"

"Bress de Lor', honey! You're drefful good."

"Now, you let me just put things to rights a little."

She spread smooth and even before the fire-place the scanty strip of carpeting. She shook the topsy-turviness out of the window-curtain, and made it hang perpendicular as a plummet-line. She arranged in order the few articles on the old table, a Bible being among them.

"Oh, there's the old lady's shawl!"

She noiselessly darted toward it, and comfortably folded it about the thinly-clad shoulders.

"There, now you feel better?"

The old lady could not make intelligible sounds. She was crying, violently sobbing as if her old heart would break. It was the crying of joy, though; and the yellow wings convulsively fluttering were beating toward heaven this time.

"You feel—sick?"

"Oh, no, chile! Feel lubly! You—so—hebbenly an' good."

"Oh, don't say anything about it! Is there not something I can do before that Don—Don——"

"Don Pedro——?"

"Yes, before he comes."

The old lady hesitated a moment. Then she asked:

"Could you read me a psalm wid dose lubly eyes?"

The young woman blushed at the compliment, and demurringly said to it, "Oh, no," but to the favor solicited, responded, "Oh, yes! Do let me! There will be time, I know. Read a psalm? I will with pleasure. The twenty-third psalm?"

"Oh, mos' any one."

"The 'Shepherd-psalm,' I mean: 'The Lord is my shepherd'?"

"Lubly!"

"Then I will begin."

She had completed the psalm and was about to begin another, when she hesitated. She saw that the old lady was violently agitated for some reason.

"You—you sick?"

"Oh—no—happy—lubly? Dis place am hebben! So changed!"

It was changed. There had been an outward improvement. That fireplace where the flames climbed up the heap of fragments of boat and ship, like merry sailors running up the rigging, transformed the little low apartment, and spread a carpet of gold on the floor, and hung with like drapery the sombre walls that would soon be deeply shadowed by the fast-coming twilight. There were other changes of which this helpful visitor was the author. Best of all these influences, was her enthusiastic, resolute personality pervading all the place. And in the midst of the warm, golden fire-light, uttered in tones rich, tender and sympathetic, had sounded the "Shepherd-psalm." Into the room He seemed to step. Amid the warm, glowing light, rose up His form, strong, confident, yet bending down in sympathy. It was His voice, speaking in response, " I am the Good Shepherd and know my Sheep and am known of mine." Was He saying it, or saying it through one of His children? He uttered it through the young stranger's voice, for quickly, delicately appreciating that which would be more pertinent, she had left the psalms, and was reading the tenth chapter of the Gospel of St. John.

Yes, through her voice He was saying, " I am the Good Shepherd and know my Sheep and am known of mine." Yes, that room was His fold. One of His flock was there. He recognized this poor one as His, by name. She recognized Him. She cried in the joy of this recognition.

The closed Bible lay in the young stranger's lap. She watched for a moment the leaping, rejoicing flames, and then fed them with a piece of a spar that came from some lone wreck in the awful sea.

Suddenly a shadow darkened the partly-curtained window. Looking quickly, the young woman thought she saw somebody who was carrying wood in his arms, then disappearing quickly.

"Don Pedro!" she said.

The old woman had caught the shadow thrown on the window, and said, shudderingly:

"Mat!"

"Who is it? I'll go and see."

"Mat, Mat! My poor boy! De Ebil One got him."

"Oh, no! and it's somebody—why, he's coming in!"

The old woman trembled. If the newcomer were her son, she was afraid of him. The young woman, though, had no reason for fear. Besides, she had her own idea about this person. "It is Don Pedro," she had concluded, "and he is bringing a very much needed article to this house."

She rose to open the door for this bearer of wood, expecting to see one of the old lady's color, one poorly dressed.

"Don Pedro—I suppose—" she called out.

She stopped. "Oh!" she exclaimed, and, to prevent any further imprudence on the part of her tongue, she clapped her hand over her mouth. No young man of color in poverty clothing, but somebody—she did not know whom—as fair as she; not elegantly, but well and comfortably dressed, a well-formed, shapely young man, good-looking, intelligent, with a certain look of decision and force, as if he could push his way through the world, and meant to do it. He touched his hat courteously, and said :

"I beg pardon—is not this Miss Eaton?"

"Yes, sir." She then asked with twinkling eyes, guessing who he was, yet determined she would let him declare himself : "Do you want to sell some wood?"

"Ha! ha! No, this is a gift. I saw you on the beach picking up wood, and guessed who it was, while I wondered what you were up to. Some fishermen saw you come into this house and told me, and you see I wanted to help. There, granny, won't that help?"

His last address was to the old woman.

"Oh, yah! you're a heap good, jes' lubly!" she replied.

He turned to Kate Eaton now.

"I am Walter Plympton, from the light-house, and it will give me much pleasure to row you over. Sorry there was any delay, but we have had much to do to-day, helping some fishermen who were in a hard place, and I was detained."

"Oh, it is of no consequence. I have had a pleasant time with granny. Good-bye! I hope you will have a very happy Christmas!"

Stooping down to the old lady, she slipped into her hand, something in a fold of paper.

"De angels cum!" screamed the old lady. "Yah, de angels cum!"

The last that Kate Eaton saw of the wings on the old lady's head, they were fluttering in a delightful agitation heavenward.

CHAPTER XIII.

THE ROW TO THE LIGHTHOUSE.

"WHY, who are those coming out of the harbor?" asked Kate Eaton, when they were fairly afloat.

"Either of them look natural? That young lady is waving her hand to you," replied Walter. "Don't you know the young man?"

"Can't be Ripley and May Elliott?"

"You have guessed right. My uncle and aunt invited her, and Ripley went after her."

Everything wavable about the person of Kate Eaton was now in a state of eager flourishing. The umbrella in one hand, and the handkerchief in the other, were tumultuously going.

"I'll slacken my rowing and let them catch up with us."

The passengers in the two boats were soon shaking hands, and the greetings were cordial.

"Going to the light, you see!" said May Elliott.

"I know it. Isn't it splendid?" declared

Kate Eaton. "You wanted to surprise me, Ripley."

"Yes, sister, I did think"—he corrected himself—" we all thought it would be pleasant to get you two young ladies here, and not have either of you know about the coming of the other. Glad you are satisfied."

There was a universal look of satisfaction beaming on the faces in the two boats, and the oarsmen now pulled vigorously for the light-house.

"Please tell me, Mr. Plympton," said the chatty Kate, " about that old woman in whose house you found me. Who is she, and who is the Don Pedro ?"

" Who is Don Pedro? Oh, he is a colored boy that used to live at my uncle's, but he is now living at that house, though I doubt if he gets much to live on. He is no connection of the old lady, but a kind of waif from the South, arriving in a vessel. And the old lady—her name is Smith, as you might guess, but people generally call her 'granny.' She has lived hereabouts quite a number of years. You were very kind to make her so comfortable. Those fishermen who told me where you went, had made up quite a story, imagining who you were and why you were here.   They thought you might be a 'fine Southern lady come to look after her negro-boy.'"

"Oh, they forget the war is over and Southern people don't come North to look after their servants, or send their agents here. Well now," continued the black-eyed, vivacious young lady, "who is Mat?   I was interested in one Mat the old lady told about and what she said about 'de Ebil One' getting him or he was 'de Ebil One.'   Now that is pitiable."

Walter hesitated.   Should he tell all that he knew?   She saw his hesitation, and rather pressed him for an answer.

"Now you need not be reluctant to speak, Mr. Plympton.   I imagine quite a tale may be connected with it, and it would be very interesting to get hold of it.   Perhaps it would make a good magazine-story."

"I think I had better tell her," reasoned Walter, to himself.   "The story will come out while she is here, and it had better come out through me than Ripley, of whom she might ask an explanation.   Yes, I will tell her."

"Miss Eaton," he said, aloud, "perhaps I had better tell you.   Do you remember De Vere's slanderous stories about Ripley?"

"Remember?" she said, indignantly. "How could I forget? What has Mat to do with De Vere? He the 'Evil One'?"

Walter knew that everything must be told now. Kate Eaton was very resolute, and having obtained one end of the clue, she was sure to draw on the thread until its entire length lay in her fair hand.

"You may remember also, Miss Eaton, that some of the slanders were about a yachting-cruise, and that Ripley had said if he could get hold of one Martin, a colored man who was on the yacht, he, Ripley, could disprove the stories?"

"Yes, and Mat that man?" asked Kate, leaping from one point in the conversation to an inferred one.

"He is the man, so people say; but I have never seen him, or if I have, I don't know him. I would like to get hold of him and make him state things just as they are."

"And he is under the influence of De Vere?"

"That is what I expect the old lady means. Mat, or Martin, and De Vere have been seen together."

"Now, Mr. Plympton, tell me all you know about the whereabouts of that De Vere. Ripley tells me some things and the important things, but not all. He is very communicative, when face to face with his friends, as you well know ; but a penholder seems to stop the flow of his thoughts, and he can't write as freely as he can converse——"

" A way with the most of us."

" My brother's way, peculiarly. Now tell me about De Vere and Martin. I have heard it said that justice is on the track of De Vere for some kind of forgery, and that he is hiding somewhere. Then I have heard that it is not forgery, but he wants money and he has gone to get it; and amid so many conflicting stories, I don't know what to believe. If he were in very serious danger, I should think he would clear out altogether and go abroad. It is risky remaining where he may be caught."

" Yes, it is risky. One thing why he has been here, I believe, has been the hope that he might get money from Ripley. He has other reasons for being here, doubtless."

Here he told about the strange night-adventure at " T'other Seal," about the call of a colored man, probably Martin, at the lighthouse, leaving behind a request that Ripley would pay what he was owing somebody.

" Now, he may be—I mean De Vere—he

may be lingering here hoping to get money from some other besides Ripley—don't know whom, it is all guesswork—for there have been rumors that if De Vere could get money, he could settle for his wrong-doing, whatever it is, and whoever may be the party that he settles with. He can't be badly chased, for they could catch him by this time. That night at 'T'other Seal,' I imagine he thought officers were in pursuit, but I don't know. Ripley was a hero that night. Did he tell you about it?"

"Yes, something. He tells me, too, he has made up his mind to lead a new life—oh, Mr. Plympton, we are so glad!"

"You well may be, and I think he is building right, on a good foundation, and he is building up steadily. My aunt has had a close connection with his case——"

"Yes, she has done wonders, from what I know. We are grateful to you all. And, Mr. Plympton, I think Ripley has been most unjustly treated by that De Vere."

"Oh, he has been. We all think so. I tell Rip the evidence is at the bottom of the sea somewhere, and it will come up sometime."

"If it only would! If that boat would be so considerate as to come to the surface some day, and bring the box which De Vere pretends to say has Ripley's confession of debt, note or something!"

"It will be found to be an empty box, or without that document at any rate, when it does come up."

"Let us hope so.   I—believe so."

"So do I!"

Walter rowed away in silence. Kate watched the sea and then the distant, dimming horizon.   Suddenly, she held up her closely gloved hand and exclaimed:

"What!—Snow?"

"I don't doubt it.   Seems to me I have seen it falling for the last hour, but I believe it really has just begun."

"Oh, these little boats sailing out of the sky! So white! Such, pure tiny sails!"

"Only to be wrecked, never finding harbor. That seems pitiable. On land they always arrive in port, but the ocean drowns them."

"So pure, and faster now!"

Yes, faster and thicker, till a dense white veil was drawn by the storm across the sea.

"Oh, hark! Where is that other boat, Mr. Plympton? Are they calling?"

"Yes! I'll answer.—Ship ahoy!"

"They have got ahead of us. And where is

the lighthouse? Dear me! Have we lost that! Must we be like that De Vere, wandering around?"

"Toot—toot—toot!" came that blatant voice of the trumpet.

"What is that? Mercy!" cried Walter's companion, springing up.

"The fog-signal! Don't worry, Miss Eaton!"

"Why, it seems everywhere! Ahead of us, around us, everywhere!"

"It is the lighthouse or signal-tower sending it out."

"Oh, I must see it!" she cried, enthusiastically, reminding Walter of Ripley.

"You can hear it now. Don't you think that enough? Imagine yourself out to sea, bewildered in a fog, confused by the dense, driving snow, and you can tell how pleasant might be such music. See how it snows now!"

The flakes were crowding down faster than ever, making a canopy of shifting, feathery particles, and it shut down on the blue sea everywhere. In the centre, was this lonely boat with its two occupants.

"What is that black thing ahead, rising up, going above your head, a huge pillar, Mr. Plympton?"

Walter turned around.

"Good! That is the lighthouse! Can't you see something black at its foot, a small object?"

"A boat? A rock? What is it?"

"Ripley's boat. He made excellent time, rowing the school-marm."

The two boats quickly rested side by side at the foot of the tower.

A voice called down from the door-way:

"Welcome to the light—lighthouse!"

It was dear Aunt Lydia, her voice worn and sharp, but expressing only a warm-heartedness acceptable as open fire to a pilgrim chilled by the December air.

"I know I shall like her," said Kate, enthusiastically.

But Kate was prepared to like everything. The kitchen was "charming," and although small, the very limitations gave it a charm because ensuring "cosiness." The watch-room was just the place for "meditation and study," and the lantern was "wonderful." The view from the platform outside must be "unsurpassed"—when it did not snow!

"Dear me, I think I shall have to be a lightkeeper!" she confessed to Ripley.

"Ha! ha! You are as enthusiastic as your

brother. When I came here, I thought I should apply for the place the moment Uncle Boardman left it behind him."

"You like me any the less because I am enthusiastic, Mr. Eaton?" asked Kate, her excitement brightening her eyes till they shone like jet.

"I don't," thought Walter.

Ripley said aloud what he thought:

"No, sister, no! A person without enthusiasm is like green grass for fuel. Go on!"

"I am going on. No, there is no view it is true from the platform, but the situation is just unique. Up here in the clouds, snow all about us, this tower of stone under us, and that dark water far, far below."

It was unique, this perch high above that wintry water and in the heart of a great travelling snow-cloud.

"Strange to think that what will make huge drifts on the land, filling the roads, hiding the fences, hindering travel and blocking the cars, leaves here no trace behind, every flake melting as it touches the water and disposed of, forever!" observed Kate.

"Yes, what falls while I am saying it, and would make an avalanche if it could be gathered up from the sea, is turned at once into

water.   But there!   It won't do for me anyway
to stay here," continued Walter, taking out
his watch and glancing at it, "for I find it is
just about lighting up time."

"Lighting!   Allow me to light the lamp?"
requested Kate.

"And you will want to know about the
light, the lamp, the lens," said Ripley.   "Just
like me!"

"I want to know?   Of course, if I can find
an instructor."

"Give me that pleasure, Miss Eaton?"
asked Walter, " soon as I have lighted up."

No, Kate wanted to light up.

"Class in optics going into the lecture-
room? Excuse me, though I know the information will be valuable. Think I will go
down and see Aunt Lydia," said Ripley, laughing.

Walter was willing to have a class of one,
and inviting Kate from the lantern to the
watch-room, showed her a little diagram he
had found in a book in the lighthouse library-
case, which illustrated this subject of the lens.

"You noticed that the lamp we lighted was
not very large?"

"I did, and was surprised to see it so small.
What you see on the head of a lighthouse

looks like a barrel of light, a big mass of fire."

"Well, what makes the flame appear so large is that setting of crystal all about it, and in shape like a barrel. We call it the lens, but it may be of different sizes. I have heard of a lens at Minot's Ledge light so big that a man can go inside of it. This here is of course a much smaller one. This lens is so constructed that it gathers up the rays of light going out in all directions, and sends them out in parallel and horizontal lines——"

"Oh, I see, I see!"

"Take, for instance, this lamp on the table which I now light. The rays shoot up, shoot down, shoot in every direction. There is a good deal of lost illumination if I want it to shine out upon the sea. Some of the light has gone up to the ceiling and some down to the floor. Now you understand the peculiarity of what we call a prism of glass?"

"Wait a moment! Let me see if I can recall my optics at school. If I had only anticipated this need of my knowledge up here in a lighthouse, I would have packed it away as carefully as a good housekeeper does her furs in camphor-scented packages. A prism is a transparent body that has generally three sides, right-angled, and the ends are triangular. The ends, or bases, might be shaped differently, quadrangular, for instance—and that would make a quadrangular prism."

Kate had been rolling round her charming eyes as if searching for information in every quarter, and her eyes or her definition gained her a compliment from her teacher.

"Very good, very good, Miss Eaton! We will suppose that these prisms are triangular. A prism has this peculiarity, you will remember, that it refracts or bends light."

"It used to be in my book on optics that light going from a medium of one density, the air say, into a medium of another density, glass say, would be bent out of its course, or refracted, teacher."

"Right again! A most apt scholar. Lines of light going from a central lamp in all directions, may be caught up by prisms and sent out horizontally. What we need to do is to arrange our prisms around our lamp so as to intercept the rays and refract them and send them out in horizontal lines. The lenses are what are called annular, made ringlike, and the light is caught up by them and sent out an immense mass of parallel lines or rays, going out on every side across the face of the sea."

"And to Fresnel, the lighthouse world is especially indebted for the great change inaugurated in lighthouse illumination. This one other thing occurs to me now as I recall my optics, one small piece of drift-wood saved from the wreck," said the class.

"Saved a good deal, I should say," replied this lantern-professor.

"Really," he said to himself, "Ripley's sister is quite a charming girl."

They went down-stairs to the small light-house world in the base of the tower. And so Christmas drew nearer, this huge snow-cloud covering and melting into the sea, but troubling not the visitors that filled the lighthouse with the music of their laughter.

CHAPTER XIV.

MAKING READY FOR CHRISTMAS.

CHRISTMAS was coming. The odors winging their way up from the kitchen and flying all through the lighthouse proclaimed the approach of some festal day, but it was now Wednesday morning and the festival would not be due until Friday. The snow-cloud had lifted from the sea.

"If it holds fair," remarked Walter, "I am going ashore to-day, and any last Christmas package that is going off in the mail, I will see that it is delivered."

The breakfast-table was still in the floor. Uncle Boardman, Aunt Lydia, Kate and May, Walter and Ripley, still lingered at the table. Walter's remark launched quite a discussion.

"I believe I have remembered all my friends," said Aunt Lydia.

One after the other said very much the same thing.

"To my mind," remarked Uncle Boardman,

" one of the best things about Christmas is the giving away of the presents."

" That is what the Bible says," replied Ripley, " more blessed to give than to receive."

" But we would be a leetle disappointed," said Aunt Lydia, " if we didn't receive."

" Oh, yes, it is pleasant to be remembered. We all like to be thought of. But there's my wife ! "

Uncle Boardman pointed proudly and affectionately at Aunt Lydia. The pointing was so direct and plain that she blushed.

" Now Lyddy begins for the next Christmas about as soon as the last one is over. She has what she calls her Christmas-bag. Any present she thinks would be fit for anyone, she puts away, that is, supposing it comes into her hands. Well, the thinking about it, how acceptable it might be to the person, the good it may do, the making of it ready, getting everything in preparation—why, that is very pleasant. I tell Lyddy, I don't care how soon she begins to fill her Christmas-bag. It sort of lays one Christmas alongside another. And then the doing up the things and sending them to the mail, imagining the pleasure they will give and the good they will do—to my mind, is very pleasant.   When it is done, a big part of Christmas is over."

"I really think," said the young lady whose eyes were so black and sparkling, "I must make sure of a Christmas-bag before leaving the lighthouse, and I'll commission Mr. Plympton to buy me cloth for a bag to-day."

Quiet May Elliott did not say anything. She had had a "Christmas-bag" for a number of years.

"Yes," remarked Aunt Lydia, "I tell your Uncle Boardman, I feel quite homesick when the last package leaves for the mail."

"But you begin to feel better, Aunt Lydia, when the Christmas packages arrive for you?" said Walter.

"Yes, Walter, she droops," said Uncle Boardman, "droops at first ; but when I bring in the bundles and say, 'Lyddy, your turn has come,' that chirks her up a good deal."

"I pity one house I can think of," said Kate, "where there will be very little sending and getting."

"Where is that?" asked May Elliott.

"Where Dom, or Don Pedro lives," replied Kate.

"There is one person in that house who don't deserve a present."

Aunt Lydia said this, and all knew whom she meant.

"As for Don Pedro, I think he does deserve a present, and—and—if Walter is not goin' right off, this very minute, I'll see if I can't pick up suthin' for Don."

"And Aunt Lydia, I'll try to think of something for granny, up at the Harbor, in one of the stores, and Walter, perhaps, wou'd buy it for me," said May. "Could you, would you, Walter?"

"Certainly, May."

Uncle Boardman was rather disposed to propound perplexing questions to his spouse, in part because he liked argument, and in part, because, while a very kindly-natured man, he liked to tease her a little. He stopped this side of provoking her, but up to that fence, he would bewilder the old lady, if he could.

"Ahem-m-m, Lyddy !"

She knew what was coming and quickly looked up, like a tennis-player when he sees the ball coming and lifts his racket.

"You say there is one person who don't deserve a present where Don Pedro lives. We don't make presents because people deserve them, do we?"

"N-n-o, but because we like them and they like us."

"I was going to say we may make a baby a present, and yet the baby have done nothing to specially deserve it—merit it, you know."

"I dunno, Boardman! You git a little baby into your arms and his fat little hands go out to you and play over your face, and the baby's voice keeps a-cooin' and a-cooin', making you happier and better. I don't know why you might not say the little thing deserves suthin' in return. I think it *does!*"

She spoke emphatically.

"Now as to that man at granny's—we all know who is meant—he has done nothin' to me one way or the other to deserve anything, but I mean in a gineral way his conduct has been what you don't like or don't approve of, and in gineral you might say he don't deserve nothin' from nobody——"

"Of course not!" murmured Uncle Boardman humbly, his head drooping, and twirling his thumbs one about the other.

"But you take a baby! Do you remember a leetle black baby once at our house—cunning thing as ever was—and he took a great fancy to you and——"

Those thumbs went twirling about one another rapidly.

"Yes, I remember he took a great fancy to you, and he played with your whiskers —you had a beard then—and he cooed and——"

The thumbs were going faster than ever.

Kate Eaton had noticed Uncle Boardman's drooping head and twirling thumbs, and suddenly on those big thumbs she saw a big tear splashing.

Aunt Lydia was very observant generally, but she had not noticed her husband so carefully during this talk. She saw everything now. She suddenly was silent. Ripley and May chanced to see her eyes before she dropped them as humbly as her husband. There were big tears welling up under her spectacles and chasing one another down her cheeks.

"Yes, I s'pose it's jest so," murmured Aunt Lydia, in a bewildered way, as if she could not remember the previous train of thought exactly, but felt that this remark might hitch on to it.

Aunt Lydia now rose from the table, Uncle Boardman also, and the rest of the wondering company. Ripley and May, who were rather disposed to seek one another's society, by design or chance this time found themselves out in the lonely engine-room of the signal-tower. Up in the clear sky, a cold sun was frigidly smiling, and the wind sweeping over the water groaned about the tower.

"May," said Ripley, who had got into a way of dispensing with any formal address, "did you see that? Uncle Boardman rather likes to puzzle his wife, but she upset him this time. Was not that funny? Did you see it all? Strange!"

"Yes, I saw it. Uncle Boardman—as we all call him—is very tender-hearted, and I understood it all. Aunt Lydia has sometimes—more than once—told me about it, and I can see how it happened that he was so affected to-day. They once had a little child. It died when very young. Soon after this, in the neighborhood, a little black baby was born. Its mother was very fond of it and used to bring it to Aunt Lydia's. Uncle Boardman took a great fancy to the little thing, and it had the greatest liking for him. And you see he was still missing his own baby, and this little thing was such a comfort to him, cooing at him, pulling his whiskers, and playing by the half hour with him. The conversation to-day brought it all up again and the memory of his great grief."

"Funny! Guess Uncle Boardman didn't know where he would fetch up when he started out."

" Not by any means."

" What became of that black baby?"

" The mother died and the father put it in some asylum for children, and I've heard granny say they lost track of it altogether."

" Who was the father? He probably did not follow the child up, and the child was given away."

" The father? There is another strange thing about it. It was Martin, granny's son."

Ripley looked intently at her.

"Not the man that goes round with De Vere? Kate says you know all about the affair."

" That is the one."

" Strange! Things are always happening in this world, are they not?"

" They certainly are."

" And you are going to send granny a present?"

" Yes, I thought I would."

" Then Don will have one, and granny, all

but the little baby's father. Say, I have an idea."

"That is encouraging."

"No, you are teasing. Beware! You know what happened to Uncle Boardman and how he came to grief when he got to teasing."

"Then I will stop here and be good."

"Now I will tell you my idea, and you tell me what you think of it. I know you are a safe counsellor."

"Thank you, for returning good for evil."

"I have been at the village which you call the Harbor, and Miss P. Green, who keeps the post-office, has some warm, thick stockings. There is nothing that goes quicker to a man's heart than something that promotes his comfort. And she has a little stock of Bibles. I will get Walter to buy some of the stockings and a Bible and you can add your gift for granny, and Walter will see that they all get to the right place, I know. Mine, of course, are for Martin. I don't know what he will say to them."

"I know what he will do with the stockings, wear them."

"Perhaps you think the Bible is the last gift to be appreciated by Martin."

"It does seem like throwing a pearl before

swine, but if I had the inclination to do it, I would gratify it. Our inclinations are not always safe guideboards, but here is one that will do no harm anyway. I would send it."

"One might ask if any kind of a present would be appreciated by such a man. I think though I know Martin. He is under the influence of another person's stronger will. He is naturally a kind-hearted fellow, but this influence warps him as heat will warp wood. Queer! One's will power over another may be very great."

Then followed a long talk about psychic influence, the strange laws of will power which we feel and obey and can yet give little explanation of, the magnetic strength of certain personalities which at a distance may fasten upon and sway us. Of these facts, the two young persons in the signal-tower now gave instances. If required to do it, Ripley Eaton could have presented himself as an illustration of the very positive yet agreeable power of May Elliott over him. He was strangely silent however before his sister Kate about any such proof of psychic influence.

CHAPTER XV.

THE CHRISTMAS STORM.

CHRISTMAS EVE, the young people ascended to the lantern to see Uncle Boardman light up. There was no sun in the western sky that could be seen, but it was supposed to be behind a thick blackish bank of cloud. This looked very much like scowling earth-works thrown up in time of war in whose rear a heavy battery had been massed, ready to let loose flame and shot at a moment's notice. Uncle Boardman stood, watch in hand, looking closely at the dial and ready to scratch a match the moment the hand said, "Sun is setting."

Kate introduced a subject that has been glanced at previously in this book.

"I suppose, sir, the light in lighthouses was just what people built on top of them, any kind of a bonfire."

"That is all, I suppose," replied Uncle Boardman. "Down to the close of the last century, they tell me, the sea-lights of Great

Britain were open coal-fires. Then, somebody got up lamps with reflectors, and these first were mirror-glass, but afterwards they used metallic reflectors. Why, I was reading that the first light of the Eddystone lighthouse, so famous, was just that of wax-candles on a chandelier, and there wasn't even a reflector to go with it. You have heard of Fresnel, though? He made a great change. Of course, others have helped."

"Since I have been here, a distinguished professor in optics has been lighting up the merits of Fresnel even beyond my previous estimate of him," said Kate.

"Ha! ha!" cried Ripley, and clapping his hand on Walter's shoulder. "Merit stands crowned at last."

"Don't be envious, Rip! Your turn will come," cried Walter.

His turn soon came.

"Kate, you would have been one to appreciate the great Pharos-tower," he remarked.

"Oh, Pharos? Let me see! That was famous, wasn't it? Tell me about it."

He repeated the information he had read one day to Aunt Lydia, that entranced listener.

"Oh have I—have I—forgotten all I ever

knew?" exclaimed Kate, her dark eyes looking away as if intently searching for something that wished to remain hidden. "What did I learn about Pharos in my school-days? Built by Ptolemy Philadelphus—yes, and thought by some to have been five hundred feet high, —and what else can I remember about it? Oh, it was said to have cost eight hundred talents, I believe. Josephus said you could see its light a great distance—how many of our miles would it be? Forty-two, I think!"

"Bravo!" cried Walter. "Professor Ripley, are you not proud of your pupil?"

"Perhaps I am, but I don't think I show it so much as the professor in optics."

"We are even. Let us shake hands."

Uncle Boardman had gone outside the lantern and he said to the others soon following him, "It does not take anything of a weather-wise to say that the storm will break upon us any moment."

"Oh, a real storm, sir?" cried Kate, clapping her hands.

"Without much doubt, Miss Kate. There is every prospect of it, and every feeling, too. The air feels like storm."

The light-keeper shook his gray hairs and

murmured, "Yes, a real one! God help those who will feel it!"

Kate Eaton and the other young people did not take this view of it. To them, the storm was an excitement to be welcomed. Any calamity to the sailor and the craft he sailed, they did not try to realize. Kate went round on the northeast side of the lantern, and looking toward the cold, hard, combative northeast, hummed several notes of defiance. May Elliott joined her, and the two twining their arms about one another, sang Tennyson's "Break on thy cold, gray stones, O Sea!"

Kate possessed a rich, triumphant soprano. May's part was that of a full, deep alto.

"Those two gals sing well together," Aunt Lydia had previously remarked. "That Kate spreads a lot of sail when she sings, but May's voice is good ballast for it all."

Their voices now beautifully blended:

> "'Break, break, break,
>   On thy cold, gray stones, O Sea!
>   And I would that my tongue could utter
>   The thoughts that arise in me.

> "'O well for the fisherman's boy,
>   That he shouts with his sister at play!
>   O well for the sailor lad
>   That he sings in his boat on the bay!

> "'And the stately ships go on
>   To the haven under the hill!
> But oh, for the touch of a vanished hand
>   And the sound of a voice that is still!
>
> "'Break, break, break,
>   At the foot of thy crags, O Sea!
> But the tender grace of a day that is dead
>   Will never come back to me.'"

An hour later, all around the brilliantly il-luminated lantern, there was a dense, deep blackness, through which drove the heavy rain and roared the mighty wind, while beneath, raged the great billows, beating their towering heads into angry, hissing foam, against the massive walls of the lighthouse.

"What of the weather?" cried Aunt Lydia to her husband, when he came from the signal-tower into the kitchen, and found a merry circle around the supper-table in the little room.

"Weather enough to-night, to suit any taste," said Uncle Boardman, removing his hat from locks, to which the rain had given a gloss. "Bad enough! About the worst night I have seen out here. I went to the door, but could hear only the terrible rage of the waters around the ladder."

"Any boats there?" asked May.

"Boats drawn up into a safe place."

"Shall you run the fog-trumpet?" asked Ripley.

"I hope not.   It will be a very serious time if the wind should keep on blowing."

Uncle Boardman ate his supper and then hurried up into the watch-room and lantern. Those down-stairs made up their Christmas packages to be crowded into, or attached to a variety of stockings suspended around the kitchen-stove.

"Dear me!" exclaimed Aunt Lydia. "These stockin's jist fill up this kitchen. People must wear small sizes if they are going Christmassin' round this stove."

"Too late to change sizes of feet now. Hark!" said Kate.

As she spoke, there was a furious burst of storm against the eastern window, while a tremendous wave broke heavily against the strong walls.

"My! Did you feel it tremble?" asked May.

Yes, there was a jar felt in that heavy house of stone.

"God keep the sailors to-night!" murmured Aunt Lydia.

Uncle Boardman came down the stairway

leading to the kitchen, and passed through the little room, lantern in hand. He would have left without a word.

"Goin' to start the fog-signal, Boardman?" asked his wife, guessing his intent.

"Yes, Lyddy, there is a heavy mist shuttin' in all about us. Awful night!"

Walter and Ripley were already out in the engine-room, having started a furnace-fire.

Soon, the heavy, hoarse, penetrating, "Toot—toot—toot" echoed about the lighthouse.

"There it goes!" said Aunt Lydia, "and I'm afeared they will have to keep it up all night."

When Uncle Boardman appeared again, he said, "The storm is furious, but everything is tight and snug."

"Boats all histed up, Boardman?"

"Yes, indeed, as I told the girls. Why, they couldn't live a minute in the heavy sea that is breaking around the light, Lyddy."

"Then I suppose there is no getting off from the lighthouse or getting into it while this storm lasts," said Kate.

"Those here are prisoners until fair weather, and those outside must be spectators and nothing more. I saw one fishing boat go by making for harbor just before dark. I was out at the door, you know. Those on board wanted to say something. One man put his hands to his mouth making a kind of trumpet, and I dare say he shouted to me, but I couldn't have told any speech from that of the man in the moon."

"The boat got on all right, Boardman?"

"I think so, hope so. It was heading for harbor and labored pretty hard, but I guess it got in all right."

"Jest hear it!" exclaimed Aunt Lydia, as the big seas continued to pound on the light-house walls. "I expect the spray is a flyin' clean over the lantern."

"No doubt of it, Lyddy! And if it don't now, it will run that high before mornin'."

"Glorious!" said Kate, her eyes flashing. "This is just what I have wanted."

"You will have all you want," Uncle Board-man assured her.

The storm increased in violence, and the women retired early, though sleep for any length of time was impossible. The noises were turbulent and incessant. Walter and Ripley sat up with Uncle Boardman to watch the lantern and keep the fog-signal vigorously going.

"Awful!" was Aunt Lydia's last word to

the young women, before retiring to her couch behind the curtain in the light-keeper's room. There she bowed long in silent, humble prayer for the poor sailors at sea.

"What a Christmas they will have, O Lord," she was saying in her soul, "and what a Christmas it will be for their families on the land!"

That night was a battle. The storm let loose all its thunders upon the lighthouse, sent heaviest charges of rain, and drove over the sea a cloud of mist big enough to keep the fog-trumpet going almost incessantly.

May and Kate knew that the forces awake and on watch must often have passed from the lantern down to the engine-room and then returned.

"Can't hear any footsteps," thought May, "but there is the light of their lanterns over the curtain about my bed. Yes, it is awful, this storm! What a Christmas! Will the night ever go by?"

Yes, at last, and a grayish light made its way into the girls' room. They rose early.

"We will go down-stairs or up-stairs and wish folks Merry Christmas," said Kate.

They stepped up into the watch-room, but no one was there. In the lantern, the light was still burning, for sunrise hour had not arrived yet.

"Wonder how it looks outside, May," said Kate, stepping to the glass. "Why, the spray would have splashed into my face if it had not been for this window."

"I know it. Can't seem to see anything very distinctly, only that it is morning. I expect it is awful. Let us hunt up Aunt Lydia."

Kate wanted to linger a moment longer.

"I am thinking, May, what if this thing should go over, this whole tower! "

"Oh, don't think! Let's go down into the kitchen! "

Two rich, laughing voices rang out a peal of Christmas greeting as the young women burst into the kitchen. Aunt Lydia looked up from her work at the stove, as she stooped to thrust a mince pie into the oven, and nodded cheerfully, then pointed at a figure in a chair on the other side of the stove.

"Uncle Boardman," thought May.

No, it was Ripley Eaton who had flung himself into that resting-place, and in his weariness had sunk himself so far down in slumber that the storm could not reach him.

"Merry Christmas!" said Aunt Lydia, in a

low tone. "Dredful, ain't it?" was the contradiction she next uttered.

"Come!" beckoned Kate to May, and they started for the signal-tower, whose lungs and throat were in active operation. The breaking of the waves under the little covered way between the lighthouse and the tower, made a furious clamor.

"What if this should give way as we are going over it?" was a conundrum that Kate Eaton shouted in May Elliott's ear.

Up in the engine-room the light was very indistinct. Amid the shadows the engine was panting away, the piston steadily driving, the air-pump forcing the air into the tank that steadily supplied the hoarsely braying trumpet.

One form stood by the engine closely watching it, while another swathed in a thick overcoat was in a chair, the head tipped back against the wall, and a wide world of storm forgotten in the blissful unconsciousness of sleep.

"Wish you merry Christmas!" cried the young women to Walter, the guardian of the engine.

"The same to you, but may there be no returns like this!" Walter shouted back. "Weather don't trouble him," he added, pointing at Uncle Boardman.

"Poor fellow!" said Kate, sympathizingly.

"Don't call me poor! If you want to direct your sympathy toward anyone, go to that window and look out," said Walter. "I am happy. Alas, for the man that is out in those seas!"

Every moment the light was strengthening, and Kate and May looked out on an indescribable confusion of dark water and white foam, black clouds above, and low, trailing folds of mist.

"Oh, what is that?" cried May. "A vessel going by? I should think a ship would put out to sea——"

"If they can get there, May. Sometimes a skipper must do the best he can, and he may make a lucky run inshore and slip into harbor. Let me see!"

The little group could not settle the question whether a struggling something on the edge of the dark shadows might be a ship or not. The young women returned to the kitchen.

"Aunt Lydia, has Ripley gone?" asked Kate.

"Yes, he went up to put out the light, for it's mornin' now."

"Such a morning, Aunt Lydia!" said May.

"I know it, but it is not so bad at Seal's Head as on ' T'other Seal.'"

"Oh, it must be murderous there. I want it to be light enough to see if they haven't got a wreck there," declared May.

"Wall, now, gals," Aunt Lydia began to remark, "we must make the day as cheerful as possible."

"Oh, yes, oh, yes!"

"And we will follow out the programme that is all made out. First, breakfast—and you can see it is going to be a good one, and then about church-time we have our Christmas-service. Now, we may have to divide up and eat in fragments, and do the same when we have service, some in the signal-tower and the rest here, but we will do the best we can and enjoy it. I wonder whenever a Christmas-service was held here! Never, I guess. However, we will have one to-day."

The programme, as thus set down, was carried out.

"In fragments," was the breakfast enjoyed.

The service at the usual church-hour was carried forward by a divided congregation, but carried forward.

"Now, Uncle Boardman, you stay here all the time!" Walter had insisted. "Ripley and

I will look after things out in the engine-room. We are going to divide up the time, he here the first half of the service, and I with you in the second."

Aunt Lydia's melodeon seemed never sweeter, though the breakers added more bass to the chorus of voices than they needed.

Uncle Boardman's reading met with a like interference from the thumping sea, but he read perseveringly on. And the *Te Deum!* May, Walter, Kate and Ripley had rehearsed this, and while they now sang it, Aunt Lydia, self-sacrificing soul, insisted on running out to the engine-room, doing a man's duty, that the four young people might sing together this triumphant ascription.

"We praise Thee, O God; we acknowledge Thee to be the Lord!

"All the earth doth worship Thee, the Father Everlasting!"

Aunt Lydia took her prayer-book out into the engine-room, and lovingly followed the chorus as she imagined, from verse to verse, round to round, in this ladder of praise up which worshipping hearts were ascending.

"Oh, I can hear 'em, yes, I can!" declared Aunt Lydia. "So sweet!"

"Toot—toot—toot!" brayed the old fog-trumpet above.

"Boom—boom — boom — boom!" crashed the sea against the tower.

No matter! Faith's ear was so sharp that it penetrated that volume of obstructing sound, penetrated all intervening walls, and heard the rich, triumphant *Te Deum* in the lighthouse kitchen.

"Oh, beautiful!" she exclaimed, her hands uplifted, the tears streaming down her cheeks. "Never thought I should live to see this day of rejoicing! Yes," she said again, clasping her hands, as she stood and watched by the grimy old engine, "beautiful, beautiful!"

"Lyddy," said a voice, "Now you just go in and get the good of that. I have had my share of listenin'. You would be wilful and come. Let me spell you! Quick, before they finish the *Te Deum!* Fly! That's a good gal!"

Lydia flew.

Across the covered way under which the sea plunged and roared, ran Aunt Lydia, into the store-room, up the stairs, into the kitchen where the four rich voices were blending into one jubilant harmony the words:

"We therefore pray Thee, help Thy servants, whom Thou hast redeemed with Thy precious blood!"

"Yes, Father," was the echoing thought in Aunt Lydia's soul, "all upon the sea, this awful day!"

"Make them to be numbered with Thy saints in glory everlasting!

"Oh Lord, save Thy people, and bless Thine heritage!"

The *Te Deum* went on, Aunt Lydia standing erect, her face lifted toward heaven, her eyes shining with tears. In her ears was only the triumphant music, the roaring sea and the hoarse fog-trumpet in vain trying to reach and disturb her soul.

Ripley read the second lesson, and after the singing of the *Benedictus*, he went up into the engine-room and relieved Uncle Boardman, who resumed his place in the little circle of worship in the kitchen.

"Wonderful!" declared Aunt Lydia, when the service was finished.

"We must have a Christmas offertory," said Uncle Boardman.

It was made, and subsequently the money was sent to the treasury of the home parish.

The Christmas dinner was at one. The hour had its special advantage. If half after one had been the time appointed, very little dinner would have been eaten.

Something happened very soon after half-past one. It was startling enough to drive all other thoughts away.

" May," said Kate, " let's take a walk round. Don't you want to go up to the lantern?"

" Agreed."

Little could be seen, for a mist brooded over the deep. As far as there was any sight, they saw only one terrible boil, as if they were in the centre of a most angry cauldron. Under the ocean, fires of most terrific energy seemed to have been kindled. It was one gigantic, perpetual turmoil that they beheld.

" Let's see how it looks from the signal-tower door," suggested May.

Down they raced, these light-hearted, nimble-footed girls, to the signal-tower door. Pushing open the door and cautiously stepping out upon the platform, they saw something that seemed to hang their hearts with weights and so fettered their feet that at first they could not stir from the spot.

"Oh, look !" cried Kate, in horror, pointing at an object fifty feet away from the foot of the tower.

"Where, where?" asked May, startled by Kate's outcry.

She did not need to ask this. Kate was pointing out the locality.

"There!" she hoarsely murmured.

May saw.

"Oh!" she shudderingly cried and clasped her hands.

Down in that awful, hellish rage of the billows, in that wild mingling of the dark green water and the bright sea-foam, was a man's face! It was white as the froth breaking in wild spray over him.

"Oh, I can see his eyes! How they stare at us!" cried Kate. "Look, May!"

"Doesn't he beckon? Isn't his arm going? See, Kate!"

Then they saw something dark reaching ahead of the man, and reaching behind him, was something long, dark, round.

"It is a spar and he must be tied to it, Kate!"

"It's *that man!*"

"What man, Kate?"

Kate was covering her face with her hands.

"Oh, he stares at us and he beckons!"

" I'll run, Kate, and tell them."

" Yes, run, both of us! They must get a boat! Quick! Let's get them!"

For the first time, the fog-trumpet was deserted and left to its own management. It did not abuse its opportunity, but sounded on.

Deserted was the kitchen where Aunt Lydia had been working.

Deserted was the watch-tower where Walter had been busy.

All came to the signal-tower door, and crowding out upon the threshold, some of them stepping forward upon the platform, they looked down with shuddering eyes to see " *that man* " whoever he was that Kate had discovered.

" I see him," cried Uncle Boardman. " He is fastened to a spar! Stand back all! Let me throw this rope."

He drew forward one end of a rope that he had not forgotten to bring with him, and wound it into a coil for slinging at this unhappy mark down in the water.

" Oh, Boardman, can't you launch a boat?" asked Aunt Lydia.

" Lyddy, it wouldn't live a minute down in that awful sea."

" But you might try it."

"Yes, try it and you would have another dead man on your hands. Stand back!" he shouted, "I want to throw this——"

He aimed and sent that rope as well as any one could have thrown it.

It was too short!

"Quick, Walter! Hand me another piece and tie it to this! No, I will get it!"

Walter though was more nimble than his uncle, and bringing the additional rope, spliced it to that first fragment. The man in the water was now farther away, for the tide was making in and it set with much violence between Seal's Head and "T'other Seal."

"Now let me try it! Quick! It is gettin' away from us," shouted Uncle Boardman.

There was something indescribably painful in this watching of the drifting of a human be-ing away from help, and into that dreary world of mist and storm whose ragged edge was descending toward and covering him!

"There, there! Right over him! No, I believe in his very face!" shouted this slinger of ropes, Boardman Blake. "Why don't he catch it?"

Uncle Boardman was drawing in the rope preparatory to a third attempt when he paused

and said in a solemn, profound awe, "I do believe he is dead!"

"Oh, try! I can see those eyes! Do try!"
besought Kate.

"I will try to reach him, but it is of no use."
The effort was fruitless.

The drifting mass was not reached, and soon
it was lost amid the confusion of tossing billows and flying spray and thickening mist.

The throwing of that rope seemed as trivial
as the tossing of a thread down into that
frothing deep.

"Awful sorry!" said Uncle Boardman,
mournfully, pulling in the rope.

"Come in now! Come Boardman! Come,
everybody! You will all git your death
a-cold!" warned Aunt Lydia.

They were now conscious that they were
cold and shivering, and closing the doors
against the storm, huddled together in the
shadowy tower.

"Well, it is my solemn opinion that the man
was dead afore he ever reached us," said
Uncle Boardman. "He could not see or
hear."

"Not out of those eyes?" asked Kate.

"No, and he couldn't hear."

"Toot—toot—toot!" savagely went the fog-trumpet, as if angry to think any pair of ears could not hear that.

"Oh, there is that trumpet!   Well, we have done our duty by the dead, and now we will work for the living," remarked Uncle Boardman, ascending to the engine-room.

As he climbed the stairs, he muttered to himself, "It is a sure thing in my mind that the man is dead. My! that rope struck him in the face and he didn't even wink, poor feller."

As he stepped forward to the engine he also muttered, "It is a sure proof to my mind that there is a wreck in the neighborhood. These folks don't think of that."

As he stooped to throw more wood into the furnace, he murmured, "Yes, we have done our duty by the dead, now we must attend to the living."

"Toot—toot—toot!" responded the trumpet valiantly, defying the elements raging about it and at it, and hopeful as long as there was a Boardman Blake below stuffing wood into the furnace.

Walter now joined his uncle. The rest of the awe-struck party adjourned their conversation to the kitchen.

"What did you mean by 'that man'?" asked

May, turning to Kate. "You said out at the door, ' that man.'"

Kate shook her head and placed her finger on her lips, and also looked toward Ripley. His back was turned. He was asking Aunt Lydia a question:

"Aunt Lydia, you don't have many storms like this?"

"None as bad as this since I have been here."

"And no such scenes as what we have witnessed?"

"Not like it, but then you may expect in a lighthouse to see most anything."

"A pretty hard place! A pretty hard place!" declared Ripley. Kate then spoke:

"Why, I thought you were enamoured of a lighthouse and wanted to keep one, Ripley."

"Well, Kate, I was enthusiastic, and so were you. I saw that if in case of vacancy I applied for the situation, I was in great danger of missing my chance because you would be likely to get ahead of me."

Somebody attempted to smile at this, but for Kate it was like trying to light a candle under water.

"Don't know that I feel so enthusiastic now," said Kate, meditatively and sombrely.

A different kind of voice was here heard. It was Aunt Lydia's. She spoke with sudden but decided cheerfulness, " Wall, now, it does seem and it *is* awful mournful. That is only one side to it, though. There is another side. If the sea brings all these dangers, all these terrors, then it is somebody's place to be *here* and do all they can to cheer and help those poor fellers on the sea. That was our purpose in comin' here. We had a purpose, yes, we did. Those that have a purpose when they come to a hard place, must not let it upset their purpose, but stand to their guns cheerfully and let the enemy have it, and think of the good they're doin'."

" Aunt Lydia is saying that for me," thought Ripley. "She is looking this way. I guess she said it for me as well as for light-keepers. I may need to remember it."

If Aunt Lydia, who was saying a resolute, cheerful word for herself, intended to say one also for Ripley, she did not make any remark to prove this. Her words, though, had an effect on Ripley. He now spoke. His tone had her courage and cheer.

"You're right, Aunt Lydia. Yes, we must remember our purpose and stick to that in a hard place, and think of the good that will come out of it. Why, now, it is a very inspiring thought, when you reflect how many light-keepers are meeting bravely this storm, each one in his place, hundreds of them, all trying to be cheerful, encouraging others, doing their best, lighting poor fellows into harbor, warning of bad, ugly rocks, making the best of things, holding up everybody about them— why, hurrah! for the light-keepers!"

And Ripley's kindling eyes and hearty tones and inspiring way so affected his auditors, that Aunt Lydia, like a girl, said, "Hoo—rah!"

And Kate said, "Hur—rah!"

Only May was silent.

Her eyes, her face, her manner, told that she said "Hur-rah!" but she said it in her soul, and Ripley Eaton heard it echoing there and was glad, and caught her hand and said, "That's right!"

Later in the day Uncle Boardman brought word that the storm was holding on hard, but the temperature had fallen.

"In the morning," he affirmed, "you will find yourselves in the midst of a big snow-storm."

CHAPTER XVI.

THE CONSPIRATORS.

THERE was a conspiracy organized at the lighthouse Christmas afternoon.

The time was four o'clock.

The place was the kitchen.

Its leader was the youngest, Aunt Lydia.

The other conspirators were Kate and May.

"Girls, girls, I have an idee!" said Aunt Lydia.

"Oh, tell it!" cried May.

"It will be worth telling," said Kate. "I know."

"This is my idee. Your Uncle Boardman is all tired out. Just think how he looked out in the engine-room, all bundled up in that chair and fast asleep! And Walter is tired, and Ripley is tired. They won't own it, none of 'em. Spunky! I like to see it, but it tires you jest the same. Now, let us spell 'em! My proposition is that we run this lighthouse until twelve o'clock, and make *them* go to bed and take a good square nap, or round one, jest as they prefer. Now I propose we run this lighthouse."

Two pairs of eyes flashed back an enthusiastic fire in response to this proposal of the youngest of their number.

"The very thing I had thought of," said May, "but I didn't know how to bring it about."

"Splendid!" cried Kate, "I am in for it! But how can you make those obstinate men bow the knee to this proposition?"

"Starve 'em out, if they git stubborn, and say they shan't eat. See here! What is that?"

Aunt Lydia went to the closet door and pointed below the knob.

"A key! a key!"

She turned the key in the lock. She put the key in her pocket.

"Now, gentlemen of the lighthouse, no bread, no pie, no cold turkey, no coffee-pot, nothin', unless you let us have our way! That will bring 'em to!"

Aunt Lydia shook her head and said again, "That will bring 'em, too. I know 'em. Take away their food! You can starve a man when he won't submit any other way. I know how to humble the lords of creation."

The other conspirators cried, " Bravo!" clapped their hands, and said they meant to try this subjugation-process in their individual households if they ever had any. They were in favor of a preliminary trial on the spot.

" Then it is settled. We will go and tell them now," proposed the conspirator-in-chief. " They are all out in the engine-room, discussin' us probably. We've got ahead of them."

" Hadn't I better take this broom, in case there is any opposition ? " asked May.

" And I this shovel ? " suggested Kate.

" And tongs is good for rebels," said Aunt Lydia.

A broom, a shovel, and a pair of tongs were soon moving toward the engine-room, and their bearers were grinning and giggling, Aunt Lydia guessing that those " men-folks didn't know what was a-comin' ! "

" Well, well ! " cried Uncle Boardman, when looking up from his watch by the engine he saw the advance of the conspirators. " Ripley ! Walter ! Leave that wood you're sawin' and splittin' and see what these women are up to ! "

" We want this lighthouse," demanded Aunt Lydia. " We want it from now until midnight."

"An unconditional surrender!" asserted May.

"And we are prepared to enforce our demand," said Kate, waving her shovel.

"Well, now!" said Uncle Boardman, grinning, tipping back his hat and thrusting his fat, broad hands into his pockets. "That's funny!"

"To arms!" shouted Walter.

"Come on, Macduff!" cried Ripley.

"No," said Aunt Lydia, soberly, "we mean business, whether this is a business method or not. We want you all to go to bed——"

"Hear! Hear!" "Ridiculous!" "Catch us doing it!" were the outcries greeting this proposition.

"We want you all to go to bed!" again said Aunt Lydia, undaunted. "We want you to have a good rest. We will run the lighthouse, keep the engine a-goin', watch the lantern, and give you a good, sound chance to have some rest. Now, submit! We can do it."

"Do what?" asked Walter. "Run the lighthouse, or make us submit?"

"Do both, sir."

Uncle Boardman laughed scornfully, while Walter and Ripley cried out their defiance.

"Then, gentlemen, you will have nothin' to eat," said Aunt Lydia.

"Not a crumb!" said May.

"Not one leetle shickun bone even," said Kate.

Broom, shovel and tongs were all brandished in support of this threat.

"Let me get the cupboard key!" cried Ripley, springing forward.

A broom was promptly laid across his pathway. The tongs spear-like were thrust at his breast. The shovel was suspended above his head, its blade threatening to come down any moment and hardly in blessing.

"The key!" said Aunt Lydia, mockingly. "I turned it in the lock and now it is in my pocket. Safer there than if at the bottom of the sea, and your Uncle Boardman knows he would have a tough time gittin' it out."

"Yes, yes, I know," said Uncle Boardman, sheepishly. "And it's a serious matter when you trouble a man's rations. I guess, boys, we had better pull down our colors and——"

"Go to bed? Never!" said Ripley.

The tongs touched his breast. The shovel approached his head. The broom was pressed against his legs.

"Pull down those colors, Rip!" cried Walter. "You don't know your Aunt Lydia. You'd better give in."

"Oh, have *you* knuckled? Then—I submit!" replied Ripley. The conspirators cried "Good!" "That's wise!" "All right now!"

The young men wanted a compromise. Ripley desired to watch the lantern awhile. This was May Elliott's special care for the next two hours.

Walter wished to assist in the engine-room that Kate Eaton proposed to superintend for the present.

"You may take turns with your Uncle Boardman watchin' one another go to sleep, but it is forbidden ground out here and up in the lantern, until twelve. Now, disperse! We want this engine-room, at once!" said Aunt Lydia.

Broom and shovel and tongs forced everything before them, and all that was masculine disappeared.

"If this ain't cute! Lyddy beats all!" murmured Uncle Boardman, making himself comfortable under the bed-clothes. "I'm resigned! Had to be! Oh, don't this bed feel good! Farewell to the world!"

Only a snore was soon heard from Boardman Blake. Over the young men now quartered in the light-keeper's room, that empress, Sleep, soon reigned as absolutely as over Uncle Boardman.

The three female keepers of the lighthouse met in the engine-room of the signal-tower before separating to their duties.

"There," exclaimed the enthusiastic Kate, patting fondly the engine that was now her care, listening with delight to the blowing of the trumpet above her, " I call this fascinating. Now I have a responsibility laid on me, I like it. I begin to be enthusiastic again about lighthouses. If you have something to do——"

"That is, a purpose," interjected Aunt Lydia.

"Yes, that is it—why, it makes all the difference in the world. Now, I stuff this furnace with food, and I just delight to cram it in. I feel quite an affection for the engine already. I think of having one of these things in my house, and if the neighbors don't object, I'll use it in foggy weather. There is no telling how serviceable it may be. Put it in a house where the man goes to a club and comes home late and in a confused state of mind. This piece of machinery will tell him where his home is. His wife can manage it."

"If that is the kind of club-house he belongs

to," said Aunt Lydia, indignantly, "I should like to have this fog-trumpet run up into the banquet-room and toot there long enough to clear out the whole of 'em."

May during this conversation had slipped away to watch the lantern. Aunt Lydia remained to assist Kate, promising soon to visit May.

"I am a kind of go-between, you know, and I will help both," said Aunt Lydia.

Kate here had a question to ask of her superior in fog-signal work:

"In lighthouses, they have steam fog-whistles and also this kind. Why are not all of the same kind? Why not have steam?"

"Wasn't it lucky that Boardman was speakin' of this, only the past week! He said this kind was very economical. It is an air-engine. There is plenty of air to run it. As long as the atmosphere lasts, there will be no trouble in supplying these tanks. What if we relied on water? You can see it is not so easy to manage that. Now we have this air-engine, simple——"

"And a good friend."

The assistant-engineer watched with pride her strong, loyal servant whose lungs were down in the engine-room, and whose mouth was somewhere above the roof and thrust out into the cold, nipping, repelling air.

When Aunt Lydia visited May, who was making occasional trips to the lantern, this assistant also had a question to ask: " Aunt Lydia, I have noticed that this lighthouse has a different way of shining from that at the ' Ledges.' Are there many kinds of lights? "

" Boardman showed me a list of the lighthouses one day, and there I saw quite a number. Ours here is what they call a ' fixed white ' and it is ' varied '—that is the word in the book—by a white flash every ninety seconds. That at the ' Ledges ' is a ' fixed white '—that is the name for it. Then off at Rocky Island is one that they say ' flashes alternately red and white '—you see I am posted—and the interval between the flashes is fifteen seconds. Now you see that difference helps sailors. Here is a coaster we will say. It is a comin' in from sea. The cap'n says, ' That light ought to be the "Ledges," a fixed white.' Then he looks off and sees one flashin' red and then flashing white. ' Rocky Island,' he says. Then he sees a ' fixed white ' a flashin' every ninety seconds. ' Ah,' he thinks, shakin' his head, ' I know where I am. Most hum! That is Seal's Head. Good! Yes, most

hum !' Now don't you see how handy it is?
Good as guide-boards ! "

These female conspirators had submitted to
a small compromise, that the male population
should be aroused at half after eleven. Then
a lunch was to be served in the kitchen for all.
At twelve, the males were to be permitted to
resume their duties, and " the other watch," as
Aunt Lydia labelled it, " would turn in."

That lunch at the dead of Christmas night
in the cosey kitchen, was often recalled by
those enjoying it.

" Ah," exclaimed Uncle Boardman, beaming
across the table burdened with Christmas
cookery, "it was wise that we submitted, boys.
That key never would have come out of the
cupboard-lock, if we hadn't submitted. I have
been round, too, and everything is in capital
order. The lighthouse never was doin' better.
Hark, hear that fog-trumpet ! It sounds
cheerful ! "

" Cheerful ! " That was the thought like an
atmosphere extending and felt everywhere.

In this mood, Ripley's sister went to her
rest. As she sank into a grateful slumber, one
of her last reflections was this, " If this hasn't
been a strange Christmas ! Never spent one
like it, and never shall again ! And yet, isn't

it a true Christmas? What is a true Christmas but the remembering of Christ in the doing for others! That is what light-keepers do! That is Christ-like! That is the Christmas spirit."

Here she seemed to behold a picture. Some patient, vigilant, faithful old light-keeper changed into One very different. Into the face came the features of One who gave Himself for men, who loved them, felt for them, died for them. Yes, up in the lantern tall, watched and waited the Great Shepherd of souls, who thought of His own on the vast deep, His scattered flock amid the valleys of the sea, those cold, cruel valleys between billow and billow.

CHAPTER XVII.

THE WRECK AT "T'OTHER SEAL."

WHEN Kate stepped to the window of her round little chamber the next morning, she exclaimed, "Oh May, it is snowing!"

"Let me see! So it is! Uncle Boardman was a true prophet, Kate."

The two young women stood at the lighthouse window and watched the white storm. White above, and the blue of the ocean below, a blue that the white flakes could not affect in the least. It seemed strange to think that on the land this same snow was changing the aspect of all the fields and roads, gardens and streets, dressing them in drapery whose folds covered up all ruts in the highway and dents in the fields, and thickened under the trees. Then in the continuance of the storm would come disaster. The highways would be blocked, lonely farm-houses besieged by snow-drifts, the great trains brought to a standstill on the iron tracks. "What a conqueror!" would be the confession of the earth in the presence of the storm hurling down its columns of snow-flakes.

How different it was on the sea! Here was a constant absorption, one by one, of the white flakes. This feathery cavalry of the sky would quickly be dismounted and submerged. As fast as they came, as readily would they be seized, disarmed and swallowed up. There was something impressive in the thought how promptly the great ocean disposed of the material that on the land became wide surfaces of crystal and huge blocking drifts. The sea was absorbing every little snow-flake, and when all was over, would hold out to the sky one unspotted surface of blue.

The two young women stood at the window and watched the white, descending cloud and the wide, devouring sea. After a season of watching, May said:

" Kate ! "

" What is it ? "

" Will you tell me something ? "

" Depends upon what it is. Guess so."

" When that dead body went drifting by the lighthouse, you said something about its being ' that man.' "

Kate shuddered.

" Oh, don't speak of it, May ! "

"Won't you tell me who it was?"

"Well, I thought I saw his face at one time, and it was just like that De Vere's! Oh, how it startled me! To see that face looking up out of the sea, and looking at me! Didn't you see it?"

"Why, no! I couldn't see anything distinctly, except that it was a man's face."

"I am glad you saw nothing distinctly. I don't want to see it again."

Kate turned about as if she were avoiding the sight of an object that would persist in coming before her unwilling eyes.

"Dreadful, Kate, dreadful! Does Ripley know it?"

"No, I think not. I don't want him to feel as I do."

"Uncle Boardman said he didn't doubt that there was a wreck somewhere in the neighborhood. I am anxious to have a look at 'T'other Seal.'"

"You think a vessel has gone on to the rocks?"

"I have that feeling."

"I wish the snow would lift up its veil. Let us see if we can't possibly detect something."

They went to a window that faced "T'other

Seal," but could see only the far-extending, dense veil of flakes that the storm threw over everything.

Later in the day, however, something suspicious was seen. The storm seemed to be growing weary. The flakes dropped feebly. There was a widening area of water visible from the lighthouse window. Aunt Lydia's spectacles were the telescope that detected something peculiar about "T'other Seal."

"Seems to me I see a-suthin!" soliloquized the old lady, as she relieved the monotony of bread-making by a long gaze out of the window. "Why, there is that 'T'other Seal'! And what are those things stickin' up from it? Looks like a bug with his horns a-stickin' up!"

The sharp, bright spectacles made another observation. Then she threw up her hands and exclaimed, "Save us! If there isn't a wreck!"

She went to the head of the stairs leading down to the store-room and screamed, "Boardman, a wreck!" She shrieked in the wrong direction to reach Boardman Blake. He was up in the lantern. Down in the store-room were Walter and Ripley. One was sawing and the other was splitting wood.

"Hark, Rip! That is Aunt Lydia!" said Walter. "Hark!"

The young men ceased work with saw and axe, and listened.

"Boardman, a wreck! Quick!"

"Oh, heavens!" ejaculated Walter. "Where—where is Uncle Boardman wrecked! Come on, Rip! Let's lower the boat!"

Walter, tumbling over the wood-pile, was aiming to reach the door of the tower, and Ripley was tumbling after him like Jill after Jack in the nursery-rhyme. A third one was rushing after them, Aunt Lydia.

"No, no!" she shrieked. "Up this way! Where's Boardman?"

"I don't know," replied Walter. "I thought you said he was wrecked."

"No, no! A wreck on 'T'other Seal'!"

"Oh! I thought Uncle Boardman was up-set in the water, and yet I might have known he had not left the lighthouse in this storm. But where did you say——"

Aunt Lydia, though, had flown up-stairs again to find Boardman, and heard none of these questions. The two young men, rubbing their bruises, followed her, laughing heartily. They reached a window where they could inspect the sea for themselves.

"Yes!" said Ripley. "No doubt about it, Walter! Some kind of a wreck is there!"

"I see it, Rip! Awful! What's going to be done about it?"

That was a perplexing question, how a wreck could possibly be reached. Uncle Boardman arrived and looked out of the window.

"That's awful, boys!" he said, solemnly.

"Don't you suppose we can get to them, sir?" asked Ripley.

"We have two boats, but not the least chance to lower a boat down into that sea and have it live. She would be upset quicker than a flash."

"Well, what *can* we do?" asked Walter, impatiently. "Something ought to be done. Hard to stand here and do nothing."

"And worse to be out there and have nothing done," added Ripley.

"It's awful, I know, boys, but I don't think we can do a thing."

"There may be nobody alive upon it, Uncle Boardman," remarked Walter.

"That is the situation, I am afraid. That body a-drifting we saw, came from that wreck in my opinion."

There was a fluttering of several females up to the window.

"Nothing, nothing can be done," asserted Boardman Blake, solemnly.

There was one minute of serious, excited contemplation of that unlucky hull thrusting up two stripped and sickly-looking masts amid the thinning snow-flakes.

Aunt Lydia spoke:

"Wall, suthin' has *got* to be done, Boardman."

"I want to do as bad as you, but I don't see that we can do anything. In my opinion, there is not any livin' bein' on that wreck, Lyddy."

"We might try, Boardman. We might shoot."

"Shoot, Lyddy?"

"Why, do as they do at the life-savin' station when they send off a line."

"Oh!"

"Yes, shoot a small line and then if there's anybody aboard——"

"I understand, Lyddy.   Yes, if we had a bow, we might——"

"You hold on," said Walter, turning away and going down-stairs, Ripley following.

"I thought I saw in the wood-pile a stick of ash," said Walter.   "I can make it into some kind of a bow.   You get me a stout string, please, and whittle me three or four arrows."

Walter fashioned a rather rough bow, which, he said, would throw an arrow, and Ripley whittled out several arrows. These two archers then went to a window looking toward the wreck. They were promptly joined by the other inmates of the lighthouse.

" Here is string," said Aunt Lydia. " I've got packthread, cord, grocer's twine and you can pick what you want."

It was decided to try the cord, and Walter carefully tied it to the arrow.

" Now raise the window, Ripley! All ready! I'll shoot! Wish me good luck, everybody. Give me a little more room, please!"

The tall archer drew hard on his bow, while the keeper and his wife, Ripley, Kate and May, stood back in a semicircle and intently watched this effort at wreck-rescue.

" Whiz-z-z!" went the arrow.

The cord flew after it, and both, caught up by a sudden and malicious gust of wind, were swept into the sea, a hundred feet from the wreck.

" Too bad!"

" Oh, dear!"

" That's a shame!"

These exclamations broke from the lips of the eager spectators. It was pitiful to see them gaze into that raging sea and endeavor to pick out some trace of that arrow. The cord dangled feebly down into this heaving cauldron.

" Haul her in, Ripley ! " shouted Walter.

The cord broke away from the arrow and this was left in the sea to be contemptibly flung from breaker to breaker. One of the party thought they saw the arrow. If seen once, this miserable little adventurer was not spied a second time.

" May I shoot, Walter ? "

" Certainly, Rip ! Try your hand ! "

" Watch your chance and wait for a lull in the wind, my boy," advised Uncle Boardman.

" Whiz-z-z ! " went the second arrow.

"I rallely think," said Uncle Boardman, squinting eagerly, and trying to follow the flight of the arrow and its attendant cord, " that—that——"

" Has hit the wreck ! " cried Aunt Lydia.

" It has hit something," said Ripley, " struck somewhere. You see the line is held up and don't give any, hardly."

" Yes," said Walter, " I can see it stretching

toward those masts, and I can't see exactly, but I should say it fell over them."

"Oh, good! Now they'll pull! You got t'other line ready to hitch on, Boardman?" asked Aunt Lydia.

"Yes, I have got a stouter line all ready to be spliced to it, but—but—do you see anybody, boys?"

Walter and Ripley shook their heads.

"Mebbe, somebody will crawl out of the cabin where we don't see 'em now," suggested Aunt Lydia.

That cord of invitation, saying, "Here's a chance! Pull on me!" met with no response.

It dangled over the chasm between the lighthouse and "T'other Seal," troubled only by the wind. This swayed it occasionally, and once gave such a pull on it that Aunt Lydia thought that human hands must have been laid upon it.

"Only the wind!" she muttered at last.

The snow had now almost ceased to fall. "T'other Seal" and its wreck could be seen more distinctly. The cord went to the wreck and invitingly stretched over it. An appeal even it seemed to make to the little rigging left, to the battered house on the deck, and to the tightly-secured hatches. Here was an invitation that somebody would please come down from the few ropes still in position, or out of that cabin so shattered, or was not there a chance for the lifting of those hatches, and might not a scared, pale face show itself? Seeing the one cord of hope hanging down, it might exclaim, " Thank God! Life may yet be mine! Let me pull on that rope!"

Nobody pulled on the cord, though. There was not the least sign of any disturbance of a hatch, or intimation that for a century there had been any life in the cabin. Unnoticed, the little cord fell across the hull.

" Mebbe," theorized Aunt Lydia, " they got out of the wreck and crawled up the rocks."

" Too much water about the bows, and then there is no sign of a human being on ' T'other Seal,'" replied Uncle Boardman. " It's an awful sea yet all about that vessel. However, we might look through our spy-glass."

No person could be seen on that most desolate, forsaken, wave-battered piece of rock and sand, " T'other Seal." Occasional breakers would roll over its solitary hummock and down into that crater in its centre which Ripley knew about.

" Oh, there's nobody there!" said Uncle Boardman, dolefully. " I know it, I know it!"

"Well, Uncle Boardman, we did all we could. We can say that," remarked Walter.

"I don't know, if anybody had been there on the wreck," said Uncle Boardman, "how we could have got them into the lighthouse, Lyddy."

"Why, pulled 'em in, Boardman!"

Uncle Boardman smiled.

"Pulled 'em in across that terrible gulf? You think of it. What we would have needed is what they have at life-saving stations. They send a line to a wreck, and by means of it rig up an endless line, as they call it, with blocks, and so on, and then they pull out to the wreck a breeches-buoy, or a life-car, and pull it back again when loaded up."

"Oh, Boardman, if we had got a line to the wreck, any poor feller could have shinned right up to this window."

Uncle Boardman shook his head, and the others laughed.

"Lyddy, we did what we could. There! We can say that. It's a great comfort sometimes to be able to say jest that, we did what we could."

"Yes, we can say that, and if the sea should be quiet, or not so bad but we could venture off, then Ripley and I are going to put off in one of the boats and see what may be the news at 'T'other Seal,'" said Walter.

"Very well. You can try that. It is going to clear off. The wind has been shifting into fair weather quarters, or is a-heading that way, and to-morrow, it is my opinion, we shall see the sun," prophesied the keeper.

It proved to be a true prophecy.

In the morning the sun broke his way through clouds like a rosy-faced boy, clearing out of the path heavy snow-drifts, and he calmly looked down upon the still, uneasy sea with an air of wondering why there had been the late fuss and tumult. Walter and Ripley could not be restrained, though Uncle Boardman advised waiting for a less troublesome sea.

"We are going to see to the bottom of all the mystery at 'T'other Seal,'" declared Walter.

Ripley said, "Go ahead! I'll stand by you. You won't forbid us, Uncle Boardman?"

"I shan't forbid ye, boys. If I was younger, I'd—I'd—go myself."

The young men lowered a boat and pushed off. They were anxiously watched from a lighthouse window, but the voyage was safely accomplished. A long inspection was made

and at last the impatient Kate reported,
"They're coming back!"

"What *are* they bringin' back, Boardman?"
asked Aunt Lydia.   "Looks like a whale's
head."

A cargo of something the boat brought
back, a very mysterious something.   The
young men looked up from their boat to the
waiting group at the lighthouse door, and
shouted, "Lower away there!   Here is something to be hoisted up!   A treasure!"

Uncle Boardman had in readiness his
"taykle and falls," as he called them, and the
" whale's head," began to rise.

"Careful, care—ful!" sang out Walter.

The women insisted on helping the keeper,
for the "whale's head" proved to be heavy.
It rose slowly, slowly, but before it reached
the door of the tower, Walter had mounted
the ladder and was pulling on the rope.
When the "whale's head" had been swung
inside the door, it proved to be something very
different from a whale's head.

"The starn of a boat!" declared Uncle
Boardman. "What under the sun and moon,
Walter, have you brought home?"

"Miss Kate Ripley, please read the name on
this relic," was Walter's answer.

"'*Water-fiend*'! You haven't brought home a part of that yacht in which De Vere went off with my brother and that Martin?" said Kate.

"Nothing less!" replied Walter. "A very, very important piece of evidence thrown up by the sea. Storms do some good."

Ripley had now climbed the ladder, and his eyes flashed as he stood beside the fragment brought home. His sister understood the reason of his excited look and her face was as anxious as his. There was so much interest in the unexpected arrival of this wreck, that the other at "T'other Seal" was almost forgotten.

Aunt Lydia did say, "I don't s'pose there was a livin' soul on board that vessel," and Walter replied, "Nothing at all! Vessel is a-breaking up. Name is the *Nancy*."

It was the "whale's head," that attracted and received the attention of those in the lighthouse. What was the *Nancy* compared with this soiled, dark fragment clutched by the sea, and now wrenched from its grasp by the storm? A mystery surrounded it. Aunt Lydia could not understand it.

"Don't see why all this fuss should be made about that thing," she murmured.

"Hush, Aunt Lydia!" said Walter, taking her aside. "Don't you remember we told you that De Vere claimed he left in his yacht proof of Ripley's debt, proof stowed away in a little tin box in the locker of his boat!"

"Oh, yes, I do remember."

"Well, that is the locker in this stern we brought here."

"You don't say! Stowed away in that! Who ever would have thought of that! Let's have that open quicker than a wink! Where's an axe?"

"Just wait a minute, Aunt Lydia! Hammer will do, if we need anything."

All stood about the stern of the *Water-fiend*. Everybody wanted to help. Half a dozen hands were laid upon the locker. Ripley, though, was allowed to begin operations with his hammer. Aunt Lydia stood behind him, prepared to offer the axe if needed. Kate Eaton was as eager in her interest as her brother, and anxiously bent over him.

"The thing sticks," said Ripley, trying to force the doors secured by a bolt that had rusted and refused to slide back. "There—there—she comes!"

Open flew the doors, letting out an odor of the depths of the sea.

"Now what have we got here?" asked Uncle Boardman, stooping to get a look into the dark, mysterious locker.

"La!" exclaimed Aunt Lydia. "Makes you think of lookin' into one of Capn' Kidd's pirate ships. Full of suthin', I know!"

"Yes, mystery will be unearthed now," declared Walter.

"Full of villainy," said May.

"Crowded, I know," added Kate, peeping over her brother's shoulder.

The end, though, of the inspection, of all the stooping and gazing and peeping, of all the sharp, close pryings into the dark, damp and decaying locker, was to see and find—nothing.

"Empty as a drunkard's pocket!" said Uncle Boardman, rising, red in the face from his search.

"That is the end of all of De Vere's talk about proof in a locker!" said Walter. "Nothing at all! Doesn't that relieve you, Rip?"

Ripley smiled and nodded his head, while Kate declared, "Of course, nothing could be found. We all knew that."

"That is the way I felt," said May, stoutly, which gratified Ripley exceedingly.

Aunt Lydia seemed a little disappointed.

She did not want to find any proof of De Vere's charges, but did wish to see something in that locker which the rusty bolt had so long secured as if holding most valuable treasure. She again and again took "a peek" into the locker. She looked intently at her husband as if querying whether he had not better try to get inside that locker, and by the closest, personal examination learn if some little box, can, or scrap of paper might not be there. The light-keeper by this time, though, had put on his big storm-coat and was ready for another kind of a venture.

"Wife, I must go ashore to let folks know that the *Nancy* is wrecked. I'll take Walter with me. Maybe I can hear something about any bodies that have come ashore or if anybody were saved alive," said the keeper.

"You got to go?" asked Aunt Lydia.

"Yes, that is one of the duties of light-keepers, to give intelligence of wrecks, Lyddy. I may not have to go far. I may see somebody who will take the news ashore. If I don't see anybody, I will land there by the school-house and find someone who will take the news. Sad enough for any family that had friends in the crew."

After the departure of Uncle Boardman and

Walter, Kate and Aunt Lydia went into the kitchen. Ripley and May climbed the successive stairways leading to the lantern.

"I promised Uncle Boardman I would wipe the lens for him and rub the brass-work," said May.

"I would like much to help you," said Ripley, and his offer was not refused.

It was very pleasant to be cleaning the lens side by side with May Elliott, and to receive her congratulations on the emptiness of that locker.

"Of course, we did not doubt that you were clear of what that De Vere charged upon you, Mr. Eaton."

It was indeed very gratifying to Ripley to hear this from so important a judicial source. In a very happy frame of mind he worked upon the lens and was very sorry that it was not one of immense size requiring a week of hard but also combined effort. It was rather chilly up there in the lantern, but he only looked to see that May was comfortable in her thick cloak, and then pursued with delight an occupation giving other light-keepers some occasion for grumbling, the polishing of a lens. He was very communicative, for somehow May Elliott had power to draw out his plans,

his dreams and aspirations even.   He told her
it had been decided by him that he had better
apply for the school she had been keeping,
that it would be pleasant to keep "the winter
term" in a school-house where she had taught;
that a letter of application had gone for the
position and any day he might hear from it.
Would she tell him about the scholars,
please, and how it was one kept school?

"For do you know," he added, "I think you
are at the bottom of all this talk about my
keeping school?"

"I?" she asked in surprise.

"Do you remember the letter you wrote to
my sister after I had been in your school?"

"Did you see that letter?" asked the blushing May.

"Oh, don't worry if Kate did show it.   Now
tell me please, how to keep school," urged
Ripley.

It took much time to give all this information, and in the meanwhile there were as many
as ten revolutions made about one lens, Ripley rubbing all the time as for dear life.   Then
all the brass-work needed special attention.

"It gets awful dirty," said Ripley.   "You
have to go over it several times to have it anywhere near right."

During this process of lens-cleaning and brass-polishing, the conversation went from subject to subject, and, at last, reached that which, naturally would have been suggested at the start to individuals thus occupied, that of lighting.

"Why don't they light up lanterns with electricity, I wonder?" asked May.

"It is the expense, I believe, Uncle Boardman says. Of course, it would take very highly skilled labor. You would need men who would understand their business fully. If any accident to the lights happened, you would want first-class help on the spot to repair the damage. I—I don't know much about the subject, anyway."

This mode of lighting is in its infancy, and other nations have surpassed us in using the electric light. France has led off in such use. At the very gates of the River Seine, rises the tower of La Heve, reputed to be the best light-station in the world. This has two towers, a north and a south. Oil was burned in these towers. For oil, in 1863, in the south tower, an electric light was substituted, and declared to be far superior. When the light itself was invisible, yet the atmosphere around it would be so illuminated that the location of the light was indicated. La Heve, as a rule, has been a success in the world of electric illumination. England has a brilliant electric light at South Foreland and at Sonter Point. At these stations, oil lamps are kept in readiness for use, in case there should be any failure of the electrical apparatus. Electricity is also used for lighting buoys in Gedney's Channel, New York Harbor. It was felt to be of great importance as a roadway at night, but it must be successfully lighted. Sometimes, the lighthouse establishment has used "buoys containing a reservoir filled with compressed gas which is fed through a pressure regulator to a small burner located in the focus of a lens supported on a frame-work at the top of the buoy." These buoys cannot be used in Gedney's Channel. Somebody hit on the device of "an incandescent electric lamp, operated by a current generated on shore and conveyed through a cable laid on the bottom of the sea." The buoys were fitted up with such apparatus. The lights were kindled for the first time in November, 1888, and were afterwards reported as lights that had gone into "successful and continuous operation." These light-pillars in the sea are very convenient for a steamer, or any vessel that wants to travel by night. The lamp-globes on different buoys can be made of variously colored glass, and thus are distinguishable, while it is said they can be made intermittent or flashing. Now, if we could only have such marine street-lights along the great highways of the sea reaching from America to Europe, how convenient it would be! This is nothing more wonderful than many accomplishments by man.

Those young people in the lighthouse lantern could not give the above information to one another, but ignorance did not worry them. Other subjects came up for attention. All the glass-work and all the brass-work were thoroughly cleaned, and re-cleaned and re-cleaned, till there was no excuse for prolonging conversation up in the lantern. There was then an adjournment to Aunt Lydia's kitchen. The view from the lantern was cold and wintry, open and wide, but dreary. When Ripley and May reached the door of the kitchen, the look into it was a much bounded one, but it was a picture delightfully cosey and domestic. Aunt Lydia and Kate were busy with cookery, whose odors were very appetizing.

"Well, well!" called out Kate, "Who comes here? Glad to see you, very."

"Thank you, thank you!" replied a voice,

that of Walter, appearing at the door that led from the store-room. "Good to be welcomed!"

"She meant, just then, somebody coming down-stairs," said Aunt Lydia.

"And not anybody coming up-stairs?" inquired Walter.

"We—we will think it over," said Kate.

"If you knew what a mail we brought with us, you would give us a welcome, I tell ye," said Uncle Boardman, who was slowly following Walter.

"A mail, a mail!" screamed the young people, rushing forward, not only to welcome the mail-carriers, but to unload them as rapidly as possible.

"We thought we would go to the post-office when we landed," said Uncle Boardman. "I sent my message off about the *Nancy*, and brought away these messages from the post-office."

Among other names he called over, "Letter for Ripley!"

"What?" said Ripley, breaking open the letter addressed to him and reading this sentence: "'Dear sir, you can have the school you applied for'—hear, hear, everybody! The school-master has arrived. I'll read the rest,

'Our terms you know, and we would like to have the school begin a week from next Monday,' and so on, and so on. A letter from the committee, you see!"

The school-master was here surrounded by a jabbering circle, all congratulating him on what he had secured, and anxious to hear what might be expected in the future. When this wave of excitement had passed by, Uncle Boardman was asked if he had learned anything about the wreck.

"I know more than anybody else," he replied. "I didn't find a person who knew anything about the *Nancy*."

"Or any that had come ashore?" asked Kate.

Uncle Boardman shook his head.

"She means that De Vere," whispered Aunt Lydia to Walter.

"All dark on that subject," was his reply.

"That's where evil things disappear," she told him.

CHAPTER XVIII.

THE HAUNTED SCHOOL–HOUSE.

THE young school-master of " Deestrick Seven " was looking out of a window of that palace of learning where he was the king. School was over for the day and he was glad of it. He had drawn on his thick, warm overcoat and taken from its nail his hat, and was about to start for his boarding-house. He halted at a window from which one could see the wintry water.

" It looks very peaceful out there at the light," he said. " Wonder what they are doing ! "

Then he imagined Aunt Lydia in the kitchen getting ready the evening meal. The sun was running low and he fancied that Uncle Boardman was saying to Walter, " Most time to light up, nephew ! "

It was pleasant to Ripley to think that, though absent now, May Elliott had been in that lighthouse. As for Kate Eaton, she had long been at home.

Then Ripley turned and faced his school-room, fast slipping into the shadows, strangely going out of sight without any going at all. He recalled his school-life and glanced from desk to desk.

"I am not sorry I came," he said, "but it has not been smooth sailing all the time. Aunt Lydia told me she liked to see one with a 'purpose,' and I suppose I had it in coming here. I sometimes have wondered why I came here. I don't believe I would if May Elliott had not taught here. It is pleasant if you can't see her, to be where she has been."

As he spoke the look of care on his face vanished.

"Yes," he said, "some pleasant things here. Yes, a number!"

Then he began to enumerate various agreeable experiences.

"Now, there is Granny Smith, though she is outside of the school, but Don Pedro who lives with her, is one of my scholars, and the whole family seems to be identified with the school. Now, that matter came out pleasantly."

"That matter," was the source of various pleasant memories. It originated in a call he made on Don Pedro and Granny Smith. Ripley resolved to call on his scholars—an excellent plan in teaching—and this visit was in accordance with that plan.

He wished he might find Martin at Granny's. He wanted to see Martin and ask him to refute De Vere's charges, and Ripley wanted also to tell him about the empty locker that the storm had plucked from the grasp of the sea. But Martin, like De Vere, was a mystery that Ripley could not lay his hand upon. Ripley made his call. Granny was delighted to see him. She wrapped her brightest handkerchief about her head, twisted those gaudy folds so as to conceal poverty's rents, and sat dignified and straight in her only rocking-chair.

"You a preacher?" she inquired of her guest.

"Oh, no, madame!" replied Ripley, with that grace and courteous deference which made him such a favorite among old people. "I'm only a school-master."

"Oh, I didn' know but ye might be bof. Some folks am."

"Just a school-master."

"Couldn' ye come an' hol' a meetin'? Ye hab a good voice for dat."

Ripley smiled and shook his head.

"Afraid I couldn't."

"Mought try," she said, appealingly.

The more Ripley thought it over, the more he ventured to look upon it as something feasible.   He was a fine singer.

"I can keep them singing anyway," he reasoned.

Aunt Lydia had heard about this invitation to Ripley to conduct services and she sent him this word, "Good to have a purpose, you know."

"So it is!" he said.   "I—I'll try!"

Ripley hardly knew how he would acquit himself, but he knew he could sing, and his singing always seemed to interest people.

"Then as for the rest, it is God's work and I will leave it to Him," thought Ripley.

That meeting, the school-master now standing at the school-house window, was recalling with great satisfaction.   He saw Granny sitting with a queen's air on a very shabby throne.   He saw the neighbors carefully listening to what he said, and to his singing still more intently.   Then before the closing prayers, he saw and heard something else.

A man arose.   Ripley had not seen him before.   He had been hidden behind Granny's broad shoulders.

"It's a colored man, and where have I

seen him? I've seen him before," thought Ripley.

" I—I—I'd like a chance fur to say a word," the man began, showing much emotion. " I didn' 'spect to say dis."

Every eye was turned toward him. The old lady threw up her hands, clasped them and screamed " Bress de Lor'; I didn' 'spect to hear dis ob my Mat! He got free from de Ebel One!"

" What?" thought Ripley, in surprise.

A number of colored people who were clustered in that neighborhood, had come to the meeting, each bringing a chair or a box for a seat, and these now joined their sister in some very strong demonstrations.

Martin went on: " I made up my mind Christmas Day, when Massa Eaton and dem folks sent me an' us dose tokens, dey were frowin' coals ob fire on us, an' dey smart, an' I don' mean to git ober de smart. No, I'se gwine to swing off clar from ebel, de Lor' bein' my helper an' begin a new paf."

When he sat down, the meeting was again in commotion.

A new path Martin did sincerely take from that time, and one proof of this was his treatment of Ripley.

He steadfastly asserted of De Vere's charges against Ripley, that as far as he knew, "Ripley were only a gen'leman."

"But how did you get away from De Vere's influence?" Ripley asked Martin.

"Don' know. De Christmas presents set me to thinkin', an' I couldn' help comin' to dis meetin', sort of curous like, an' de meetin' was too powerful fur me."

"Where do you think De Vere has gone?"

"Dunno. Gone somewhar. I lef' him, I broke away."

"Were you off in the big storm?"

"Oh, no," said Martin.

"What did he come down here to the coast for, do you think?" asked Ripley.

"Jes' to get hol' of some money. He come off to 'T'oder Seal' dat night you foun' him cos he had an' idee de officers were after him, an' he did tink he might see you an' get some money from you. Oh, I were a fool to hang by him, but I couldn' seem to break away from him, not until de Lor' came dis way an' broke my chains. Dat am all I can say. A heap sorry for all de trouble I gib ye."

To have this consciousness of an effort put forth in God's strength and to know it had had power in breaking those chains that had held Martin, gave a pleasure to the school master's meditations at the window the night of the opening of this chapter. As he still lingered there, recalling his experience as schoolmaster, various things gave him pleasure. He remembered the many tokens of attachment his scholars as a whole had given him. There were signs too, of their positive improvement in study.

"I am getting something in return for my purpose which Aunt Lydia spoke about, and yet—and yet—" he murmured and ceased.

Little gusts of scandal would sometimes blow upon him and at him, involving charges of misconduct in previous years. Why these should spring up again and again, when so much had been put to rest through Martin's assistance, he could not understand.

"Seems as if somebody must be going round keeping stories in circulation," thought Ripley.

Then had come a foolish statement, ridiculous and unworthy of notice, it seemed, and yet compelling notice; the school-house was haunted! It was said a mysterious presence was seen going out and coming in at hours very late or very early. Who was it? What was it?

Martin in a friendly way first mentioned these stories.

"Ha! ha!" replied Ripley. "It makes me laugh. Who believes in haunted houses?"

What though came first to him as an outside rumor, unpleasantly intruded itself upon his notice as an item in school-life. This very day of our story, Ripley was inquiring of a boy why "Johnny Geddes," a neighbor, was not coming to school now-a-days.

"His marm says," replied the scholar, as plainly as he spoke promptly, "that she is not going to send her boy, Johnny, to a haunted school-house."

"Ridiculous!" said the master. "It makes me laugh. Ha, ha!"

The scholars were laughing also.

"If anybody mentions such stuff to you, say it is absurd. Nobody in these days has faith in such absurd notions. Say that, scholars, and laugh at the nonsense all you wish. We will think no more about it."

No more?

The school-master said this and then acted like many other people and people generally; he kept thinking upon this subject.

"Very foolish!" he said, looking round upon the school-room that night when all had been dismissed. "To think this innocent old place is haunted! Absurd!"

Hark!

He gave a little start, and Ripley Eaton, the daring gymnast, the invincible, was conscious that his heart thumped rather violently when he heard a noise above him. "The wind rattling round the roof," he ejaculated. "Think I won't stay any longer."

He whistled, buttoned up his coat, stepped out of the room, fastened the door, and then gave a look at the roof.

"Oh, I see! A bough of an old pine flaps down against the roof!" he said. "That explains the noise I heard. Other absurd stories could be explained as easily, I doubt not. We will think no more about this."

The next morning, he was on his way from his boarding-house to the school-room.

"Ah!" he said, chancing to look up. "Here comes Seavey Loud, one of my boys. Wonder why he has not been in school lately? I will ask him."

Seavey was a colored boy, one of a little colony of his people on the edge of a dusky patch of woods which on stormy nights, Seavey's mother and other timid souls peopled with all kinds of mysterious, raving, howling beasts.

Seavey's mother could not live there in any kind of peace of mind, and yet she would not have moved from such a fascinating quarter for any small consideration.

"Seavey," now asked the school-master, "why have you been absent from school lately? I have missed you."

His face assumed the look of the tragical. His voice dropped down into his boots. His eyes began to wildly roll.

"My mudder," he said, in awed tones, "she don' wan' me to go whar de school am haunted."

"Fiddlesticks!" said the master, a little impatiently. "Your mother does not believe in such nonsense. Why, laugh at it, Seavey!"

But Seavey did not laugh. He did not change his look or tone of voice. The subject was too awful.

"She—she—she won' let me!"

"Well, tell her I say 'fiddlesticks.' Ha! ha!"

The two separated.

"Such stuff is not worth thinking upon," said the master, and kept thinking upon it.

"Poor, abused building!" was his address to the old school-house now appearing in sight. "Too bad they should talk about you! I am not going to dishonor you by having any such foolish ideas about you. Catch me thinking that way about you!"

And he kept thinking upon this very subject.

When he entered the school-room, he was not in a mood that could be called contented and cheerful. The subject of his thoughts annoyed him more than he cared to confess.

"That old pine bough," he said, looking up, "keeps rattling and rubbing away! It is cold, too. I will light my fire. It will make me feel better."

He felt worse before he got through. It was a wood-stove, and the night previous he had piled a quantity of wood by the side of the stove in readinesss for the morning fire. Not a stick was now left!

"That is queer!" said the master. "Could I have been mistaken and put it into the stove all ready to light? I believe the fire was out when I left."

He opened the door. He saw no wood, but an abundance of ashes. He touched these. They were still warm.

"Haunted school-house!" flashed into his mind.

"It begins to look serious," he muttered. "What a bother! It is very annoying. It makes so much talk, too, in the neighborhood. I don't see why I should have this fuss. However, I will have a fire."

When he had kindled the fire, and enjoyed for a few minutes the pleasant music a fire always makes on a cold morning, he turned toward his desk.

"Hul—lo!" he shouted, as if spying and addressing a friend there in the school-master's seat. It was not a friend, but an old enemy, and planted there on the very desk. It was a wine bottle. It was not empty. A wine glass stood near it. "Help yourself!" was the invitation written on a slip of paper stuck into the glass.

"If that isn't the strangest thing," declared the school-master, stepping up to the silent intruder. "That looks convivial! Looks as if somebody had had a good time in here! Left an invitation for me, too!"

What a magician's wand may be in a word! "Convivial," how that winged the school-master's thoughts back to college days! "Good time!" How complete did this phrase make the transformation! And with it came a sudden temptation. He was invited to help himself. Why should not this harassed school-master first fill and then empty that glass? He was surprised later in the day when he recalled the temptation. He was ashamed, also, of his weakness.

"I ought to have taken it and pitched it out of the window," he said.

He did not, though.

He looked at it.

He said, "How it used to exhilarate me!" For a moment, he forgot the after-shame, the regrets, the heart-aches, the disgrace of other days. Temptation, though, does not show us consequences. It only hangs up the evening-cloud and paints it with the light of the sun as we tread some dangerous mountain-path. It is the present glory we see, and the night is hidden, the night of regret that will surely come, the night when we stumble in the dreary mountain-path, the light gone out of the western sky, and the clouds that fascinated us, settling about us in cold, dreary, bewildering vapor.

Ripley was looking at the bright, fascinating light; not down at the unsafe mountain-path in which he walked, and which the night would chillingly cloud.

He saw again the invitation, "Help yourself!"

"That looks like writing I have seen before!" he said. "It looks friendly."

It was the opposite of friendliness.

He seized the glass, seized the bottle, when a noise detained him in the act of opening the bottle.

"That noise overhead? Anybody looking?" he asked, turning toward the school-room.

If he had known what evil eyes were fastened on him, he would have shuddered, but he saw nothing. Turning toward his desk, he saw something that startled him. It was a text-book, an arithmetic, that the previous teacher had lent him, and instantly he seemed to see the teacher herself, May Elliott! She rose up behind the humble desk, such a grieved—and also, rebuking look on her face? Not rebuking, but extremely sorrowful, a look that seemed to say, "I pity you, and I wish, oh, I wish so much I could help you!"

Another moment, she was gone. The temptation, too, was gone. All the deceiving cloud-lustre was swept away. Through a clear air Ripley saw his danger, the risky path he had been treading, and trembling he turned away. He was glad to hear the sound of a youthful voice, echoing outside.

"Don Pedro!" he said. "A relief to have somebody come. I don't want him to see this bottle though. I will get him to sweep away some snow that has got into the path before the door, and in the meantime I will hide this bottle."

He went to the door.

"Good-morning, Don!"

"Good-mornin', sah!"

"You are early, Don. I'll get you the broom and please clean out the path for me."

"All right, sah!"

When he had brought the broom to the door, he halted on the step long enough to turn the key in the lock and thrust the key into his pocket.

"That is to make sure no one goes into the school-house until I have put that bottle away. Don might get in before I thought," reasoned Ripley.

He gave Don the broom, and Don went to work. Ripley may have stayed with him, overseeing the job, five minutes. He then unlocked the door of the school-house and went into the little entry, closing the door and locking it that he might not be disturbed until he had hidden away that tempter on his desk. He stamped off the snow from his boots. He lifted the latch of the door of the school-room. He entered it. He strode toward his desk.

"Now I'll take care of that bottle and hide it."

He suddenly halted.

He exclaimed in surprise, "That bottle is gone! The glass too! Haunted school-house! I begin to think it may be! If this isn't the strangest thing!"

CHAPTER XIX.

A BOAT THAT WENT TO SEA.

"WELL," said the school-master, "I might as well unlock the door and let that poor Don Pedro in. I will say nothing about this unfortunate affair. Some scholar may know about it. Yes, it is possible that a scholar might have put it here, might have got in a window while I was with Don and cleared out through the woods with his bottle. Yes, it is possible—no, it isn't! Anyway, I will say nothing about the affair, and if I keep still, I shall lose nothing by it anyway."

He went to the door and called, "Don Pedro!"

The shivering Don Pedro looked up.

"You may come in now. Let the rest go!"

Don wondered why the master should be willing to leave thus incomplete a work he was so anxious Don should begin. Rolling his eyes about in wonder, showing his white, chattering teeth, he came gladly into the school-house and stood by the roaring stove. Other scholars came in. The sun entered the old-fashioned windows and gave a gilding to the plain, defaced seats and desks. School life began once more. A chapter from the Bible was read. The room was hushed as Ripley's clear, full voice rose in prayer. A chorus of scholars' voices ascended in the repeating of the petition "Our Father." After this opening form, Ripley sometimes would lead off in a "general exercise" as he termed it. He would talk upon some subject, giving items of interest and information. While he talked, the scholars would be required to note down on their slates what they could, and then Ripley would examine them upon the subject. He was expecting soon to take up and talk about the subject of lighthouses.

"I'll do it, this morning," he said to himself. "I want something to take up my attention and drive from my thoughts that unpleasant matter of the morning."

He looked out of a window in the wall toward the sea to get what he called a "little inspiration." The water had a hazy look and he noticed that the sun at first so bright and golden, was shining with a dull light. There was a threatening bank of clouds between the sun and the sea.

"Foul weather coming in? Maybe. I believe the vane on that barn opposite—a wooden ox—is sticking its horns out toward the east," reflected the school-master. "There is the lighthouse, though!"

Yes, its two towers rose steadfastly from the water. It was a pleasant sight. It suggested the past. He thought of Uncle Boardman, Aunt Lydia, Walter, his sister Kate, and fondly dwelt upon that other member of the former lighthouse circle, May Elliott.

"Yes," he thought, "it will help me drive out of my mind all unpleasant thoughts. It looks so home-like and encouraging out that way."

Fastening his eyes upon the lighthouse that a thickening haze would soon obscure, he said cheerily, stimulatingly, "Now, scholars, we will have a talk about lighthouses. I'll put a picture on the board. Take up your slates and copy my work."

There was a prompt, gratified clicking of pencils.

"Here is the lighthouse at Fowey Rocks, Florida. You will see it is very different from the style we can see from our window. It is what they call an iron-skeleton, frame-work light. They have this advantage. They can be made in all their parts at a foundry and then shipped to the place where needed. They are all ready to be set up. On the Florida reefs, you will find some fine ones, Fowey Rocks, Sand Key, and so on. Let me tell you about the screw-pile lighthouse. What would you think of an iron pile five inches thick, with screws three feet in diameter? Bore into what, you say? Into a sandy foundation. It would be hard to build a tower of stone there, but you could bore with a screw-pile even as with an auger. Take the light at Brandywine Shoal, Delaware Bay. It is described as a red screw-pile structure."

We will leave the school-master and say that they have another way of managing sandy foundations. They sink deep a hollow cylinder by pneumatic or air pressure. At Fourteen-foot Bank Shoal, such a cylinder was sunk twenty-three feet below the surface of the shoal.

' Ripley now told about Minot's Ledge Light, how it was built once and how constructed subsequently. Then he made a picture of Minot's Light and that at Spectacle Reef in Lake Huron near Mackinaw. This is like Minot's Light. Its base is said to be seven feet under water. It is out in the lake eleven miles from land.   Its special foe is the ice.   In packs, this is driven against the tower.   That winter, the school-master could not tell his pupils of a fine lighthouse on the Pacific coast, for it was lighted up as recently as 1887.   It stands on Tillamook Rock, which is eighteen miles south of the entrance to Columbia River.   Tillamook Rock is distant from the shore only a mile and has tripped up many vessels.   The Pacific beats furiously against it, and those at work upon the lighthouse were cut off at one time from the main-land for a fortnight.   The rock rises out of the water on one side bold and prominent.   The great difficulty in the construction of the lighthouse was to prepare the rounded crest.   The foundation-stones were set in place when the rock had been cut down thirty feet.   Blasting, while unavoidable, was hazardous.   As the men were working on a surface that was limited, they could step aside but a short space when a blast was made.   The roughness of the sea about the rock can be inferred from the fact that the men used in landing and in embarking a life-line and breeches-buoy.   The school-master exercised his scholars on such statistics as the number of lightships employed in localities where a lighthouse is not or can not be planted.

Then he drilled his pupils in such an exercise as this:

"What was the first light established in the United States?   Speak up distinctly."

"Boston Light, 1716," yelled the scholars.

"Is the original structure there or has it been rebuilt?"

"Rebuilt!" came in a chorus.

"Name some old lighthouses still standing."

"Baker's Island, Salem Harbor, 1797."

"Another."

"Cape Hen-lo-PEN, 1789."

"Very old, you see.   Now, another!"

"*Gur-r-r*-net, Plymouth Harbor, 1769."

"Still older.   Another."

The school hesitated.

In that moment of silence came not a knock so much as a pound on the school-house door.

Bang—bang—bang!

"Who's that!" involuntarily exclaimed the startled school-master.

He generally sent a boy to the door, but such a peremptory succession of thumps brought the master himself. Opening the door, he almost ran into a rather short, compact, thick-set man who was pressing his way in.

"I want to see what you've got inside," said the man, abruptly.

He had a brusque, incisive way of speaking and his face had a sharp, cutting look.

"I am the man who means to make his way through something," was his air. "And particularly am I going through this school-house."

"W-w-w-well!" said the astonished Ripley. "W-w-walk in!"

The stranger was dressed in citizen's clothes, but Ripley caught sight of a little badge tucked far under his coat.

"Police! Detective!" were words flashing through the thoughts of the startled school-master. "Does he want me?"

"This the door?" asked the detective, pressing toward the door into the school-room, which Ripley had shut after him.

"Y-yes, sir."

The man had laid his broad, thick thumb on the latch. He turned and said:

"This the haunted school-house?"

"Well, n-n-no, sir. They give it that name, or some foolish people do."

"We will find out about it. I am an officer," and he exposed his badge.

With the air of one who had assumed command of the premises and relegated the school-master to a very subordinate position, the detective now pushed into the school-room and wholly disregarding the students making their profound investigation into the subject of lighthouses, looked about the walls, and then down at the floor, asking suddenly:

" Any cellar?"

" Never heard of any," replied Ripley.

"Attic?" asked the man, glancing up at the ceiling.

"Some kind of a hole, but I never looked up into it."

" Is there?" asked the man, excitedly. " Oh, I see!"

There were two holes in the low, flat ceiling. One was entirely occupied by the funnel that shot up into the darkness under the roof and then made its way to a chimney at the end of the building. The other hole had been cut for a similar purpose. It was larger than necessary and had never been used. A circular grating had been thrust into the hole and left there.

" Could a man get up there?" asked the detective. " Got a ladder? I couldn't get through that hole, but *you—you* might by squeezing."

"I certainly haven't tried it and shouldn't care to be asked to try. I will have the ladder brought and—and *you* can. Don, please fetch that ladder out in the entry!"

"Yes, sah!"

Away sprang Don, delighted to be of service, and quickly brought the ladder. The man planted it against the rim of the grated hole and climbing it, halted half-way up, exclaiming:

"What's that!"

There was a noise on the outside of the building and it seemed to begin up above the funnel and then descended toward the ground, ending in a thump as if something had fallen.

"What's that?" asked the man, emphatically, excitedly.

"Sounds like snow falling from the roof," said the school-master.

Several scholars here went to the window looking out upon the road. They broke out into a chorus, "Oh! oh! oh!" They stood pointing out of the window, their eyes and mouths wide open in horror.

"What is it?" said Ripley, going to the window.

The detective followed him.

"Somebody running off!" screamed one of the big boys of Ripley's flock.

"Heigh, heigh!" shouted the detective, then rushing to the door. "Where's Emery? Thought I left Emery out there. Emery!" he bawled and ran out of the building, almost falling in his haste.

Ripley halted a moment at the window. He was just in season *not* to catch a glimpse of the mysterious somebody who had cleared the road and had already disappeared among the thick firs of a large grove that came close out upon the highway. He quickly saw somebody else as he was turning away.

"Guess that's Emery," said a scholar.

"Where?" asked Ripley, turning back.

"That man up the road!" was the reply.

If Emery were a brother-detective stationed outside to intercept any fugitive, he failed to intercept. He had not stuck to the school-house, and as the school-house would not stick to the fugitive, the latter had escaped into the woods. But how had he escaped from the school-house? That was to be shown.

"Let's go out, scholars! Quick!" said Ripley.

Never was a school-house cleared of its

pupils more quickly than Ripley's domain. Bare-headed, bawling, the boys and the girls flew out amid an excitement never before known in that district.

"Stop, thief!" bawled Emery, as he came flying down the road. "Look out for him, Nason!"

"Where, where did he go?" asked the other detective, now addressed as Nason.

"*You* know!"

"No, I don't."

"You was here."

"No, I wasn't. You should have been," said Nason, testily. "I had my hands full, looking through the school-house. I started the game and you ought to have headed him off."

"You sent me up the road to see if Blodgkins was coming."

"I didn't think you would go as far as the North Pole. Here is Blodgkins!"

A third man was now seen. He came running down the road, shouting, "Got him?"

"He is in here—these woods. Now chase!" said Nason.

But just where?

The snow after a late rain had frozen, and on its crusted surface one could walk and not

leave any imprint more than a scratch. The
fugitive must have had on slippers, for there
was not even a scratch on the crust. The
three men, though, plunged into the dense
thicket noisily. If they did not know where
their game was, the game had no difficulty in
deciding where they were.

"Well," said Ripley, "the woods have
swallowed them all up. Shall we——"

"Teacher, oh, see!"

This voice of a pupil recalled Ripley's
thoughts from the grove and suggested what
it would be interesting to notice next.

It was a girl that spoke, and she pointed at
the rear wall of the school-house.

"That—that window!" exclaimed Ripley.

It was an opening not generally designated
as a window, for it seemed too little. It was a
small circular opening covered with a green
blind. No one had ever seen the blind removed before, but it was thrown back to-day.
This hole was only three feet below the ridge-
pole.

"He—he—he came out ob dat!" said Don
Pedro, pointing excitedly at the round little
window.

"Yes," said another scholar, "and tumbled
down here."

"Yes," added the teacher, "this big dent where this snow is crushed in, is 'his mark.' I suppose he lived up there. I don't wonder people thought the school-house was haunted. Well, now we will see what he left behind. Let me see? Shall we get up here? Might bring the ladder out and try to get up here."

Into the school-house they ran.

When the ladder's foot was reached, as it was already planted against the hole in the ceiling inside, Ripley thought he would make an investigation from that point. He climbed up the rounds. He lifted the little grating in the hole above.

"A very small hole! Wonder if I could get up through it!" he exclaimed.

"No, sah!" affirmed Don Pedro.

"Yes, sir!" said one of the little girls.

"I should say 'no,' but I will make myself small as possible and see if I can get up here!" said Ripley.

The school-master wormed his way upward, screwing on this side, screwing on that side, his scholars looking on wonderingly and enjoying the sight far more than any exercise in arithmetic or grammar or even upon lighthouses.

" Fraid he'll get thuck!" shrieked one little girl, an admirer of the teacher.

" No, I—I—I'm through," he shouted down the hole. " One of you hand me some matches, or better if Don will please go to my boarding-place and get me a lamp. But what is this?"

He had touched a mass of rope which seemed a tangle, but holding it up to the light that came in through the little window beyond, he saw that it was a kind of net-work.

"Can't be a rope-ladder!" he thought. " One end is fastened to a rafter or something. Let me drop it down this hole."

He called out, "Heads from under!" and down rattled the rope.

"Oh! Oh! Oh!" came up in a wondering, delighted scream from his pupils, for there dangled from the hole a neatly-constructed rope-ladder.

" Ah!" thought Ripley. " Now I see how that bottle of wine disappeared so mysteriously this morning. I dare say I shall find it up here. That ghost, who has been haunting the place, was watching me."

Yes, if he could have peered then into the dark, Ripley would have seen two eyes, sharp and hateful, looking down at him through the grating. The eyes saw his refusal of the opportunity to arouse an appetite that he had nobly put down, and the sight made the hidden tempter exceedingly angry. He nimbly took away this dangerous property during Ripley's absence from the school-room.

When Don arrived, lamp in hand, the master promptly relieved him of the article, and lighting it, began a search in those places that the window could not brighten. He found very little save in one corner. "There!" he exclaimed. "Ah, a bed!"

It was very imperfect. A few boards had been laid upon the beams, and hay thinly strewn on the boards.

"Ah, here is that bottle!" said the master.

This had been left behind, and Ripley found, also, a small bag.

"Nothing in it!" he reflected, shaking the bag. "It is the dwelling of a very poor man, and just think of it, what a hiding-place! I wonder who it was and why! Somebody that was not here all the time, and yet that rope-ladder shows he meant to have everything ready for emergencies. Now I'll go down and leave that rope-ladder. No, I'll close the blind first, and make the little window tight."

He shut out the light and made the window

secure.   Then he turned his back on the cob-
webs, the dust, the dark, and crawled toward
the rope-ladder.

"I will let the rope-ladder hang here for
the present.   May want to use it some time.
Hark!   What are those noises?"

A variety of suppressed noises came up the
hole, and the master saw something round and
dark popping up above its dusty, grimy rim.

"Don, that you?"

"I—I—I am only one, sah!"

"Only one?   Hullo!   That string of you
on the rope-ladder?"

Below Don were others, looking up with
grinning faces.

"You'll—you'll break——"

The master's prophecy came true with a
violent abruptness.   Down went the rope-
ladder, and with it a string of boyish rogues
went tumbling in a heap.   A crash, a shout
from spectators, shrieks from those on the
string, ended that display, and ended the rope-
ladder.   It was not put up again.   That of
wood was soon raised, and Ripley came down
in safety.

"Now, scholars, we will keep school again.
You may take your seats.   I hope you will
never again believe in haunted buildings.   You

see that ghosts making noises and going in and out of buildings are flesh-and-blood personages. They are the ones that make rope-ladders."

Don's face was all awry at this point, and he rubbed his bruised legs. If he had ever given any support to the theory of haunted houses, his ideas all had a tumble when this work of ghosts gave way and the ladder came down with a rush.

It was Friday. The rest of that morning, the afternoon, also, passed without event. Different scholars brought word to Ripley that "those men were round a-huntin' still but they hadn't ketch't anybody."

At the close of the afternoon school, Ripley went to the shore. It was Candlemas-day, a season that was a favorite with Aunt Lydia.

In her plans, she reckoned forward to it. In recalling results, she reckoned back to it. "Last Candlemas" and "next Candlemas" were frequent landmarks that she set up in her life's journey.

"I want you to come out, Candlemas-day," was the wish she sent to Ripley. "It will be Friday and there will be no school Saturday, so you can stay all night. Walter will be glad to come for you after school."

Ripley stood upon the wintry beach, waiting for that expected boat from the lighthouse. It was a desolate scene before him and behind him. Back of the shore extended the snow in fields white and spotless, but chilling. If the sun had been shining across the snow, it would have glorified that white desolateness into dazzling crystal. No sun, though, was shining. It had been trying to shed a sickly light out of the clouds piled up in the west, but these had finally smothered the sick luminary and only a dark, lustreless mass of vapor could be seen at sunset. At the base of the hummocks skirting the beach, the ice had accumulated in masses that daily grew through the washings of the surf, here wasting its strength and its life. At sea there was a thickening fog. Any moment a blast from the fog-signal might be expected. Beneath the mist tossed a restless sea, a cold, icy green underrunning the white, frothing caps of the waves. It was a relief to Ripley when two fishermen, leaving a neighboring fishhouse, came to him and asked him about the late exciting event at the school-house.

"Strange! 'Mazin so!" remarked the older, Skipper Joe Wherren. "Did you see the man that ran?"

"Queerest thing ever happened in this neighborhood!" declared Skipper Joe's son. "I s'pose you saw it all."

"Very queer!" replied Ripley. "I see that my boat is coming from the lighthouse, but there will be time to tell all I know about it."

Ripley then detailed what he knew of the affair. He was about closing his account, regulating the length of this story by the approach of Walter's little craft to the shore, intending to end one as the other was beached, when he saw a man shoving a boat down the sands about two hundred feet away. It was high tide and the distance to be traversed was short. The man was using rollers to expedite this journey of the boat and he was soon shoving it into the water. Then he slowly pulled it through the surf.

Ripley abruptly broke off his narration to the fishermen and asked them, "Who is that?"

The face of the man in the boat was turned toward the shore. Ripley thought he knew the face. He was about to cry, "I know that is—" when down the lane came a shout:

"Stop! Stop!"

"Who's that a hollerin'?" asked Skipper Joe.

The two fishermen turned toward the lane. The school-master could not take his eyes off from the man in the boat.

Skipper Joe and his companion saw three men running down the lane. If Ripley had been looking that way he could have told them that the first of the runners was Nason, the second Emery and the third Blodgkins.

"Stop! Stop!" bawled Nason, and, as they ran, Emery and Blodgkins considered it to be their duty also to bawl," "Stop! Stop!"

Nobody, though, seemed to stop, except Nason, for he was in advance, and, having reached the surf he could not help halting and there he stood on the edge of the restless, frothing swash, puffing and blowing and looking disgusted. The man in the boat paid no attention to the invitation to halt, but rowed all the more energetically. To add to the general tumult, the fog-trumpet was now hoarsely, vigorously snarling, as if it also said, "Stop, stop, stop! You'd better. Fog is bad. Stop! Stop! Stop!"

The man, however, kept on rowing. Ripley still watched him. He could not seem to take his eyes off from that lonely boatman, pulling away into the cold, dismal, thickening mist.

"That is De Vere!" he said to his companions. "Looks like him! He has De Vere's height, his shoulders, his head, and, I could almost say, his face! Yes, it is De Vere!"

"De Vere if it's anybody! That is his name," cried the wheezy, testy Nason, who, still panting, had reached Ripley's side. "Been a-huntin' for him all day. Where's a boat?"

It now occurred to the fishermen that the only boat on the beach was that in which the fugitive was rowing off as fast as possible, into the fog. The boat which Ripley thought was Walter's proved to be that of a fisherman bound for the harbor. It had already been swallowed up by the fog. De Vere had taken the only boat just then on the shore.

"None of you fellers got a boat?" frantically asked Nason.

"Sorry!" said Skipper Joe. "Would like to obleej ye and ketch a reskel, but our boat went this mornin' up into the river and won't be back for an hour. Guess you've lost him."

"Pshaw-aw-aw!" exclaimed Nason, prolonging his outburst of disappointment.

It was like the blowing of a disgruntled whale.

"Pshaw!" said Emery.

"Pshaw!" said Blodgkins.

The two subordinates having fully attended to their duty by imitating their chief, now watched calmly the receding boat.

Nason stormed up and down the beach, fuming testily and growling, "Too bad! Got him and didn't get him! Wanted only two minutes more! A pesky shame! Jest look at him!"

"Whar's he goin'?" asked Skipper Joe.

Nobody could tell him.

"I wouldn't want to be rowin' off so on a winter's night, not knowin' whar I was goin'," observed the skipper's son.

It was a fascinating yet chilling picture, that fog dropping lower, thickening steadily, the cold winter sea darkening, that solitary boat with that solitary man ready to vanish any moment. It was a scene of utter loneliness. The land had rejected that man, had cast him out, had exiled him. The land rejecting him, the sea waited to engulf him, and the fog was about to shut down upon him and hide every trace of this castaway.

"Going!" said one of the fishermen.

"Gone!" said the other.

Yes, only the sea, and the shadows of the twilight, and the winter mist were there now.

Such a scene of cheerlessness, solitude and despair!

"Well!" testily remarked Nason. "Justice is cheated out of its due. Within a few weeks, he has been robbing, defrauding, and I don't know what. Hiding away like an outcast, and now what has become of him?"

Yes, what?

The event not only in its morning features made a deep, serious impression on the neighborhood, but its close seemed never to fade away from the recollection of men. When people talked about the strange and the marvellous, they mentioned De Vere. His name became a familiar one in the neighborhood. It seemed as if he must have been born there, and that too in every home, and had been guilty there of all his sins of omission and commission, and before the windows of every house, had alone, sullenly, persistently pushed off into the sombre, chilling twilight. He was never seen again, and yet it seemed as if somebody was always seeing him running down the beach, shoving that boat along, pushing it off, and so disappearing.

Children playing down on the beach, frightened one another by saying, "That man will come ashore for ye, that De Vere! Look out!"

Some of them running the syllables together, made it sound like Dev-il. Fishermen, when off in their boats they might see a fog coming, would ask one another, "Whar' do you 'spose that feller went who hid in the school'us and put off in the fog?"

"Dunno, one might say! Never hearn of his bein' pickt up, or his body rolled ashore nuther. Guess as how he's off here, rowin' round somewhar', comin' in with this fog, mebbe!"

Women seeing a storm approaching, and noticing the water darkening with mist, would say to one another, "Jest sich a storm that second of February when that De Vere was hunted by them detectives down to the beach and put off. 'Spect he keeps goin' round in the fog all the time. Nobody ever hears about him fetchin' up anywhere."

Old men, when the drift-wood fire sank on the hearth, would pull closer to it their clattering chairs, hold out to the embers their hands, and rub them energetically into warmth, quickening their vitality by saying, " Now, that's a dreadful dismal story 'bout that ere chap who got off in a boat and 'gin them officers the slip! Never hearn of to this day! Some folks think they see him, a-lookin' out of the fog, kind of a-peekin' out, and hear his oars agin' every time there's a speck of fog on the water!"

The party on the beach that had watched De Vere row away, broke up when Walter arrived in his boat, Ripley going with him to the lighthouse. The fog-trumpet seemed to change the tenor of its message, blowing and bellowing, "Come—come—come—m–m–m!"

"We are coming!" was Ripley's reply.

The two men were warmly welcomed by Uncle Boardman and Aunt Lydia. The detectives' visit and De Vere's escape made a very exciting subject for discussion at the supper-table, and Aunt Lydia was very sorry when supper had been dispatched and there was no farther excuse for sitting at the table and talking about this fascinating mystery.

"The curiousest thing!" she exclaimed, while bending over the dishes she was washing. "Why, I shan't hardly ventur' to look out of the lighthouse day nor night, lest I should see that De Vere a-rowin' by. He must be somewhere a-rowin' still, and there is no tellin' where he may turn up, on sea or land. Don't know as I shall close my eyes to-night!"

There were others who had no difficulty in

closing their eyes for a sound sleep, and they shut them very soon.

Returning to the kitchen after a search in the store-room for "suthin' for breakfast," Aunt Lydia found three mute, unconscious figures sitting about her stove.

"I declare," she said, softly, "if these men, all three, are not fast asleep! If that ain't a pictur'! The three heads a follerin' one another, Boardman a-leadin' off, Walter tryin' to catch up with him, then Ripley agoin' it! If I ever see anything like it!"

There she stood, smiling, shaking her head, then wonderingly looking at them, like a gray-haired old prophetess watching the subjects of her predictions, and she gave these in her positive way.

"Three good men and true! Can't tell me nothin' new about that man, Boardman Blake. He will do well, I know. Had a purpose and came here. I am glad of it. Nothin' like it. Boardman is one of that kind sure to have a purpose. I can see that Boardman will do a lot of good, and will save enough out of this ventur' here to give him a good start in life once more. And Ripley! I somehow yearn over that boy. He's not a-goin' to be the same kind of a chap he has been. And I shouldn't be surprised—stranger things happen —if he settled down to this, that the best thing he can do, and the only thing he ought to be, is a minister. They say he handled that meetin' masterly when he brought that Martin to hisself. I mean to lay it on Ripley that his purpose is jest there. He will want somebody to help him. Oh, I can see! I've been a-watchin', sayin' nothin', a-keepin' still, but thinkin' all the time. May Elliott is the one he will want, and she will want to be the one! And Walter, good, steady boy as ever was! He will go back to college and finish up and turn out sometime a doctor, a lawyer, and, mebbe, a minister. Shouldn't wonder! And —and—Kate Eaton will be the one to help him. Sartin true! I've got an eye for watchin', two of 'em. I haven't been here for nothin'. Now, here they are, all three of those men, jest where I can see 'em, and isn't it a pictur'?"

The old lady was amused by this view of the three sleepers, and remained some time grinning, wisely shaking her head, and shrewdly tracking their lives into the future.

Meantime, the tall lighthouse tower lifted its crown of flame steadfastly toward the sky, illuminating a wide area of ocean, for the fog

had recently lifted its folds. It was Candlemas night, and was not that tower a true
candle in the sea? In half an hour there was
a change. The lantern was brilliant with light,
but the fog had come back. Uncle Boardman was awake, and the fog-trumpet was sending out over the waters its far-echoing "Toot
—t–t–t——!"

THE END.

HISTORY.

Stories from English History.

By LOUISE CREIGHTON, author of "First History of England," "Life of the Black Prince," etc. With numerous illustrations. 12mo, cloth, $1.25.

In these stories from English History no attempt has been made to increase the interest by incorporating imaginary conversations or adding fanciful illustrations. The stories are either extracted from Chronicles or woven together from well authenticated historical facts. They are intended to serve as an amplification of the ordinary Child's History, where considerations of space and a due attention to the relative importance of events must often make it impossible to tell with full details those very facts most likely to interest children. It is hoped that, if used as a reading-book, these stories may serve to awaken an intelligent interest in English History, and also to impress events upon the mind of the reader.—THE PREFACE.

Tales of the Saracens.

By BARBARA HUTTON (Mrs. Alexander). 12mo, cloth, illustrated, $1.00.

Castles and their Heroes.

By BARBARA HUTTON (Mrs. Alexander). 12mo, cloth, illustrated, $1.00.

Heroes of the Crusades.

By BARBARA HUTTON (Mrs. Alexander). 12mo, cloth, illustrated, $1.00.

The above three volumes are excellent specimens of what historical tales should be. The stories in each volume are thrilling and are given with rare descriptive power and simplicity of style.

Story of the Discovery of the New World by Columbus.

Compiled from accepted authorities, by FREDERICK SAUNDERS, Librarian of the Astor Library. Handsomely illustrated and attractively bound in white vellum and red cloth, with gold stampings, $1.00.

Mr. Saunders' story of Christopher Columbus has a charm and literary flavor often too rare in biographical literature. It is just the life to read for those who care not for the more elaborate and discursive histories.

TRAVEL.

Leaders into Unknown Lands.

Being Chapters of Recent Travel. By ARTHUR MONTEFIORE, F.G.S. With fifty-six illustrations, maps and portraits. 12mo, cloth, $1.25.

The volume contains the story of six of the most famous journeys of modern times: Livingstone's March across Africa, Burton's Pilgrimage to Mecca, Stuart's Journeys Across Australia, Wallace in the Malay Archipelago, Stanley's Descent of the Congo, and Nansen's First Crossing of Greenland.

Half Hours in the Holy Land.

Travels in Egypt, Palestine and Syria. By NORMAN MACLEOD. 341 pages, 12mo, cloth, $1.50.

Dr. Macleod was an observant traveller as well as a famous preacher. His keen descriptive power and ready wit combine to make this volume bright, readable and satisfactory.

Glimpses of Europe.

Edited by W. C. PROCTOR. With one hundred illustrations. 12mo, cloth, $1.50.

A number of bye-places on the continent of Europe interestingly described by a number of writers and a corps of artists. The combination is a happy one, and the result is a decidedly readable book.

Round the Globe.

Through Greater Britain. Edited by W. C. PROCTOR. With eighty illustrations. 12mo, cloth, $1.50.

A number of well-known writers describe in turn the various countries of the British Empire that circle the earth. The volume is very entertaining and rich in illustrations.

From the Equator to the Pole.

Adventures of Recent Discovery. By Eminent Discoverers. With forty-five illustrations. 12mo, cloth, embellished, 90 cents.

Young folks are treated in this volume to a spirited account of Thomson's Trip to the Heart of Africa, Graham's Ascent of the Himalayas, and Captain Markham's Journey in Search of the Pole.

Sunny Days Abroad

Or, the Old World seen with Young Eyes. With Sixteen Illustrations of famous places. 12mo, cloth, $1.00.

WHITTAKER'S
Revolving Planisphere